THE ISRAELI BETRAYAL

A DALTON CRUSOE NOVEL

RICHARD TREVAE

The Israeli Betrayal / Richard Trevae
First Edition Paperback: July 2011
ISBN 13: 978-1-936185-39-9
ISBN 10: 1-936185-39-3

Editor: Ralph Gallagher
Interior Design: Roger Hunt
Cover Design: Jennifer Colon

Other books by Richard Trevae:
The Tarasov Solution

Readers may contact the author at:
Richard@trevae.com

Published by Charles River Press, LLC
www.CharlesRiverPress.com

10   9   8   7   6   5   4   3   2   1

AUTHOR NOTE

As a fiction writer one enjoys the luxury of blending history, current events and possible future events into a tease about our reality. The more convincing the story the more *real* it all seems. Sometimes even little known events of the past when twisted to an altered outcome provide a rich template for an intriguing thriller novel.

After I created James Dalton Crusoe and began to detail his persona, the trials and triumphs of his life, his interests, strengths and weaknesses the possibilities for story-telling exploded. Placing him in circumstances taken from history gave rise to The TARASOV SOLUTION, my first published novel based on Dalton, where his emotions and resourcefulness are tested in a crisis. Likewise in my second novel, The ISRAELI BETRAYAL, a battle-seasoned Dalton is called upon to address a volatile matter confronting the world today—the political and economic tension arising from energy concerns—just as Dalton takes control over a new slow fusion discovery promising to revolutionize weaponry and energy. Rival factions drawn from today's headlines take dangerous actions to control the technology and alter world power. Dalton reveals his decision-making skills, courage and intellect to manage the outcome for political advantage while taking down the conspirators.

After working through a plausible plot line for the novel, the story outline, and character creation the story development flowed... as I *knew* how one James Dalton Crusoe would proceed. The final result is truly reality-inspired-fiction. I hope you enjoy this next chapter in the Dalton Crusoe saga.

ACKNOWLEDGMENTS

To Jonathan Womack, who initially saw the good and the less-than-good in the original draft. His encouragement, guidance, writing advice, and commitment to the story allowed me to improve the novel.

To Chris Markley who made me very happy when he enthusiastically notified me CRP wanted to publish the second Dalton Crusoe novel.

To Jessica Colon for her cover designs.

To Ralph Gallager, whose thoughtful revisions and commentary pulled me through the copyediting effort.

To Roger Hunt for giving the book interior so much character.

To Jim Yates, whose constructive reviews of my earlier drafts tightened the story throughout, and also to Barb Yates, his real life supporter, encourager as well as a college literature instructor. Their friendship is a blessing to my family and me.

To Vicki, my wife, who steadfastly encourages me to write and enriches my writing through our exciting travels. Her first reader reviews are my *reality check* for my story's appeal. I truly rely on her support and encouragement for my musings.

To my extended family, friends, and business associates who have, and continue to express their joy in my writing journey.

DEDICATION

To Megan, Tyler, and Jacqueline

CAST OF CHARACTERS

NSA Prodigy
Jameson Dalton Crusoe
Special Opts Commander
Colonel Brad Ronet

NSA Field Agents
Wilson
Cotter

Secretary of Energy and defacto NSA Leader
Ed Kosko

President of The United States
Jerome Conner

KCG Members
Sang Huchara, Japan
Dr. Eli Weiss, Israel
General Yong, North Korea
Defense Secretary Kytoma, Japan

Contract Assassins & Mercenaries
Khamal
Gilles Montrose

Others
Carolyn McCabe, Dalton's love interest
Jane Holman, Research Manager, Enertek
Toro Nagama, Lab Technician, Enertek
Major Kunghee, North Korean Military
Susan Wallace, Toro's girl friend
Mohammad Hatta, (Benjamin Glickman), covert Israeli spy
Jack Tucker, CIA Section Chief

PRELUDE

MOHAMMED Hatta had yearned for this moment every day for the last thirty-four months. Masquerading as a nuclear engineer at the Iranian Energy Research Laboratory in Jefrah, Iran, Mohammed lived a contrived life. His espionage efforts for Israel were now complete; the bomb in place, his deep cover was intact. Once he was safely back in Tel Aviv he could discard his alias and return to his life as Benjamin Glickman. His Israeli handlers ordered his return to Tel Aviv within thirty-six hours. The event, close at hand, meant he had to be beyond Iranian borders.

OPERATIONS CENTER, SITUATION ROOM
ISRAELI ENERGY COMMISSION, OUTSIDE TEL AVIV

The first test of the new weapon, on a real target, was underway once the security door locked shut. Inside the Israeli Energy Commission (IEC), Dr. Eli Weiss, its managing director, studied a large wall clock displaying 8:45 p.m., local Jefrah Iran time. The clandestine IEC organization appeared as a blend of national energy policy, procurement functions, and an applied research

PRELUDE

center to explore and develop new alternative forms of energy. Deep within the research section a secret alternate command center functioned for surveillance and mission control of all Israeli national defenses.

Dr. Weiss stood locked in the IEC operations area of the situation room with his manager and ten key technicians, each busy positioning satellite data onto screens. Weiss watched the real-time downloading imagery over northwest Iran. Joining him in the operations area were a few high level researchers who worked tirelessly over the last few weeks. The objective required them to establish the specific parameters under which a powerful detonation from a new custom bomb would occur; a nascent technology, stolen weeks earlier from the U.S. firm Enertek, located outside Seattle. In moments the success, or failure, of their efforts would be known.

Israeli Defense Minister Dyan stood next to Weiss and whispered, "When did you hear from Hatta?"

Covering his mouth as though he were about to cough, Weiss answered. "He called me early yesterday morning to say the bomb is in position. He also confirmed uranium enrichment is approaching full production." Weiss's face displayed his hatred for the Iranians and their stated goal, eliminating the nation of Israel. Dyan's mouth contorted to an angry set.

"Then this is it, Eli. We have no choice but to act." Dyan looked directly at Weiss, searching for hesitation.

"Yes, that's correct. We must proceed. Delaying longer could endanger Israel and put our research in jeopardy. I ordered Hatta to leave Jefrah no later than last evening. He should be close to crossing into Jordan now."

"And what about our American scientist counterparts at Enertek? Have they not discovered the secret power of the technology as yet?" Dyan's nervous eyes fixed, waiting for an answer to his question. Weiss looked around the command center now buzzing with activity.

Smiling he said, "No, the Americans assume it's merely a low grade catalyst. Their test protocols, we believe, lead to a dead end. They have no idea we have the raw technology, or how far we have advanced it for weapon's use." Dyan smiled shaking his lowered head to hide his joy.

The elite security group watched as the satellite controlling the impending bomb attack provided vivid coverage of the area on screen. Seconds passed as the huge wall screens displayed images focused through the atmosphere, sometimes loosing clarity as clouds obstructed the view to ground. Other screens displayed the area within a 150-kilometer radius of the target showing the encroaching darkness line as the earth rotated away from the sun.

Watching as the satellite scanned, focused and magnified details, a young lead operator swung his chair, looked to Dr. Weiss and said, "Device is programmed

PRELUDE

sir, and the Local Detonation Controller awaits detonation code in."

The target came into clear view, filling the entire main screen. Several buildings appeared, connected with massive underground tunnels and railways to move weapons components around the site. Dr. Weiss nodded and said, "Enter detonation code to the LDC."

The console operator entered the eight-digit code, turned a safety key, and opened a clear red protective cap on a button that read *Detonation Start*. The operator, looked again to Dr. Weiss for approval, and pressed the button. Seconds later, at precisely the expected moment, a huge controlled blast filled the screens, along with many secondary explosions that erupted throughout the Iranian weapons complex. Billowing yellow and white clouds boiled over the demolished structures encompassing a quarter-mile radius. The wall clock showed local Jefrah Iran time at 8:59 p.m. Iran was out of the nuclear weapons business, and its Iranian Energy Research Laboratory (IERL), a misnomer for the actual purpose of the facility destroyed.

Weiss looked out to his team and said, "It is over, the technology works and the Iranian threat is eliminated."

Moments later the secure situation room erupted in applause and cheers over the successful explosion. Photographers snapped a dozen photos as Weiss received congratulations from all. Defense Minister

Dyan said, "Eli, you have opened a new era of security for Israel." Dr. Eli Weiss felt like he stood at the pinnacle of his career . . . and he loved it.

Enjoying the epic moment, and withholding tears, Dr. Eli Weiss smiled. "This effort could not have been accomplished without the dedication of my research team at the IEC. Over the next few months, we will completely change the world's respect for Israel. May the God of Abraham bless us all."

EARLY THE NEXT DAY, NINE HOURS AFTER THE EXPLOSION, TEHRAN IRAN

Hasid Khamal opened his phone to a new text message. *Interrogate Mohammed Hatta about the explosion at Jefrah. Investigate suspected involvement with foreign enemies to position bomb. Use all means necessary to confirm our suspicions. Report to command by 1800 tomorrow.*

Hasid Khamal, an assassin for hire, received training and education in France and the United States. Although out of the glare of Middle Eastern public political displays, he always operated either near or part of the action. He became the Iranian's first choice for covert operations. Over the last decade, Khamal had worked for several Arab countries and political groups

PRELUDE

within those countries. Each time Khamal accepted an assignment, he took care not to violate the trust and confidence of his prior clients lest he become a target. This time it became clear the Iranians suspected a mole, deep in their nuclear research program, and likely connected to the west.

Therefore, he had a no real worries about upsetting former clients. The priority placed on this assignment was also clear, as the Iranians had doubled his usual $5,000,000 USD fee and deposited it in his Swiss numbered account within four hours of him accepting the assignment. They wanted answers fast, as world opinion was already forming, and delays would make even more difficult the task of drawing sympathy from the world community over the explosion, and publicly blaming Israel and the West.

Khamal had completed his initial assignment within seven hours of first contact with Mohammad Hatta. The deep cover Israeli mole failed to escape from Iran posing as a Jordanian businessman returning home. A random check by Iranian security personnel delayed Hatta boarding the last flight to Amman, Jordan before the detonation. He failed to make the flight out. After the explosion detonated the government sealed the borders and halted all flight departures, leaving Hatta stranded.

Intercepted outside his rented room near the airport,

RICHARD TREVAE

Khamal uncovered and confirmed Hatta's espionage role for Israel while working at the IERL as a nuclear engineer. During his torture, Khamal extracted much information from Hatta. After he finished, Hatta died from a lethal injection and would never be found. Next, Khamal began his way to the Waldron range in Montana with enough knowledge of the Enertek discovery to suggest direct involvement of Israel and the U.S. in the blast at Jefrah. One name came out of Hatta before his quick death — Dr. Eli Weiss of Israel.

ONE

THE fourth day of September was cooler than usual in Seattle, although under a brilliant sun, and Jameson Dalton Crusoe pulled his sport jacket tight around his neck as he hurried to The Elliott Bay Crab House. He didn't want to be late for his lunch meeting with Ed Kosko concerning the Emerging Energy Technologies, Inc., or Enertek, the shortened name for most acquainted with the premier technology firm. The official start of fall had not yet arrived in the northwest, although the air felt crisp and refreshing, and the leaves had just begun to show a bit of color. The bank sign across from the harbor restaurant read sixty-four degrees on its electronic display. Ed had arrived early, following his usual style, and was anxiously watching for Dalton, or JD, as his closest friends referred to him.

Dalton loved to meet at the Elliott Bay Crab House. It was sprawling, much of it open and it overlooked the Puget Sound area. Ed and Dalton had met many times at the restaurant to brief each other on their activities, and they usually sat outside on their open deck with umbrella tables and propane heaters when the air turned cool. The other attractive feature was the privacy afforded Ed and Dalton, as the tables were spaced far enough apart and the water activity, road traffic and even the mild wind made adequate background noise to muffle their words from prying ears.

"Been waiting long, Ed?" Dalton asked as he sat down across from Ed.

"No, just a few minutes. I'm enjoying the weather anyhow. It gave me a moment to reminisce over the great times we've had in past September's when we went fishing at the lodge." Ed's relaxed mood could not hide the serious expression overtaking his face.

"Yeah, those were always great diversions and fun times," recalled Dalton. "I have the draft mineral rights leases here on the Montana and Canadian land, if that's what you wanted to discuss. They arrived in yesterday's mail from Enertek's attorneys."

"Thanks, we'll get to those later," Ed said dismissively. "Actually, I need your help on some interesting events of late at the Emerging Energy Technologies in Seattle."

"Enertek, Okay, what's up?"

The waitress delivered two small cups of the house special clam corn chowder with warm bread, and fresh coffee. Ed thanked her and said they were fine for now, his polite way of saying don't bother us. He then focused in on Dalton. "A recent find at the Elko mine in Montana appears to have extraordinary properties."

This part of Ed's makeup always intrigued Dalton, for Ed, a non-scientist, monitored a highly technical research and development company. As a former Enertek board member, he forever looked beyond the science and into the political, economic, and subtle business nuances of this company's activities. Eight months earlier, stepping away from his deputy director role at the NSA, Ed became Secretary of Energy for the President of the United States; his very public, visible and primary responsibility. In fact, the reason for the arms length involvement at Enertek allowed him to stay tightly connected with one of the country's leading applied research facilities in the states, and to keep an eye on the $1.8 billion, or so, the defense and energy departments spent each year supporting Enertek's research. His earlier NSA connections remained active sources of information when needed. Ed enjoyed a long-time relationship with his friend, political ally and confidant in President Jerome Conner.

Educated as an engineer, Kosko moved through his PhD in record time, and at twenty-four years old had a full professorship at Princeton. Academia did not suit Ed Kosko well, however, and he took a jump at age twenty-seven to the FBI, and after a short stint, left to join the NSA. Always part of republican administrations Ed Kosko operated as a loyal, innovative and creative guy, connected at the highest levels of government, and yet had access to academia and industry leaders.

A short stocky man with intense eyes and a large smile, Ed was not opposed to telling a joke at his own expense, yet he had a very serious side as well. At fifty-eight, he reached the pinnacle of his career, a cabinet post, reporting to a President he had known as a friend for twenty-two years, and most impressively, a part of the inner circle of influential men counseling the President. Being married with no children allowed him and Irene extensive travel opportunities, even when working, and to maintain a committed if not particularly intimate marriage. It evolved into a comfortable relationship for both. He felt the happiest and most satisfied with his role in life than at any time in the last five years.

Pausing for a moment to survey the surroundings, Ed began, "Eleven weeks ago the Enertek excavation contractor in Elko, Montana opened up an unusual vein of a lithium crystal-quartz aggregate which has a density and crystalline structure like nothing we've ever seen before. Being so new and unique you can imagine how our research group responded; they promptly began a series of evaluative tests and screening studies to see what it does, if anything. We thought it may have application in prolonging solid battery life and allowing them to be recharged almost indefinitely." Ed whispered as though the entire restaurant was trying to hear him.

Dalton interrupted, "You mean to say this stuff is naturally occurring and it is still unreported in the scientific literature?"

"Yeah, that's about how I see it, at least for now," replied Ed. "Its origin may date back to a meteor impact tens of thousands of years ago, we just don't know. However it is a sizeable vein." Ed paused for a moment, sipped his coffee and spoke softly. "Last week Jane Holman, the senior lab manager directing this work created a new novel test protocol which is under way now."

Dalton sensed the tension in Ed as he leaned closer and spoke in a soft whisper.

"I, and Jane, and some of her team leaders, believe this may be a catalyst for slow fusion. The next few weeks should tell us more." Ed paused, sipped his coffee again and continued, "Perhaps you can see my concern, JD?"

Dalton ran Ed's words through his mind once more, trying to fathom the full impact of his statement. He studied Ed and in a very serious tone answered, "Absolutely, this discovery, if real, could forever change the world; bad guys and good guys would kill for control of the technology. Who else knows of this?"

Dalton reflected for a moment, as Ed organized his

next thought. "No one knows except you, Jane and I, so far. And yes, if this is a true breakthrough in the energy development field we must control the release of findings until we are confident of what we have and," Dalton's gaze froze on Ed causing him to pause speaking, and then Dalton finished the thought. "Secure the mine site and the mineral rights in Montana and Canada."

"Right," whispered Ed as he again looked around the restaurant. "This entire issue could quickly become a matter of national security, if we are right about its potential. If it works to control slow fusion it may also lead to a new generation on nuclear bombs. I need you to take charge of this entire project from a management and security standpoint, while I keep the Feds from stepping into this and screwing it up, okay?" Ed hoped for the right answer.

Dalton thought intensely for a moment, and then told him what he needed to hear "When do I take control?" A calm settled over Ed just as Dalton's adrenaline kicked in.

"Tomorrow at noon in a conference call, I plan to announce it to the executive committee and insist they let us lead the effort from here on out. Can you be up to speed in three days?" Ed asked with authority. Dalton nodded agreement as he finished the last of his Seattle's Best coffee.

RICHARD TREVAE

Ed reached in his coat jacket and retrieved a zippered, leather case the size of a large envelope and moved it across the table under a newspaper to Dalton. In a very low whisper Ed said, "Here are the XR-211 project files on encrypted disks with the original scope, justification, and budget, as well as the new test protocols. Get up to speed fast. Only Jane Holman has seen the new slow fusion predictions, as she wrote the new protocols to test the feasibility of achieving the predictions."

"So what does Jane think about this?"

"Well, she sees so many experiments with high hopes that fizzle; I think she's just waiting to see what develops. The new test protocols should definitely tell us in the next several weeks if there is potential here to produce slow fusion . . . and a new weapon."

"I'll be ready," Dalton offered. "I'm returning to Washington tonight for the long weekend, but I'll be at the Enertek site Tuesday morning." Standing to leave the men shook hands and without uttering another word knew the awesome responsibility they now shouldered.

"Thanks, JD, I'm counting on you."

Jameson Dalton Crusoe is now the guardian of an

emerging technology that emboldens a powerful shadow government consortium to destroy avowed enemies and alter the balance of power in the world. Unknown to Crusoe and Enertek its first test in Jefrah, Iran was an epic success!

Two hundred yards away the driver door window of the Cadillac Escalade slowly raised and closed. Gilles Montrose stowed his small binoculars, removed his earpiece and dismantled the listening antenna he had been using to eavesdrop on the conversation between Ed Kosko and Jameson Dalton Crusoe. Unable to hear all the whispered conversation Gilles did conclude Kosko had the project encrypted disc files on him. Dialing his cell phone Gilles instructed, "Proceed to intercept Kosko now and retrieve disks."

A reply came forth, "On our way."

Jameson Dalton Crusoe stood out as one of those special individuals whose life and career had vested him with more knowledge and experience than his years revealed. As the only son of Jonathan David Crusoe and Elizabeth Louise Crusoe, Dalton had grown up in the Chesapeake Bay area. He played on the high school tennis and football teams and was always looked up to as the acknowledged leader of his teams. In addition to his athletic skill, JD excelled as a natural leader and could think his way through most situations and have the physical skill to carry it out to completion.

His striking good looks were evident even at a very young age. He had chestnut brown hair, always cut just long enough to allow a part, clear bluish grey eyes and a perfect broad smile that made an instant impression on all he encountered. When his father took an assignment in Brussels as IBM's European Sales Vice President, he was a senior in high school. Young JD, nicknamed after his father, welcomed the experience as he learned about European culture and became fluent in French, German and some Flemish tongues. A year-and-a-half later, JD's father died suddenly of a massive stroke. However, JD continued on to college at the Annapolis Naval Academy and graduate school with the strong encouragement of his mother.

The loss of his father at a young age matured Dalton quickly. As an only child, he felt a responsibility to his father, after his death, to protect and care for his mother. Fortunately, Elizabeth Crusoe, a strong and resourceful woman, made certain Dalton worked hard to fulfill his clear potential. Never having remarried, she moved to the balmy shores on the outer bank of islands in North Carolina, bought a beautiful three-bedroom condominium on the beach and always welcomed

Dalton for weekends when he was nearby. She spent her time becoming a short story writer and liked to have Dalton review her work. She had met Carolyn, Dalton's "special friend", and very much enjoyed her company, since it meant she could tell embarrassing childhood stories about young JD. She unexpectedly died four months later after Dalton joined Ed Kosko as a consultant.

Trained in engineering at the Annapolis Naval Academy, JD worked for Sylvania in San Francisco one summer between semesters and became a key asset in the assessment of new technologies with implications for national security. Bright and articulate Dalton quickly drew attention to himself. His father had first introduced JD to Ed Kosko when JD was starting at Annapolis. Kosko worked as a technology expert and section head on the National Energy Policy Group, a quasi-governmental organization loosely connected to the NSA. Following Jonathan Crusoe's untimely death, Kosko became a personal friend and mentor to Dalton. They enjoyed a robust professional and social life involving sailing, golf, and running. The relationship had taken Dalton all over the world and he had direct access to many high-level diplomats and foreign agents, some managed by Ed.

It took Dalton less than two years to get his MBA in International Finance at Wharton, and after that he became a paid associate/consultant of Ed's in several clandestine operations in South America and Europe looking into various oil and natural gas projects. Always active and athletic Dalton kept fit and strong at 6'-1", 190 pounds, and solid muscle. He was never combat trained, but the black belt in karate he had earned made Dalton a formidable companion when Ed needed to show a physical presence in troubled locations.

Now at twenty-eight, Dalton operated in essence as Ed's unofficial right hand man. Formally designated a Consultant to Kosko, who now held the Secretary of Energy cabinet position under the President, Dalton received high exposure. In reality, Ed pushed off most of the day-to-day department stuff to his deputy under secretaries and functioned more as an ex-officio part of the President's national security team. Ed kept Dalton close and informed about every serious issue confronting him or the President as it related to energy throughout the world.

Dalton had proven his capability and resourcefulness several times when on special operations overseas to untangle delicate situations. His resume involved a Foreign Oil Minister trying to close down a shipping port in an extortion scheme and a South American eco-terrorist flexing his military muscle at mining and oil drilling firms hoping to get political recognition from the U.S. and his country's leadership. On occasion he would lead a small insertion team to undermine a target or lead a quasi-military group on a "snatch and grab" mission.

Immediately after joining Ed's team Dalton uncovered and foiled an assassination attempt on Russian and U.S. presidents by a mad arms merchant, Yuri Tarasov. With strong intuitive skills, a decisive nature and somewhat risk averse he had proven himself several times leading teams on very clandestine assignments to retrieve information vital to national security. Dalton could go from a business suit in the boardroom to combat fatigues and weaponry in a jungle, as the situation demanded.

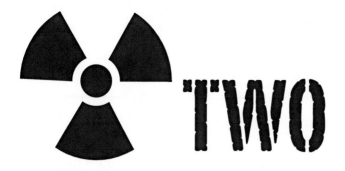

TWO

SHE grew excited and ready to start her long Labor Day weekend with Dalton in the Virginia hill country. It had been five weeks since the two of them had taken time for themselves, and Carolyn McCabe was ready for some romantic time away from academia. As she strolled down the concourse to the visitor area and waved to Dalton, she noticed that he appeared relaxed and ready for the weekend as well. He smiled with obvious excitement as she neared, then grabbed her waist, looked in her passionate eyes. "Hello darling, how have you been? I sure have missed you."

This followed with a brief, firm kiss, sent Carolyn to the next level of arousal. Dalton could really affect her in ways no other man had ever done. In addition, it extended far beyond just sexual; it was very emotional, and vividly sensual. Holding and then releasing her he could feel her body submitting to his control of her waist - he too became excited. Carolyn's face beamed with joy at seeing Dalton again; she could feel her pulse quickening.

"I've missed you too, but you are the one flitting around the country, Mr. Hotshot!" Carolyn smiled as she teased Dalton about his schedules and then returned for another kiss.

As they left the airport and drove to one of their usual bed and breakfast getaways, Dalton first shut off his phone and then buried the thoughts of his meeting on the Enertek find. It had been two days since that meeting, although his mind couldn't seem to forget it. Carolyn knew that their time was too precious to waste on trivial questions about their business lives. As she snuggled as close to him as she could in the front seat of Dalton's Audi, she rested her arm lightly on his right shoulder. Watching him, more than the road captured her desire. A partial smile remained a permanent feature on Carolyn's face the entire time in the car.

She wanted nothing more than a few relaxing days with the man of her dreams. JD had always been, and would forever be, the man Carolyn needed, wanted, and waited for every day of her life. However, she knew enough about the high access, yet low profile, role JD played in the administration not to expect that she could gain more than these few infrequent getaways, at least for the time being.

Women came and went in Dalton's life, not that he lacked opportunities, although the travel and the break-neck pace of some of his assignments made lasting relationships awkward. Carolyn McCabe however was special, a drop-dead beauty originally from North Carolina and now an associate Professor at Wharton's finance school. She had just started at the university when she and Dalton became acquainted. He pressed on through the last of his MBA while she finished her first year of graduate school in international finance. Within a year, they became very close.

When Dalton graduated with his MBA, they were a known couple around campus. They had maintained a strong, albeit episodic love relationship, which they both accepted as the way it had to be, at least for now. As a college student, Carolyn had excelled as a runner for the track team and helped take her school to the national semi-finals as a senior. Strong yet without an overdone musculature, she had maintained a healthy 117 pounds of solid, yet curvaceous, toning. At five foot, six inches she appeared as commanding and sexy in a tailored business suit as she did in a Lycra top and running shorts. Naturally a brunette, she typically kept her medium length hair shaded to almost blond most of the time. Bright and charming, she epitomized the ideal mate for Dalton, for she could compete with him intellectually and yet arouse and satisfy his sexual desires. Marriage had never been discussed as both were on fast career tracks that had to be played out a few more years; although because both understood their situation, they were willing to maintain this random schedule of intimacy.

One Hour Later
Rural Virginia

JD and Carolyn unloaded the car and then checked out the room and the grounds. The day had grown warm and yet at the same time more fall-like. A brief walk around the park like setting that was the bed and breakfast provided a time for playful teasing and total enjoyment of being with each other. They held hands and Carolyn thought about how much she truly loved him.

Both were beginning to feel the tempo of their day slowly changing as the thoughts of big city life melted away. Later that day they sat on the deck of their room overlooking a winding lake stretching to the west. The view their room provided framed the sunset behind the mountains as the sky displayed the rich oranges, reds, and purples of the early fall in the Virginia countryside.

As the afternoon gave way to evening, they both settled back and took in the beautiful fall colors, the deep, rich blue sky, the glistening water, and the soft breeze silently releasing leaves to the ground. Dalton held her hand with their fingers almost interlocked. By the end of the first wine bottle, Carolyn drew JD into a deep wet. Their hands roamed over each other bodies and the night become one ruled by emotions. The arousal triggered many memories where he and Carolyn had stolen away to a romantic location and enjoyed each other for a few passionate days. This getaway had potential to be another great encounter. Several hours later, as they were falling asleep in their bed, Carolyn whispered, "Promise me you'll always want me with you."

Exhausted and nearly asleep JD whispered, "I will always want you with me, promise."

Moments later they were both sound asleep and captured in each other's arms.

THREE

MOST research had been slowed or halted during the early part of the week in anticipation of the long Labor Day holiday. Only a few Section Chiefs and eager young researchers were around to oversee the few experiments that could not be interrupted over the long four-day weekend. The New Energy Technology Group (NET-G) within Enertek, under Jane Holman's direction, had only two experiments active in the lab. The first involved a new prototype electric car battery regenerated by a highly efficient solar cell system. The second experiment was different. Labeled XR-211, it was designed to systematically program the variables of temperature, concentration, laser wavelengths, and electromagnetic fields through an array of combinations and measure the ratio of energy output versus energy input.

What made this unusual involved the "host catalyst" supplied to initiate the energy release. While hundreds of "host catalysts" were available, and most had been tested under these type scanning experiments, only a very few produced a positive energy ratio, that is, one which yields more energy than it consumes. Nuclear fission being the most notable example of a thermonuclear reaction yielding vast amounts of energy relative to that required to initiate the release. Ostensibly, Project XR-211 explored the properties of this mildly radioactive composite of lithium quartz salts in an unfamiliar dense crystal structure.

The raw material had been discovered by accident, weeks earlier, as a brilliant, nearly clear, hard crystal, during strip mining investigations in the Waldron mountain range by Enertek's subcontractor, Mitsui Construction and Mining Limited, of Vancouver. They were working the range for evidence of nickel, copper and shale oil deposits when the huge vein of unknown ore was discovered. Except for the high security given the project through its "XR" classification, it appeared not much different from dozens of other similar lab exercises at Enertek.

Work stopped until a research group examined the site and took samples for the experimental work going on in the lab. Mitsui was directed to seal the excavation and place light security at the dig until the research indicated whether Enertek had further interest in the leased land on the Waldron Range. That occurred eleven weeks earlier and very little had been said or done about the find except for the property scanning experiments now underway.

Gilles Montrose, however, also followed the mining activity concerning this find for eleven weeks, and had secretly arranged for six fifty-five gallon drums of the ore to be packaged and labeled, "Drilling Waste Sludge", and be shipped off site to a landfill location.

Once off the mining site the drums were re-directed by Gilles's "foot solders", Ted and Jeff, to another site, Haifa Israel, for delivery to a Dr. Eli Weiss. Several other groups had a serious interest in the properties of the new, rare ore discovered at Elko.

LATE FRIDAY AFTERNOON, BEFORE LABOR DAY
NORTHEAST SEATTLE — ENERTEK'S RESEARCH LABORATORY

Jane Holman sat frustrated at her desk, trying to sort out the huge pile of paper mail obscuring her work surface. It seemed bad enough as a Lab Unit Manager she had to work the Friday evening and Saturday before Labor Day when the majority of her seven-person lab team were out enjoying the fantastic early autumn weather of the Northwest. Nevertheless, Ed Kosko himself had requested Jane and her two senior people cover the weekend to keep from delaying the test work on XR-211, the project code number for the recently discovered deposit.

Jane would have to brief Dalton, on Tuesday morning. She had not fully studied the original test protocol outline because it seemed like so many other fast track, quick screening experiments that came and went a dozen times a month. Curiously, the project had been given a high-level security status with a very limited distribution list. This caused Jane to further study the background information and testing results thus far and she concluded there might be more involved than meets the eye.

Typically, this meant the government had a piece of the work, or all of it, under their direction. Acting on a hunch Jane proposed examining the unique ore as a catalyst for energy release. Her test protocol copied only the top scientific minds at Enertek, including the 'overseer' Ed Kosko. No one except Kosko held privileged status to the security reasons or the 'players' behind the research work request when the project number began with an 'XR.'

As the chestnut surface of her desk began to appear from under the paperwork, Jane turned her attention to her computer, which monitored the data results flowing from XR-211. She had organized the computer to record, analyze trends, predict optimum conditions, and design new test combinations extrapolated to improve results. A few keystrokes and Jane saw that after four-teen hours only 17% of the programmed combinations of the entire array had been completed with nothing notable to report. Moreover, the trend predictor showed only a 3.2% improvement expected on the series of tests planned for the next eight hours. Jane sighed as the monotony of her work sometimes got to her. It began as a very long afternoon and evening for Jane.

FRIDAY 10:15 P.M.
OUTSIDE ENERTEK'S LABORATORIES

Toro Nagama watched the sunset melt away two hours before and crouched ready to make his move down the grassy hillside toward the Enertek Laboratory. His attire looked very different from the lab coats and safety goggles he wore earlier. However, tonight was different; he felt life would never be the same for him again.

Originally recruited direct from USC after complet-ing his M.S. in energy physics, Toro had been with the company for seven years. After being promoted to Jane Holman's group, Toro figured he had finally arrived and would soon lead his own research staff and move on up to more and more responsibility and money. Almost three years had passed since Toro joined Jane's group, and he still remained stuck as a second tier researcher — a lackey, if you will, in his eyes. Despite being recognized as a competent researcher, he never got the job he really wanted . . . a Technical Group Leader, with his own staff, budgets and respect.

Tonight would be the big equalizer, thought Toro. Once he retrieved the XR-211 test protocol and physical property results, along with Ed Kosko's project scope and justification, another $275,000 cash would be handed to him.

Over the last three years, Toro had "earned" over $380,000 for his special services to the intelligence unit at Mitsui. In an email to Sang Huchara, CEO of Mitsui, and Toro's secret partner in his plans to get rich at the expense of Enertek, Toro reported, "Extraordinary mineral find at Waldron Range, may hold breakthrough promise." Sang Huchara promptly set in motion a long string of events as a 'Plan B' to Toro's efforts. Gilles Montrose was the contact Sang Huchara depended on to oversee field operations that were, shall we say, outside of the scope Mitsui had been assigned from Enertek.

Toro left his car and slipped silently into the woods that created a buffer around the 1,320-acre Enertek site. As an avid runner, Toro felt the initial warmth in his lungs as he sprinted through the open woods to a small hill overlooking the site. He felt confident and strong, dressed in black jogging sweats, a jacket, and gloves with his nine-millimeter Beretta tucked snugly in his shoulder holster.

The cool weather seemed perfect for Toro. He was energized, felt exhilarated and very much alive; all his senses were peaking. He reached the site perimeter fence at 10:42 p.m., knelt down low, and scanned the huge complex. Security was tight in the building, yet Toro was able to scale the eight foot high fence with ease. On occasion, the security team would patrol the fence from their car, yet they seldom stopped to scan the forests and fields around the plant. Because no one expected a security breach, precautions were sloppy. The real security resided inside the building and throughout the computer systems. When Toro reached the rear of the building where deliveries were made, he located the kite string taped down and obscured to the casual observer of the building.

The string withdrew a climbing rope prepared by Toro earlier this very evening. Once on the roof Toro swiftly covered the three hundred feet to the roof scuttle used by the building mechanical staff. The scuttle hatch remained unlocked just as he had left it two days earlier. Once inside, Toro found himself in the boiler room. He crouched motionless for a moment and collected his thoughts, everything now running at hyper-speed.

RICHARD TREVAE

This ranked as the most ambitious assignment Toro had ever taken on for Sang Huchara, however the rewards were great. Sang originally approached the young researcher at a summer party four years ago sponsored by the Mitsui organization in appreciation for all the mining and security contracts they had received from Enertek over the years. Over four hundred people attended, including just about everyone at Enertek and most of the field personnel with Mitsui, along with construction engineers, supervisors, technicians, and office support types. Sang only spent a few minutes with Toro, however they both had family and history in Japan which broke the ice and made a connection.

Sang then began with small, seemingly innocent requests, such as capital budgets, new spending priorities, patent work and major equipment purchases. Toro received a $10,000 check and a paid weekend in Vancouver for his initial task of copying the capital budget for an upcoming year. It seemed so easy to provide these low security documents, Toro was drawn to the money and not the ethics or legality of his deeds. His appetite grew for more money as well as his disdain over his job status. He wanted more and he wanted it now. He began asking exactly what else Sang wanted and how much he would pay for it. Sang pulled him along slow and steady, as he had done with many other "associates" to get the information he and other friends wanted.

Once in a dark, empty lab, Toro turned on a network computer connected to the server and began to access Ed Kosko's secure electronic files, updated daily and transmitted to him over the internet. They were password protected of course, though Toro had earlier loaded an invisible program onto the local network in the applied research lab offices to record the passwords and related files during one workday, store those in a dummy experiment file on a remote computer, which could then only be opened by Toro's password - 'RECOMPENSE.' The screen flashed through various numbers and symbols and then froze with six passwords as headings showing twenty-two protected files. Scanning with growing excitement, Toro found XR-211 under the heading - Slow Fusion.

Toro's hands shook and his heart raced as he read the file title over and over. Could this be what it implied? Had Enertek stumbled onto something of incredible proportions? His anxiety gave way to fear, an adrenaline rush and then to greed. Toro reasoned, *I will demand more for my efforts; they will have to give it to me, once they know what I now know.*

Six sub files appeared including the experimental scope, expectations, schedules, and meeting notes with the Board all copied to Ed Kosko; though no experiment results were known yet.

"Damn," exclaimed Toro in an uncontrolled response to the only setback he had seen thus far. In a matter of moments, he had copied the six files on to a disk, deleted his password capturing program and shut down his computer.

It showed 11:22 p.m. on his laptop and he needed the test results, which were still grinding away uneventfully in Jane's lab. Toro decided to hide until early in the morning, around 3:30 a.m., before once again trying to access the computers in Jane's area. Toro knew Jane and two staffers were roaming about. By that time, some of them would certainly have tried for some naptime . . . or so he hoped.

Toro was not about to give up when he stood so close to cashing out big and kissing off Enertek and their ungrateful management. He remained hidden and allowed his mind to rehearse a new demand for more money from Sang Huchara. He could not restrain a smug smile forming across his face. The night fell darker and quiet as he waited for the lab results to be generated and uploaded to the server. He drifted in and out of a light sleep while he fantasized about his good fortune.

Sunrise would never again come for Toro.

FOUR

NORTHWEST SEATTLE — OUTSIDE ENERTEK

BY midnight, the black four door Buick had come to rest about two hundred yards behind, and hidden from, Toro's car. The two men inside were 'soldiers' for the Mitsui Mining organization, seldom seen with the top management, yet definitely on the payroll. Ted South and Jeff Harding were both well dressed, clean looking, business types, but were in fact skilled young assassins working for the Mitsui management behind the bamboo door. Identified as security management, few knew they had other high risk clandestine assignments.

"He should have been back by now," Ted said as he finished the last of his cold coffee.

"Let's wait till at least 1:00 a.m. before we give up trying to get the information tonight. Once we know he's got the data we can retrieve it and eliminate him as planned," Jeff coldly concluded. They continued to sit in silence waiting for their prey to appear.

At 12:45a.m., Jane had just left the laboratory to find a comfortable couch in the employee lounge when Jason said, "I'm fresh and ready to oversee the experiments till three if you want to relax Jane."

RICHARD TREVAE

"Jason, you're an answer to prayer." Jane smiled as she entered the lounge while Jason headed toward the lab. Jason was one of those bright, pleasant, eager lab techs worth twice the money Jane paid him for his work at Enertek and she had come to rely on him.

Jane's computer continued to setup and report on the methodical experiment variations being scanned in the lab. Jason had not noticed the steadily increasing trend line attempting to predict, and then pursue, a better combination of parameters for the upcoming experiments. Each experiment required about eighteen minutes to complete, and with twelve separate setups operating at once, the data flowed into the computer very fast. At 12:53 a.m., the trend line rose abruptly to 79%, then 85%, 88%, 95% and then a loud explosion occurred engulfing the entire laboratory, spreading heat and flames instantly throughout the lab and its adjacent technician offices.

Jason was ejected from his chair and hurled against a glass wall as it blew out. He died instantly. Expanding flames sent everything on fire. A brilliant orange cloud began rising from the lab site, and boiling flames erupted everywhere in the adjacent labs. A forty by eighty foot section of roof ripped open from the blast and released churning clouds of hot vapor and flames. The network computer monitoring the experiment recorded the last four seconds preceding the explosion and calculated a 100,000% energy yield compared to the energy inputted to the experiment. Results downloaded into the server network file XR-211 before the computer controlling the experiments was destroyed.

Toro never escaped his hiding place next to Jane's lab. The force of the blast killed him in seconds, followed by a wall of flames which overtook the laboratories on either side of the explosion.

Jane's eyes opened from her attempt, moments earlier to sleep, with an overwhelming sense that dramatic life changes were underway. Amid the security alarms, fire suppression systems, and general chaos in the laboratory, Jane finally saw the devastating damage which had destroyed three labs, killed four coworkers and cut her left arm from flying glass. Shaken, confused and frustrated Toro's co-conspirators were now frantic, driving away from their clandestine waiting location.

On his satellite phone, Ted speed dialed a Vancouver number. "Enter your password," the phone asked. Ted punched in 36.51.4189 and waited for a short tone, and then he said in disguised words, "Explosion at library, high order detonation. Asset likely lost, information not retrieved. Please advise."

Gilles Montrose received the message and immediately called Sang Huchara on his secure satellite phone. Sang Huchara listened to the message, and then dispatched an email, in encrypted format.

RICHARD TREVAE

```
To: The Knowledge Consortium Group
From: Member One
Subject: Urgent Meeting

Recent events require an imperative
meeting to discuss new near term
planning. Please plan to meet at the
standard Zurich location at 10:00 a.m.,
Friday, September 11, local time.
```

Within minutes, the four "members" were preparing their travel plans. The four members were Dr. Eli Weiss, Sang Huchara, General Yong of North Korea, and Defense Secretary Kytoma of Japan's cabinet, and all suspected the world had just changed.

The Knowledge Consortium Group, sometimes abbreviated in conversation between members as the 'KCG,' functioned practically as a hidden government with enormous access to technology, funds, international connections, and military forces all under a near impenetrable screen of security and privacy. Originally formed to identify, control, and provide energy technology for Japan and Israel without the direct or visible support of either government, it moved toward an interest in weaponry technology as the avowed enemies of both countries made their political intentions known — abolish Israel from the face of the earth and deny Japan oil for its economy.

Each member contributed a key element to the group and its objectives for their constituent members and countries. Sang Huchara personally committed $1.2 billion to initiate the organization and its endeavors. Secretary Kytoma controlled another $1 billion in Japanese government hidden budget funds for the group. Dr. Weiss, with arms length support and funding from the highest and singularly dominant leader in Israel, Defense Minister Hyriam Dyan, directed the technical and tactical field operations along with Sang Huchara. General Yong provided deep covert intelligence and operational direction in North Korea.

Passive members, referred to as 'associates,' received emails on activities and got a briefing every quarter on their overall activities, some legal and some not so legal. The associates were important for specialized knowledge, access, insight, or funding, for the day-to-day decisions largely handled by Huchara and Weiss. Many associates held powerful political positions in various governments with personal connections to Weiss and Huchara. Over the seven years of its existence the group had developed a group of associates and contractors numbering one hundred and fifty, with the potential to quickly assemble another five hundred on short notice.

Equipment, technology, weapons, transportation and, access almost anywhere in the world was achieved in the early months of operation. Banking from the foremost banks in Switzerland assured absolute security and protection of their assets and credible cover for the legitimate, as well as illegal, operations. Embedded and compromised sources of information such as Toro Nagama provided the Knowledge Consortium Group with information and data they had used many times to capture control of energy or military assets.

Through their network, they won the only bid on a Russian pipeline for natural gas serving Eastern Europe after they had eliminated the wealthy owner of their only competition for the pipeline. An electronics laboratory in Munich had been quietly purchased after the corporate parent got forced into bankruptcy, just as research obtained revealed they had a novel laser/radar imaging weapon system that could penetrate material much further and deeper than previous technology.

Details of something as important as the Elko find were never disclosed in general emails, so the few necessary messages were always cloaked in vague wording. However, when they achieved a real success a full-sanitized summary of the effort followed and on occasion a celebration meeting provided at exotic locations. The Russian pipeline project of 2002, which consistently yielded $800 million a year in positive cash flow, celebrated with the thirty-eight associates and their spouses in the south of France for a week, directly on the Med and all expenses paid. This kind of extravagance always fronted by Sang Huchara and his Mitsui Construction and Mining Company shifted the visible impressions away from the real entity, the KCG.

The prospect of controlling a slow fusion technology grew too enticing for the members and their participating countries to forego. They would have this for their own regardless the cost or obstacles. Their ability to project and deliver power and influence was unrivaled except for the major economies of the world.

WEEKS EARLIER
WALDRON RANGE MINE

The Mitsui Mining Company had earlier discreetly filled six fifty gallon drums of mining samples with the center portion containing the new ore find that Toro and Jane's group were evaluating. Now having retrieved the ore from the Haifa port, Dr. Weiss and his team were aggressively conducting their own series of investigative experiments.

RICHARD TREVAE

Mitsui and the Israeli energy unit, IEC, had an unusual pact. Sang Huchara of Mitsui was critical to the group for his ability to extend staff, equipment and technology to all ends of the earth. The Japanese, totally dependent on oil and swimming in U.S. dollars, were funding the Israeli research efforts in secret to stay atop energy developments, which helped both of their countries. Admitting the clear need for an oil alternative, Japan had the financial clout to become a partner, and Israel had the clandestine skills and will to secure and contain whatever new knowledge arose.

Moreover, Israel and Japan feared the emergence of a radical Arab group in the Middle East controlling oil and eventually nuclear technology. Years earlier the two groups, Sang Huchara's Mitsui Mining and Dr. Weiss's IEC, with support of Japanese Secretary Kytoma agreed to expand the Knowledge Consortium Group to include General Yong of North Korea.

General Yong had many years earlier made his political feelings known to the Japanese Defense Secretary Kytoma in a bold move to assist in taking down the oppressive North Korean regime if he would be welcomed and rewarded by the Japanese and the modern western capitalistic countries. His political leanings were not displayed openly in North Korea, and for that reason he continued to be advanced and rewarded with increased command assignments. At fifty-two years of age, Yong looked fit and formidable in his military garb.

He exhibited a commanding presence, even though he stood just five foot, nine inches tall, because of his penetrating voice, strong verbal skills, and a keen strategic mind for solving problems. Still he was content to remain a mid-level general and work in secret on his foremost desire to take down the current regime.

Yong obsessed to be the leader of a new democratic North Korea and re-establish the union of the north and south. The working relationships were all directed through Dr. Weiss and Sang Huchara who were the most forceful members of the consortium, and oversaw the day-to-day issues, keeping a pulse on their collective interests. The Enertek discovery of late represented the ideal technology advantage this group and their two countries needed for the future.

SATURDAY MORNING BEFORE LABOR DAY
RURAL VIRGINIA

DALTON Crusoe tried to ignore the vibrating cell phone next to his bed. After several seconds, recognizing the faint sound, Dalton awoke enough to realize that a call at 6:27 a.m. on a Saturday morning must be serious.

"Hello." Dalton groaned as he straightened up and cleared his eyes. A voice mail message prompted Dalton. Entering his pin to access voice mail, it played,

"Mr. Crusoe, this is Marjorie, Mr. Kosko's assistant. Yesterday Mr. Kosko's car was forced off the road near Seattle; he's injured and unconscious much of the time from a mild concussion. Doctors want to keep him sedated to reduce the swelling. He wakes every half-hour or so and struggles to stay awake, yet he has said, "Find Dalton, find Dalton" several times. He's at Seattle Claremont Hospital in room 279 under federal security, and would like you to call him." Dalton sat up quickly, punched in a few commands to his phone and the screen displayed, Message received Friday September 4, 3:40 p.m. PST.

Damn, Dalton thought as he looked back at Carolyn sleeping soundly. *This is a half-day-old already.*

A second message flashed, indicating it came from Ed Kosko. Message received Saturday September 5, 5:45 a.m. PST.

"Dalton, this is Ed. We have had an explosion last evening at the Seattle lab. I assume you are not on your way yet, so call me as soon as you get this. I'm in the hospital, and must remain here awhile. . . . I'm banged up a bit, kinda groggy with a concussion that hurts like hell, but I'm going to be okay. They ran me off the road and may be looking for the disks, be careful."

A third message followed by thirty minutes, it was Ed again, "We suspect problems have occurred with the fusion tests, perhaps sabotage, we just don't know. Can you get up there as soon as possible and meet with Jane Holman on XR-211? Call me in Seattle here by noon Monday after you've heard from Jane as to what's going on, and what she thinks happened. Okay? Sorry to mess up your weekend."

Dalton sat silent for a moment trying to focus his thoughts; Carolyn lay still asleep beside him so he went to the kitchen area and logged on to his laptop to make flight arrangements for Sunday morning. This was not what he and Carolyn wanted to deal with right now; though he knew had to get back to Seattle as soon as possible. Trying to compose his thoughts Dalton slipped back into bed, pulled Carolyn to him and held her close. She began to stir and instinctively burrowed her face into Dalton's shoulder. He kissed her forehead and said, "I have some bad news darling." Carolyn opened her eyes and sighed.

By 8:00 a.m. Saturday morning Dalton had explained to Carolyn the calls, with the shortened version background about Enertek's find, and they were packed and on the road by 9:00 a.m. A brief and frustrated embrace ended the short weekend for them that they both needed and wanted. Fighting back tears Carolyn made JD promise to call her when he could. He said without hesitation, "Yes, I love you and I'm sorry."

SUNDAY MORNING
WASHINGTON D.C.

Dalton had made the flight many times before, a non-stop Reagan International to Seattle/Tacoma that left at 10:40 a.m. local time. With luck, he would be in by2:30 p.m. Seattle time. The 767 lifted off with noticeable acceleration, a good sign Dalton thought — light load, fewer travelers, and faster air speed.

As he closed his eyes and tried to relax, he thought back to the troubling events surrounding Ed Kosko. He focused back to the fantastic single day and night with Carolyn. Surprisingly, he found Jane Holman in his thoughts; the single PhD senior lab manager at Enertek's Seattle laboratories. Jane loved her work and she made her skills very evident on several other priority applied research projects. Pleasant yet tough, she could operate in a man's world, manage teams toward results and still maintain her feminine nature. Everyone liked her and her team of researchers was the best in the northwest. Dalton wondered how she handled the stress of the explosion and what her thoughts were on its cause. The plane leveled out at 37,000 feet cruising without even a bump to disturb Dalton as he slept.

By 3:03 p.m. in the afternoon Dalton drove past the main entrance to Enertek toward his hotel two miles away. After unpacking, he jumped back in his rental car and headed to the site. The entire site was swarming with fire and rescue personnel protecting the damaged lab areas. As he approached the entry gate he was directed to the security team leader controlling access to the plant. The tall, disciplined man immediately scanned Dalton's security badge and verified his identity, offered a hint of an approving smile, and motioned him through to the lobby. Jane waited just inside and recognized Dalton from many previous meetings at the site with Ed.

"Ed called me last evening from the hospital here and

indicated he was planning to have you come up today," said Jane, fighting back tears. She offered her hand in a professional yet feminine manner, confirming his earlier impressions of her. Without hesitation, she led Dalton to the laboratory wing, down a long access corridor, and into the applied research section. The devastation looked massive, very intense at its origin and producing a one hundred and twenty foot diameter crater with everything in the blast area burned to a melted charred pile. The heat and force of the explosion were tremendous. Much more damage would have been done were it not for the fire rated walls and explosion relieving vents in the lab's ceiling.

"What was going on in here, Jane?" inquired Dalton. "Were you dealing with dangerous materials in your experiments that could explode?"

"Not really," proclaimed Jane, "we were running two experiments, all with tests involving property protocols, which usually does not favor reactions of this force." She wondered how much Dalton knew of the new test protocols.

"Well, perhaps this was sabotage; a political statement, environmentalist movement or something." Dalton's mind avoided the direct question concerning the suspected fusion capacity of the ore.

"I don't know. The work we were doing appeared routine, certainly nothing to warrant this kind of destruction. We detected no radiation however, so it does not appear to be a terrorist dirty bomb. Based on the devastation I'd say it was a standard fast combustion detonation."

"Can you retrieve the test procedures for me and take me through them? I must call Ed this afternoon and he would like to know our opinions on the cause. Can you help me with this?" Jane could not halt her involuntary expression about where the discussion was heading.

"Yes, of course, although one of the experiments was classified and only the summary file on the test purposes can be accessed by my level of security. Only, Ed Kosko can enter the full test protocol and tell you precisely what the objectives were." Jane studied Dalton, testing his authority to know her security concerns.

"Ed has asked to take complete charge of this problem. He gave me the full test protocols along with access codes. I need you to get me up to speed on slow fusion." Dalton remained humble and restrained. "Can you do that for me?"

Breathing a visible sigh of relief Jane said, "Okay, that's a comfort. I have to talk to someone who can see the big picture here. It's tearing me apart trying to sort out why or who made this happen." Forging a fearful expression she continued, "This discovery, if real, could change everything, right?" Dalton smiled and tried to settle Jane's nerves.

"Yes, that's true and we must keep the possibilities about this technology absolutely confidential until we know facts and have a full understanding of the discovery, meaning completing research on the Elko mine find."

Dalton withheld nothing and confirmed the fact he had the entire test protocol on the catalyst. He needed her full focused support and decided to wait and see what Jane returned with before compiling his assessment for Ed.

"I'll examine the explosion area and take some pictures while you're retrieving those experiment protocols; then you'd better get some rest, you look exhausted," offered Dalton.

"I'll get right on it. I hope the network is still operating, and yes, I need some shut eye, thanks." Jane smiled at him.

Dalton began to fear the worst when they removed Toro's body still carrying his Beretta nine millimeter in his shoulder holster. Toro was not listed on the roster of admitted employees for the weekend. Dalton's security badge fluttered in the light breeze, as it hung around his neck. A heavyset man with a full beard approached Dalton.

"Are you part of security here?" the large paramedic handling Toro's body asked.

"Yeah, that's me," said Dalton in a quick thinking response.

"Well, this guy's got a gun on him, and I don't know exactly what to do about it."

"I can take it with me, really. No problem," said Dalton. "He's part of our security; I'll take it for you."

Dalton retrieved the Beretta from Toro's shoulder holster and wrapped it in his handkerchief before stowing it in his soft briefcase. The paramedic seemed satisfied he had done the proper thing and began to secure Toro's remains in a body bag for transport. Dalton appeared to be overseeing and approving the activity as he slowly moved away from the ambulance and paramedic team.

Dalton worked hard at maintaining his focus while considering the facts and circumstances at the site. He had been previously introduced to Toro, and by all accounts, he was a valued and trusted researcher for Enertek. Yet Dalton's mind still reeled with questions. *Then why had he hidden in the laboratory, without being signed in . . . a complete mystery. Could he part of something bigger or just trying to steal secrets for his own gain or was he being blackmailed?*

Jane positioned herself at a network computer in the administrative area, far removed from the destroyed labs. She was able to log in to the main computer serving the laboratory that controlled the experimentation. After several false starts to access the protocol programs, she was finally able to enter the data collection and analysis memory. The data files were full, a very unusual event; however the lab exploded for some reason she concluded. Through a special command, she eventually accessed the results from all the experiments running at the time of the explosion. However the XR-211 files could only be downloaded to disks using encryption, which could be read only by her, Ed Kosko and a select few others, now apparently including Dalton. She reasoned Dalton would rather open and review the data together with Ed. A strange feeling overtook Jane — part scientific curiosity to examine the explosion data, and yet a real fear of unveiling a potential new weapon technology.

Moments later Jane located Dalton outside the security gate reviewing the status of the safety crews tending to the destroyed labs. She walked over and handed him the disks. "Here are your experiment files. The XR-211 files are encrypted, of course, and there's an enormous amount of data stored here. My God, this is scary, maybe our theory on slow fusion is real." Jane's voice had begun to tremble. Her technical training forced her to accept her earlier assumptions might be correct.

Dalton took the four small disks she held. "Thanks, you and I will get into these later"

"Do you think the experiments have something to do with causing this explosion?" Jane was persistent with her question. "Or did someone decide to halt our efforts by staging an explosion? And I can't figure why Toro was here." Her face began showing severe stress and some responsibility for the loss of life amongst her staff.

Dalton starred at her wondering how much she may need to know and how much he needed tell her. He paused to organize his thoughts before continuing. "I can't really say. We'll know more after we all review the results for answers. You know I'm not the scientific type." He had put on a calming smile to ease her nerves. Jane's face still looked torn over the power her experiments may have exposed.

"I can help you with this and I would like to since this was my lab and my staff lost in this disaster. I feel responsible." Her face turned determined, voice still trembling. A tear formed in her eye.

"All right, let's meet for dinner later and we will review what we know. Okay? Besides you really do need some rest."

"Fair enough. Can we meet at the Sheraton lobby around seven this evening?"

"That's fine. It's where I'm staying."

Dalton figured he would report to Ed prior to meeting Jane later. Back at his hotel, sequestered in a small business conference room, Dalton called Ed who had just received, via encrypted email, the files and opened the data. While waiting for the files to load and be opened, Ed told Dalton of his encounter leaving the Elliott Bay Crab House following their lunch meeting. Minutes after leaving the city and heading to the airport, his car was run off the road by a delivery van. He went over a steep wooded hillside leading to a fast river and rolled the vehicle several times. The car came to rest about fifty feet down the hill, wedged against a large tree, and Ed went unconscious.

"When I awoke the paramedics were tending to me. Strange though . . . my jacket, coat, pants and small brief case had been searched for something, yet all my cash and credit cards were still there. The rescue crew had arrived minutes after the crash and saw no one else nearby, just a silver Cadillac Escalade 'rubber-necking' the accident."

"You said earlier they were after the disks from Enertek . . . right?"

"Exactly, why go to the trouble of nearly killing me, leaving my valuables while searching? It had to be the disks I gave you they were looking for." Ed's left forearm suffered a cut and he was treated for a concussion, though expected to be released some time the next day.

The phone set to speaker mode fell silent — too silent, too long for Dalton to be comfortable much longer. Now both men were looking at the same data on their computer screens.

"Ed, it appears to me that this XR-211 test protocol in fact produced a combination of parameters which triggered this huge explosion, in milliseconds, what is it? Did the experiment go bad or what?"

"No . . . it found the optimal combination of reaction

parameters . . . and then went on to yield a huge energy release. The damn stuff catalyzed slow fusion! We've got a situation here for sure."

Both men froze in astonishment at the data before them. Ed continued in a controlled voice saying, "Dalton, I need you to meet me tomorrow afternoon at the Seattle administrative offices of Enertek with Jane after I'm released. I am ordering our security forces to monitor you and Jane until I arrive tomorrow. We should not talk anymore now on this line; do not take those disks outside your room and do not leave the hotel. Until we can arrange ample security you and Jane we must assume the folks who went after me for the files will next target you two."

Suddenly Dalton became aware of a heightened alertness. Ed Kosko was a man of clear thought, controlled decision-making and above all not an over reactive type. Therefore, he alerted Dalton that something very significant had occurred and the disk data might just put his and Jane's lives in danger. He reasoned that perhaps the new ore is in fact a catalyst for slow fusion . . . and led to the explosion! Finishing his call with Ed, Dalton said, "I'll connect with Jane shortly, stay with her, and let her know security is coming."

Dalton began to reflect on the recent events:

Could the disks Jane retrieved contain critical data about the explosion? If so would that be a valuable commodity, beyond sorting out the insurance matters concerning the human loss of life and the physical property damage. Dalton went over and over the information he had at hand: a new ore find; Toro dead on site without registering and armed; and then the actual explosion, its power and massiveness of destruction. Maybe the world did change with the lab explosion arising from a new fusion technology.

DALTON'S ROOM AT THE SHERATON

At 4:47 p.m., Dalton settled into his room and thought about alerting Jane without alarming her needlessly. As Dalton thought about his next move, the camera across the courtyard recorded his nervous pacing and tension.

The surveillance activity, by the Mitsui intelligence team, was being directed by Ted and Jeff, who were in constant communication with Gilles and his superiors operating out of Canada. Their assignment was to keep Dalton and Jane under surveillance and search their rooms, cars, and offices for information on XR-211. Dalton's activity had perplexed the surveillance team in that they knew he had met with Jane, the lab supervisor, over XR-211, although they did not know what they had learned if anything about the explosion or experiments. Without the ability to establish a 'bug' in Dalton's car or hotel business center, they did not know he had spoken to Kosko and been alerted to possible danger. Still, without the disk's data leading up to the explosion, Gilles and his men were no further along in their understanding of who knew about the potential of the new discovery.

Jane arrived about 7:10 p.m. and called Dalton in his room. Ed's security detail of two plain clothed NSA agents followed Jane's car from a safe distance as she drove to the Sheraton. They would hang out at the bar area away from Dalton and Jane yet visible from their dining location. Taking no chances Dalton hid blank disks in an empty laundry bag in his room closet. The original protocols from Ed and the disks obtained from Jane after the explosion were in the leather case and placed in Dalton's sport coat pocket. He left his room with the TV playing and lights on, however this provided no deception to the Mitsui security team. Watching Dalton leave his room, Ted called Gilles, "We are moving in now."

Gilles responded, "Leave no trace you entered his room, clear?"

Ted and Jeff moved fast, entered the room, searched for the disks and planted a bug for listening to Dalton's phone conversations. Uncertain of the time available,

Ted and Jeff made a brief, although neat search of Dalton's bags to not leave clues of their presence.

Jeff grabbed the laundry bag, and feeling the weight of the disks inside, opened the bag and said, "Got 'em, let's go." They called Gilles and said they had the experiment disks with the explosion data.

As Dalton waited at the lobby heading to the restaurant, he saw Jane approaching the front door.

"Has anyone followed you here Jane?" Dalton asked as he scanned the bar area and saw the security men.

"Well I don't know. I don't think so, why do you ask?" Jane said showing increasing stress.

"I talked to Ed and the security men assigned to us earlier are here. Although we have to be very careful what we say and where we speak, Jane. We need to find a quiet table away from everyone and I'll explain what I know." Jane's expression went solemn as Dalton suggested a sequestered table near an outer wall.

Dalton disguised his words and kept his voice very low as he explained how Ed nearly died in his car when it was run off the road following his meeting earlier last week, and that he became concerned about their safety and the security of the disks. He surmised something on the XR-211 disks during and after the explosion, held such significance that others would resort to desperate means to achieve it. He summarized Ed's remarks in a whisper, "The lab explosion data may well hold the key to an energy breakthrough so significant others may kill to own it."

Jane began to feel very uneasy and vulnerable about their predicament. The reality of the disks exposing a new, perhaps deadly technology jumped forefront in her mind. Dalton feared she may overreact.

"What should we do? I'm scared to death about what's on those disks, and where are they anyhow?" Starring straight at her, Dalton gently tapped his lapel, and Jane's face went pale.

"Shouldn't we put them in a bank vault or something?"

"No, Ed has security staff in place to protect us. He is due to leave the hospital tomorrow about three in the afternoon. All we have to do is stay low until then. Please don't worry; I'm not going to let anything happen to you . . . or these disks." Jane's expression could not hide her anxiousness over the predicament she was in.

Dalton remained calm and focused yet tried to keep the dinner conversation light as if they were on a date, although his eyes kept scanning every other patron in the room. He kept reassuring her the precautions were likely overkill arising from Ed's ordeal on the highway. Privately, Dalton felt just as nervous protecting the valuable disks. Jane appeared tense yet ate well and seemed to enjoy Dalton's company and his attempts to keep the conversation off the Enertek matters.

Undetected, Ted and Jeff sat far across the room disguised by scattered silk plants and stacks of papers and reports on their dinner table. They played a ruse appearing to be reviewing technical material. The innocuous looking tape recorder and its internal directional listening antenna which lay disguised on their dinner table continued digitally capturing sentence fragments as Dalton and Jane spoke.

After dinner, about 9:45 p.m. Jane and Dalton walked out with Ted and Jeff still carrying on the charade of a business meeting. Dalton walked Jane to her car.

"Go straight home and call me when you arrive, so I know you're okay," Dalton insisted. Jane started to cry and apologized for her emotions at the same instant. The security team would follow Jane home and monitor the house from their vehicle.

"I won't let you get hurt, don't worry. Call me when you get home okay?"

Dalton returned to his room and checked to find the laundry bag now empty of the blank disks just as he feared. His subconscious awoke, and initially broke into a small smile while thinking boy *are they ever in for a surprise.* Then the fact that someone *was* following him, and Jane, heightened his concern. Trying to be practical, yet not paranoid, Dalton questioned why anyone would go to the extremes necessary to retrieve the explosion data regarding the new catalyst. Maybe the explosion *was* the result of some new reactions never seen before and did present a new energy technology; and why attempt a killing on him or Ed Kosko to get the raw data? After all, the essential key was the raw ore at the Elko mine, managed by Mitsui, now being secured by a team Dalton could direct. Without the unusual ore, the research data reduced to only an intellectual exercise. It all seemed like too much attention, way too soon. Then a thought occurred which left him cold.

Maybe someone is ahead of the curve on this research. Maybe someone or some group already knew the power of this technology and did not want Enertek to complete its understanding of it using the explosion data.

He began to think perhaps Jane still might truly be in danger. Dalton checked the rest of the room. His TV and all the lights were on just as he left them. He began to wonder about the true power of the technology he held in the zippered leather case, now resting in his hands. A nervous chill fell over him for a moment, while starring at the leather case. He concluded it wise not to let the disks out of his reach. He slipped the case back into his jacket breast pocket.

Jane proceeded to drive the twenty minute route to her home. Traffic was heavy and an accident four cars back halted the traffic flow. Her security team followed an uncomfortable distance back as traffic bunched up. She moved along cautiously, nervous and tense however, trying to make no mistakes causing a missed turn or another accident. From nowhere, flashing lights appeared behind her and she trembled overcome with fear. *Had I been speeding, went through a light or what?* she asked herself.

The car behind her had two uniformed men in it and appeared to be a city police car. The driver got out and wore a short police type jacket and a badge displayed on the front. Jane felt a measure of relief as she watched the officer appear to her window. Seven car lengths back and stopped at a light, the two man security team looked through binoculars at the police car behind Jane. "It's just a local black and white. Maybe she needed directions. I'll get out and walk up to her, okay?" The younger agent looked for approval from his senior partner behind the wheel.

"Yeah, let's be certain she's okay. Be careful." He nodded and motioned to him to get out.

Approaching from the driver's side the uniformed officer leaned in. "Good evening ma'am, I noticed your tail light was out and I felt you should know since it is a violation. May I see your driver's license please?"

Jane fumbled around her glove box and then her purse for the information requested. The officer strolled around the car and shined his light into every part of the car interior.

"Here you are officer; I hope this doesn't take too long since my husband is expecting me home by now." The officer shown his light in Jane's face and did not see through her bold lie.

"Well ma'am I must check this out, I'll be right back." As he walked back, Jane watched in the rear view mirror. Ted South had done a good job of convincing Jane he was a policeman; although he wasn't, for he was part of Mitsui's security group. Within minutes of celebrating their good luck in finding the "explosion disks" Ted and Jeff learned they had been duped, and they were not about to let Jane Holman escape without checking to see if she had them in her car. Ted South returned to his car frustrated, "Damn things don't appear to be laying inside the car, maybe in her purse, or the glove box, or hell, the trunk." Jeff checked the rear view mirror. A man in a suit was slowly walking toward their cruiser replica.

"We can't keep this police impersonation up much longer without attracting a real cop. And there a several converging behind us less than a half mile away at the accident. I'll get in her car and drive away where I can do a thorough search," declared Jeff. "Turn off the damned flasher."

Jane became nervous, for the time had extended

beyond two minutes, and the flashing lights had been turned off. Her first emotion sprung to drive away, although as she thought about her fears she decided to wait quietly and endure whatever was going on. She retrieved her cellular phone and called the Sheraton, "Room 345 please and please hurry." Moments passed and Dalton answered.

"Dalton, this is Jane, I'm not home, and I've been stopped by a police car. . . . I guess my taillight is out. Wait, something isn't right. Dalton, the flasher light is off and it's taking too long." Dalton's worst fears flooded his mind.

"Jane, don't hang-up this phone, just keep it open while they return. Tell me what else you see unusual about the police car."

"Well, I don't know, although it looks different somehow. Oh my God Dalton, my taillights are both on. They said they stopped me for a burned out taillight, but I can see both rear lights reflecting off their bumper in my mirror."

Dalton's eyes then froze on two deep foot imprints in the thick carpet opposite the small table holding the phone and a lamp. The table legs revealed a similar visible imprint because the table had been nudged slightly from its original position. Dalton dropped to his knees as he said, "Jane I think you're probably just imagining things. I am sure it is a real police car. Before you hang up, I need you to return to the Sheraton and pick up a file I forgot to give you. Can you do that now, Jane?"

Jane's mind raced in confusion and she sat stunned for a moment. Dalton repeated and said, "Jane I need you to come now to the Sheraton. Can you do that now? Don't worry about the police car, I'll handle that matter."

Jeff Harding opened his passenger door and began to get out of the bogus police cruiser.

"Okay, I'll leave now." Jane reached for the gearshift and released her foot from the brake. Jane put the car in gear, pulled out into opposing traffic, turned left onto a side street and disappeared. The "police car" never moved or attempted to stop her. Jeff returned to the car and decided to call Gilles Montrose and update him on their fumbled attempts to retrieve the disks. Gilles listened in disgust and then demanded they continue surveillance on Jane and Dalton until they knew something. He forged a fist not happy with the news.

Dalton was taken back as he looked at the small black case, with a two-inch antenna fixed to the underside of the table. He hung up the phone and looked at the window. "Damn," he mouthed in silence and thought,

My theories on this catalyst might be right. Someone could be way ahead of us on this.

In a room two floors up Gilles Montrose listened, planning his next move while sipping a brandy, and smoking his fourth Marlboro of the evening. This was not going to be as easy as he thought. *This Dalton Crusoe character outsmarted me a second time. First, my men can't locate the disks on Kosko's almost dead body after running him off the road, and now they are suckered into grabbing blank disks from his room. I am starting to not like Crusoe.*

Jane was frightened, now certain the police car, and the officers, were not real. She drove with her eyes glued to the rear view mirror, checking to see if she was being followed. The accident scene, visible in her rear view mirror, complete with a fuming car stalled with its hood open, held traffic to a standstill in the opposite lane. As she approached the Sheraton, her body began to shake uncontrollably. Her phone buzzed alerting to a missed call; it was Ed's security men stating they had lost sight of her after the accident site. Her thoughts taken over with fear, *Could I be a target for murder?*

Jane arrived at the Sheraton entrance and left her car in the canopy area near the lighted front entrance. As she ran into the building, she looked about trying to see if she had been followed. No one in sight, she breathed a sigh of relief. As Jane approached the elevator, she tried to reason what caused Dalton to insist she return to the Sheraton for additional files; this did not make sense. With almost a frantic feel overtaking her Jane punched the up button many times. As the door opened and she stepped in, a hand grabbed the door and held it open as a rough looking, yet smiling man entered the elevator. "Thank you for waiting, what floor do you need?" he said with just a hint of a French accent.

"Three, please." whispered Jane, still shaking.

Gilles Montrose gleamed internally, now alone in an elevator with the woman overseeing the lab experiments. As the elevator slowed to the third floor, Jane moved to the front of the cab, and just as the door began to open, Jane squeezed through and ran into the hallway almost knocking over Dalton as he came out to look for her.

"I'm so scared, what is going on?" Jane's words were filled with fear.

Gilles Montrose released his grip on the nine-millimeter Glock and removed his hand from his jacket pocket. Remaining in the elevator car, he stayed out of sight of Jane and Dalton as the door closed. The elevator moved upward and Gilles thought to himself, *not here, too many people, too great a risk. Another time, another place.*

Dalton took Jane by the arm and ushered her out to the back area of the building near the conference rooms. Sensing his tension, Jane proceeded in silence. She walked with Dalton as though he were an upset boyfriend ready for an argument. Stopping abruptly, Dalton looked back at their route. "Jane, my room was bugged with some kind of listening device. I'm afraid they may have heard my conversation with you in your car. I just felt we were safer together here at the hotel than you being alone."

Dalton tried to speak in a calm voice even though he feared for their safety.

"What is going on? Why are we being followed? And this cop thing? What do they want?" Jane whispered.

"This all relates to the explosion at the lab," Dalton stated. "But I don't know who is behind all this surveillance and harassment. In any event, we are not going to take chances with these disks or our lives, this I assure you. We'll sit tight tonight and I'll have a new plan by tomorrow when we meet with Ed."

Dalton felt deep concern for Jane because the group following them must assume she has the disks and other valuable information about the lab experiments.

Dalton dialed Ed's cell phone, heard it ring once, and the call was sent right to his voice mail.

"I'll call you tomorrow at 8:30 a.m. sharp at your hospital room phone; we need to speak. Things have gotten more complicated." Dalton hung up and looked at a weary Jane.

"Look, I've arranged for another room, and you and I are going to spend the night together for security reasons, okay? The security team is back here and will be nearby all night." Nodding her approval Jane was still trying to understand how all the day's events connected to the Enertek explosion.

Jane went quietly into the bedroom of the two-room suite, and tried to sleep. Dalton checked out the phone stand, the bed, the wall hangings, and the television as he pondered the next steps to take in the morning. He eventually spread out on the couch with an eye on the bedroom door purposely left ajar. For a brief instant, he recalled his aborted weekend with Carolyn then focused back on the perplexing issues before them now.

As he hoped, Jane fell asleep in the bedroom. Dalton began to consider his next steps to get to the bottom of the trouble surrounding the Elko mine find. On the floor, just below his hand, lay the fully loaded Beretta pistol Dalton took from Toro's body. He held it, familiarizing himself again with the weight, feel, balance, and action of the weapon. He was good with handguns and had practiced at various ranges to maintain his competency. He dropped the fifteen shot clip from the weapon and noticed how much lighter it felt without a full magazine. In familiar fashion, requiring one second, he slammed in the clip, dropped the safety and aimed at the hallway door - *bang* he thought, *you're dead*. He was ready for the next day's round of trials.

Gilles Montrose left the Sheraton before 6:00 a.m. Monday morning and headed to the meeting place he'd set up for Jeff and Ted.

NEAR SEATTLE

JEFF and Ted made quick work of searching Toro's apartment before the police had arrived. Since the Seattle community had been led to believe that the explosion was an accident, no police were yet connecting Toro's presence at the site with his hidden agenda. Ted located Toro's laptop computer and stored it in a box of articles he gathered from the apartment. Proficient at their craft, Ted and Jeff left no trace of their activities.

As Jeff drove, Ted powered up Toro's computer and began to scan the files, scrolling through the typical timesheets, expense reports, staff memos, and the like. It appeared that Toro had not really stored much technical information about his work on the machine except for three files, all password protected. Unable to copy the files, Ted decided to call in for further instructions. Gilles Montrose answered the call as always.

Still in the mode of masking his words Ted said, "Gilles, this is Ted, the examinations we made are complete and nothing involving our business with the subject has been found. We have his computer, however, and three protected files are in memory which appear quite extensive; we've been unable to locate passwords, what would you advise?"

"Bring the articles you've located to me now. I want you two in Elko Montana this Thursday. Can you get here that fast?"

"Yes," replied Ted. "We will be there at 5:00 p.m." Gilles phone clicked off without further response.

"He sounds pissed, don't you think," inquired Ted.

"Yeah, Thursday's meeting should be interesting."

Gilles Montrose operated as the Director of Security for Mitsui Mining in North America; at least that was his public title. In actuality, Gilles was a fifty-one year old soldier of fortune, having led half dozen mercenary assignments over the last twenty-five years following his training in the Marines and duty in Somalia, Eastern Europe, Bosnia, and Iran. Murder for hire and strong-arm tactics utilizing new technology, communications, weapons, and explosives were the skill sets Mitsui found of particular interest in Gilles. Never one to make lasting friendships, Gilles was a big man at six foot, three inches, and built like an Olympic decathlon thrower; strong legs and upper body allowed him to overpower most men in hand-to-hand combat.

Operating from a field security office outfitted to connect Gilles with his employer through the Internet and satellite uplinks to vast data, he scoured every detail of Toro's personal and business activities. His computer had been delivered by Gilles's men, and he sent them for specialized supplies and equipment prior to their next meeting in Elko. Already he had learned Toro was a man with expensive tastes and desires. The money given Toro for his services to date was half-gone, and large debts were outstanding on credit cards and bank loans. Gilles discovered Toro's e-mail files and learned of a Susan Wallace living in Seattle and on occasion sharing her wilderness cabin in Montana, very near Canada and only a few miles from the mining site.

This smacked as too coincidental for Gilles to ignore. Toro had a girl friend and they probably vacationed at the cabin on Toro's frequent trips to the mining site. Perhaps he had hidden files with her at the cabin. Gilles played with the computer keyboard and soon had her addresses and phone number for Seattle and directions to her cabin. A visit very soon was an absolute certainty.

Susan Wallace had not heard of Toro's fate or the explosion at Enertek three days before. She had been in San Francisco for five days at a teacher's conference. Susan was an elementary school teacher, with special training in the learning-disabled child. She had particular skills in signing for the deaf, and had one class of fourth graders that were all deaf. She taught all general education subjects to this group including sciences, which were hobby interests of hers.

Susan and Toro had been seeing each other for about

two years. Theirs grew to a close, though not smother-
ing relationship. They had met at one of the many after
hours social haunts along the Seattle waterfront that all
of the well trained twenty and thirty somethings migrat-
ed to each evening after work. They had no special common interests except running and hiking, and it became
the basis for their first date. After that, Toro's charm and
Susan's caring personality kept them an item.

They both had their separate lives and interests,
although they each were committed to the other within the relationship. They spent most weekends together
and frequented Susan's wilderness lodge at Elko several times a year, particularly in the summer when Susan
had time-off and Toro used the good weather to com-
bine a mining trip with pleasure. Susan had been coming to the lodge for almost twenty of her twenty-seven
years. It had been her Dad and uncle's hunting and fishing retreat, and many wonderful memories were made
at the lodge. It sat secluded on a scenic one hundred and
eighty-five acre lake fed by mountain streams.
Surrounded by hundreds of miles of wilderness in every
direction, it was assessable only by seaplane; or for the
more adventurous, a rugged four-wheel drive vehicle
driven two hours over poor roads. Only two other, seldom used cabins were visible on the lakeshore. A sea-
sonal dock, extending from the lodge, allowed the

adventurous couple to fly in from nearby Elko in a rented seaplane for their long weekend getaways.

Susan loved to come to the lodge and had hiked and camped the area for many years. Although not a hunter, she loved to fish and live off of the land, if only for a week at a time. Toro's interest, of course, moved toward being with Susan who with her athletic stature and striking good looks, made for very romantic escapes. Susan's Dad and uncle had run outfitting and guide tours to hunters and explorers for much of Susan's teenage years. Eventually, the effort became too much for the two men and following the unexpected death of Susan's uncle, her Dad lost all interest in returning to the lodge. Only Susan, along with her companions, now exclusively Toro, were visitors to the area.

Susan returned to her apartment, collected her piled newspapers and mail, inserted her key and entered. The three-day-old headline "Seattle Lab Explodes, Killing Four" made Susan's heart race and pound. She dropped her bags and the rest of the mail, and then ripped through the paper to read the story. A photo of the destroyed lab smoldering in a twisted pile of steel and concrete made her well up and start an uncontrollable sob. Her mind went into overdrive. *Could Toro have been killed? Was he on or off duty at the time of the explosion? Was he all right?* Susan pressed the play button on her phone answering machine — three messages, one solic-itation, one hang-up, and one call from a female co-worker. Not a word from Toro or anyone at Enertek. Fumbling with her phone, she tried to call Toro's home phone. No answer came forth except his usual short phone greeting. "Toro, it's Susan calling please pick-up" Several moments passed. "Please call me as soon as you get home, please." Fearing the worst she called Enertek, only to get a recorded message stating all communica-tions about the explosion were to be directed to an information number. Dialing the phone Susan began shaking, fearing the worst.

"Good morning Enertek information center, may I help you?" replied the pleasant female voice.

"Yes, I'm a friend of Toro Nagama and can't locate him. Can you tell me of his whereabouts?"

The information team had been alerted to the possi-bility of Susan Wallace's call and directed it to Dalton, in his hotel room at close to midnight. Jane had slipped off into an uneasy sleep. Dalton heard the receptionist announce Susan Wallace on the phone. He believed Susan may have known why Toro checked in the lab so late.

"One moment please." The phone clicked.

"This is Dalton Crusoe; to whom am I speaking please?"

"I am Susan Wallace a friend of Toro's, is he all

right?" Dalton sensed the concern in her voice and spoke softly.

"Ms. Wallace I have some bad news concerning Toro. I'm so sorry to tell you Toro was killed in the explosion. He has been moved to the Callahan Funeral Home on Lexington Avenue. Do you know the location?"

Susan stood frozen in shock and felt faint.

"Ms. Wallace, are you all right?"

"No I'm not alright," she screeched. "How did this happen to him? I thought the explosion happened late at night; was he working?"

"Ms. Wallace, I don't know the reason why Toro was there. Could I meet with you at the funeral home some-time in the morning?" Dalton's voice was sympathetic.

Susan wiped her face of tears, and quietly said she would be heading there at daybreak.

"I'll be there when you arrive, Susan, and I'm sorry for your loss," replied Dalton.

Dalton figured Susan might lead him to clues as to what Toro was up to at the lab. He wondered if she knew about his weapon and unregistered entry into the lab that fateful evening. Then again, she may have known nothing of Toro's plans. They were close and an item, though Dalton felt Toro had somehow become involved with serious espionage issues, for significant money. Yet Dalton seriously doubted Toro would involve his love interest in the details. However, she may know things which meant nothing to her, yet were crucial to Dalton's understanding of what happened. A trip to the mine and the cabin was worth it, and Susan Wallace had to come along.

Susan arrived early and sobbed over the closed casket holding Toro. Dalton approached from a distance and took notice of her slender, athletic frame, short straight hair, and very caring face. She composed herself as Dalton came near, and quietly introduced herself, offering a warm though quivering handshake. Dalton extended his condolences and offered to sit with her on a sequestered couch. The hasty search Dalton ordered found no living relation for Toro in the U.S.

"Ms. Wallace, are you aware of living relations of Toro?"

Susan looked up and studied Dalton's face for a moment. Comforted by Dalton's apparent sincerity and concern for her loss, she replied, "Toro was alone in this country and the only extended family he had, not close relatives, were living in Japan." She began to sob uncontrollably.

Jeff and Ted sat motionless in their car at the back of the parking lot at the Callahan Funeral Home and watched Susan walk to her car along with Dalton. As they approached the car Ted could just overhear the conversation of Dalton and Susan through the micro listening antenna aimed at them from some sixty yards away.

"Susan, we can't account for Toro's presence in the lab at the time of the explosion, do you have an idea why he was there working late?" Dalton saw only confusion and questions on Susan's face.

"I have no idea, Dalton. He never seemed to be that interested in working extra hours."

Carefully thinking how to phrase his next question, Dalton proceeded with caution. "Susan, did you ever visit the mining site in Elko, Canada with Toro?"

Susan reacted with surprise "Yes, several times, over this summer. Why? Does the mine have something significant to do with Toro's death?"

Dalton studied her face attentively. Dalton looked into Susan's eyes as he spoke. "I believe it may well have, Susan. When you last visited the mine where did you two stay?"

"We most always stayed at my family's cabin, near Elko."

"You said your family has a cabin at Elko?"

"Well, yes, it was my uncle's and dad's hunting cabin for years, now it's mine."

"Did Toro have work papers or files at the cabin?" Dalton pressed.

"Ah, yeah, sometimes I guess, on his laptop, but

there were no outside communications, not even a phone line."

"How near is the cabin to the mine Susan?"

"What? Oh, about eight to ten miles by car, but through the wilderness only about five miles; we used to hike it for the exercise and beauty of the trail. We even camped out when we had time."

"Susan you need to take me there tomorrow."

"Well why, I have school to teach and Toro's funeral, and—"

"Susan, this is very important. And it may pose a risk to you if we cannot find out what Toro was doing at the mine. Go home now, make plans for being gone several days, and I'll arrange for you to be taken to the airport tomorrow at 9:00a.m. This is very important."

Bewildered, yet convinced through Dalton's sincerity, Susan agreed. "All right, I guess I can do that, but I'm still confused." Susan nodded and then walked away to her car. Jeff and Ted shut off their listening devices as she drove away. They called Gilles Montrose to inform him that they were on their way to Elko that evening.

SEVEN

THE SEATTLE SHERATON

JANE Holman never slept well at night, even at home, and hardly at all in a hotel room, yet that night she had managed to sleep until 10:05 a.m. Dalton had awoken much earlier and stationed the two security guards at opposite ends of the floor corridor. A note to Jane from Dalton stated he would be back before noon; that he had talked to Ed Kosko and then had gone to see a Susan Wallace.

She was thinking about the horrible events of the last three days when Dalton returned, ordered an early lunch in the room and explained the information he had gained from Susan. Jane agreed to wait for Ed Kosko's security team to escort her first to her home for a fresh set of clothes and on to the airport at 12:20 p.m. Jane looked relieved she didn't have to carry the disks she retrieved from the network computers monitoring experiments during the explosion. That task became Dalton's responsibility.

The dark glass limousine appeared at exactly 11:59 a.m. and she was escorted down by Kosko's security team. Dalton drove his own car to pick up Susan who seemed to be still perplexed about Dalton's interest in the cabin and her stays there with Toro.

The twin engine Beachcraft Kosko had provided Dalton with for their trip to Elko from Seattle was ready to go, with the engines purring. Dalton and Susan arrived moments before Jane did, along with Steve and Kirk of Ed's special security team — tough, heavily armed and fitted with the latest intel and communications gear. Ed was taped up; moving in slow motion and a little sore from the car crash, however no further concussion pain. The pilot, Harrison, welcomed everyone aboard and announced preparations for take–off. Steve and Kirk took seats in the rear and secured their weapons and gear. The business jet hit the runway, gained speed and lifted off into the morning sky.

Ed Kosko, with help from Dalton, took the flight time of eighty minutes to explain the circumstances of Toro's death. However, they were careful to keep the reasons for the explosion from Susan. Dalton had earlier warned Jane about giving Susan too many details.

Susan looked out the window to the beautiful sky, clouds, and forested mountains below as the approached northern Montana. She began to sob; Jane moved to a near vacant seat and tried to calm her. Toro's death was a painful loss for Jane as well.

"How could this happen, Jane? I thought Toro's work

was just normal research; how does someone die from that?" Susan held her face in her hands and continued to cry.

Jane comforted her, unaware of the connection Toro had with the Mitsui crime organization. Ed and Dalton were genuine in their sorrow for Susan without exposing their fears and concerns about Toro's involvement in the explosion.

Eventually Susan settled into a near sleep and let her mind drift back to the many wonderful trips she and Toro had at the cabin. Her heart ached and she fought back tears. She could not understand how Toro's work could have possibly endangered either of them. After all, he was a mid-level research scientist, working as part of Jane Holman's team. Susan was not aware of the nights, together at the cabin, when after she fell to sleep Toro would summarize and store his stolen data for Sang Huchara. All she could imagine involved her lover working extra hours allowing them, over time, to marry and start a family. That is what she really wanted; and Toro remained supportive, although not rushing to premature schedules. Susan recalled he used to say he was "waiting for his ship to come in." Whatever that meant.

Susan thought maybe his work provided special opportunities to jump ahead in his career and that's why he worked those late hours. More questions began to rush through her mind. Why did he dress in a black running outfit, when he was at work late in the evening? Then it occurred to Susan, maybe Toro knew something about the company or its work that others would pay him to divulge. She began to reflect, her heart started to beat faster, her mind snapped alert and running through awful scenarios. Maybe Toro was selling information or blackmailing someone for advancement or money. What could he know that others would pay for or even need?

In a burst of consciousness, she straightened up and realized maybe Toro was doing his own research and selling information to others. Dalton's words came back to her. "Toro's work at the mine may pose a risk to you...."

She had heard Toro mention the new ore found at the mine site when she and Toro met after work, weeks earlier. Several of his co-workers had briefly discussed the find with him. Nothing more than standard shoptalk she reasoned, although it seemed like the only link to the mine — and the new ore.

Susan managed to calm her nerves and tell Dalton her theory on Toro's action's the night of his death. Dalton listened carefully, he allowed Susan to hold onto her idea without divulging too much information about what Toro had stumbled upon. He allowed her to think he was just in the wrong place at the wrong time in his search for information to sell.

Dalton tried to comfort Susan again by telling her

about Jane's high regard for Toro. Susan felt as though she betrayed her feelings for Toro by not attending the brief committal service following his cremation later in the day. Again she broke down. Jane assured her that other Enertek workers and friends of Toro would be in attendance for the committal. Right now her critical issue focused on finding out how Toro came to be in the lab during the explosion and what he may have learned about the test results. She settled down somewhat and relaxed as she looked out the window.

The sky at the horizon began brightening as the plane glided lower and lower toward the small unmanned airstrip near Elko. A mist drifted above the thick pine forest and the small lakes and wetlands glistened with the low sun angle. The rolling forests were everywhere it seemed, and they were showing the first sign of fall with the tree tops changing color and reflecting the early afternoon sunlight through the thin clouds now disappearing just above the horizon. The entire group became somber as the plane drifted lower and lower toward the tree tops. Susan had tears sliding down her checks as she looked at the beautiful views and recalled her times with Toro.

Ted, Jeff, and Gilles sat watching in the Jeep Grand Cherokee with the engine off and windows up in the thick woods surrounding the airstrip as the Beachcraft made a smooth landing and came to rest at the small parking area at the end of the strip. Jeff took long distance photos of Jane, Susan, Dalton, and Ed as they deplaned.

Gilles had arrived a day earlier and hiked it back to Susan's lodge. After skillfully working the locks open, he had gone through the entire eleven hundred square foot cabin in search of anything Toro may have hidden there concerning his earlier work for Mitsui and anything about this newest mineral find. Gilles efforts found nothing, yet he could not get too aggressive and tear open walls and floors with Susan and the entire Ed Kosko entourage coming in. Doing what he could, he examined and videoed the entire place, as well as planted a minute listening bug in the main sitting area of the cabin. He and his fellow soldiers could listen in from a half mile away and learn any plans Ed and Dalton were arranging.

Toro was an amateur, though not stupid, so he had recorded all his communications with Sang Huchara. Whether it was emails or memos he scanned, photos of the Enertek building and grounds, an outline of his entrance and escape, Swiss financial accounts, passwords, or other records, they all were summarized exactly the way a researcher would organize for a new experiment. This was a "grand experiment" as far as Toro was concerned and he wanted no trail anywhere, he might occasion. So he stored the data on a small

4GB flash drive, password protected and hidden in the zippered cover of a small pillow always sitting on the overstuffed living room couch. A place he and Susan had made love on many times. It gave him a smug sense of power placing the pillow under Susan's head as they lay on the couch. Careful to avoid unwanted questions Toro always toiled on his "work log" late in the evening when Susan had already fallen off to sleep. She had no clue as to Toro's reckless undertakings.

By 3:30 p.m. Ed, Dalton, Susan and Jane arrived at the cabin. Susan broke down again as they approached the front door. Dalton stopped instinctively a few hundred yards from the entrance to the cabin and surveyed the perimeter with his binoculars. Visibility was limited except when one scanned the beautiful one hundred and eighty five acre lake located in front of the cabin.

"Looks like we're all alone," Dalton said in playful voice, trying to put a happier mood on the group. Nevertheless, Dalton pressed his forearm against his side to sense the unmistakable feel of his handgun.

As Susan opened the door, Kirk pulled out a small black box the size of a pack of cigarettes with several LED lights and buttons. As he stared at the device he pointed it around the rooms, listening to the comments of Susan as she gave the group a mini-tour.

Ed whispered something into Dalton's ear. "Kirk's picking up a listening bug, somewhere in the main living room."

Dalton's face grew tight as he considered the implications.

Once familiar with the cabin interior, everyone began to wander back to the Jeep to retrieve their light luggage. Ed halted the men near the car and said, "Listen carefully and say nothing. We've been compromised by an unknown party who has planted a bug in the cabin. Keep all conversation light and Dalton and I will explain our plan. I want Steve and Kirk to sweep the perimeter for signs of intruders." The two combat-trained security men nodded in full understanding.

"I'll alert the women to avoid discussions of our plans for tonight and tomorrow," whispered Dalton. Ed nodded in agreement.

Jane listened to Dalton's warnings and just about fainted. She wasn't able to speak even if asked to. The thought that someone, some group, had invaded their every conversation and location was too much to absorb. Susan just focused on Ed then Dalton, realizing it must be related to Toro's death. She strained at remaining calm.

Returning to the cabin, Dalton suggested they relax

for the evening and set out in the morning for the mine. Ed said nothing however he winked his understanding to Dalton. Time was needed for Steve and Kirk to do the surveillance. All conversations were orchestrated to comfort Susan about Toro's death and make it appear as if tomorrow's mine visit was routine. On paper, Dalton explained that the disks Jane had provided revealed that some sort of intense energy release occurred to cause the explosion at Enertek. It was a massive explosion considering the amount of material involved, and had come to the researchers as a sudden surprise.

It was close to four o'clock in the afternoon, fifty-five degrees and a light cool wind in the fall air. Steve and Kirk removed their business suits and donned black commando uniforms with plenty of firepower. Trained in the Delta Force unit of the military, Steve and Kirk were right in their element. Eager to begin a perimeter search Steve said, "Let's stop radio talk for about two hours while we make the loop around the cabin." Kirk looked and nodded. Synchronizing their watches they confirmed a meeting or "call in" at 5:50 p.m. if they had not made visual contact with each other.

The terrain was covered in forested hills, though not dense. They headed out opposite each other — one north then east, the other east then north until they encircled the cabin and met up on the eastern side. From maps of the area, both men knew they would have to cross two small creeks feeding into the unnamed lake where the cabin sat. Various sections around the lake were dense, covered with new short cedar and fir trees, tightly packed and running near the lakeshore most of the time. Other areas were covered with mature beech and aspen, which left the forest floor somewhat open and covered in bright yellow leaves. Pockets of low thick brush and hard woods blocked views and passage about every two hundred yards. The only easy path through and around this forest maze were on the deer trails seen everywhere circling the lake. Steve and Kirk never saw each other again as they left to search the cabin perimeter.

Meanwhile Gilles Montrose had hunkered down in a perch some twenty-five feet in the air amongst a thick stand of cedar and fir very near the eastern creek that one of the two Enertek security men would have to cross. At less than one-quarter of a mile from the cabin, he was in an excellent position to monitor the conversations in the cabin and yet have his presence hidden in the dense cover and the sound of flowing water fifty yards from his perch. Gilles was well stocked with rations for days, a nine-millimeter handgun, two hundred rounds of ammunition, a special scope equipped H&K assault rifle as well as explosives. His dull black camouflage backpack provided a heavy, although comfortable, back rest for his stand. Ted and Jeff were still in their vehicle listening to the cabin conversation and using a radio link to keep Gilles informed. They were situated on high ground with a distant view of the Waldron range and able to see if unwanted visitors came down the blacktop road and turned onto the two track trail leading to the cabin.

Gilles was a high paid covert operative, available for hire by the highest bidder. He had no political allegiances or emotion, except his own survival and continued lavish lifestyle when not on assignment. Born to French Canadian parents working in Syracuse, New York at his birth, Gilles became an immediate dual American and Canadian citizen. He always maintained his dual citizenship and spent leisure time, when not on an assignment for Sang Huchara, at a remote hunting lodge thirty miles north of Montreal.

At fifty-one Gilles had gone from ten years as an American military operative working for German Special Forces, to disappearing, to taking on one or two lucrative assignments per year. He wanted to be out by fifty-five with ten million dollars in Swiss accounts and living on his own Mediterranean island. This job, if fully completed, would put him over the top. A clean three million dollars, a quarter already received and the rest after completion. There in lay the challenge. He had to capture the disks intact, neutralize, or kill, all those pursuing the source of the explosion at Enertek and plant a bomb to consume the mineral catalyst in place with a small yet effective nuclear package. As he listened to the staged chatter in the cabin, he saw the careful moves of Steve maneuvering his way north. He was about three hundred yards out and heading straight toward Gilles.

Dalton wrote a note to Jane and Susan that he and Ed were going to step out on the front porch for privacy. They were to keep chatting as though nothing had changed. Both women nodded in somber acknowledgement of the frightful state in which they found themselves.

In a low voice Ed said, "Tomorrow we'll all leave early and head to the mining site operations office. It is the safest place since it appears we aren't alone out here. Someone else is also looking for these disks." Thinking for a moment both men were perplexed.

"Ed, who else even knows the XR-211 tests were evaluating this mineral find?" Answering his own question, Dalton spoke in hushed tones, "That's where Toro apparently came in. His financial records show deposits not attributable to his employment, family gifts, or lottery winnings. My guess is he's been turned by some group trying to infiltrate our general energy research and caught wind of this find leading to the explosion."

Ed nodded his agreement.

While enduring a mock discussion between Jane and Susan about her many trips to Elko with Toro, Dalton was busy writing notes to Susan to find out where Toro may have hidden anything. Susan pointed Dalton to a piece of trim wood around a living room window. The wood, a 1"x 6" piece of rough sawn cedar, looked normal enough though upon careful examination was hinged on the backside, unseen from the room. Using a small knife blade, Dalton was able to flip a small hidden brass latch, which held the board tight to the wall. Dalton's face froze still as he slowly opened the trim board. He motioned to Susan who had written that this was a spot her grandfather had kept rifles and ammunition secure from possible looters. Tucked into a small cavity built into the outer wall were two deer rifles, a Winchester 270 bolt action and a 30-30 Marlin lever action. Two boxes of shells for each gun were stacked and stored in a plastic bag in an effort to keep them dry.

Susan approached and whispered to Dalton, "This is all that has ever been stored in here."

Dalton took a small flashlight from his jacket pocket and aimed it throughout the hidden cavity. At the top of the opening, was a large envelope taped to the ceiling of the opening. Dalton retrieved the envelope and motioned to Ed. Susan looked on with complete surprise. He motioned to the women to keep up the idle chatter. Inside the envelope were several check stubs, copies of emails, and one sheet of almost blank paper containing, a phone number, a street address, and an e-mail address. The phone number was an international number to Vancouver. Curiously at the bottom of the page was a phase in quotation marks:

"Rest Comfortably."

Dalton pondered the message. Clearly, this was something Toro had left, although what did it mean?

Ed and Dalton headed to the back bedroom after making a few harmless remarks for the benefit of possible listeners, motioned to Susan to continue her discussion with Jane. Both women nodded affirmatively.

Gilles Montrose listened for clues suggesting the cabin occupants knew of his bug or prior search of the cabin. Convinced his presence was unknown, he positioned his silenced assault rifle sight on Steve who now was within one hundred and fifty yards. It was 3:25 p.m. and the woods were full of the sounds of birds, bugling elk, rippling water, and a mild breeze. It could not have been better for his plan to kill his opponent while he approached. Moving the trigger lever to single-shot action rather than automatic Gilles steadied the rifle against his shoulder and cheek, looked through his cross-haired scope and found Steve stalking slowly through the woods and looking into the sun as it slipped lower in the bright sky. Gilles saw through his rifle scope the extent of Steve's equipment including his communications headset and knew his prey was not a lone wolf; perhaps connected to someone else, or worse, to someone else also in the woods.

Gilles moved the scope to a position ten yards ahead of Steve's walking route. The ground was covered with leaves and nearby small pines afforded a partial sound barrier between the target and the cabin. Maneuvering the rifle and scope back on the prey, Gilles took a deep breath, held his crosshairs on Steve's face and squeezed the trigger. One muffled shot at ninety yards caught Steve in the left cheek bone of his face, exploding in his head and killing him instantly. Steve fell to the ground limp and lifeless. His weapon was silent, and he never alerted Kirk through their headset radios. Gilles settled in to await nightfall when he would sneak up on the cabin, kill the inhabitants, secure the disks he presumed they were carrying and collect his remaining fees. The isolated setting was perfect, the targets were all there, and he was ready and would not be denied. Emotionless, Gilles lit a cigarette and settled back to rest.

Kirk continued to stalk about three-quarters of a mile to the north and was unable to hear the muffled single rifle shot killing his partner.

4:45 p.m. came and went after Kirk reached the meeting point with Steve about five minutes ahead of schedule.

"Scout one to scout two, come in," Kirk breathed into his headset speaker.

"Come in two," Kirk said with a fraction more urgency. *What could this mean?* thought Kirk. The equipment used never failed and the weather was perfect.

"Scout two, come in please," Kirk tried again. Training always taught Kirk to suspect the worst. Retrieving his radio Kirk called Ed Kosko.

"Kosko here Kirk, where are you?" inquired Ed, moving to the front porch area away from the known bug.

"I'm about three clicks north east of the cabin waiting for two. But he hasn't appeared nor responded, over."

"Come into the cabin, one, I'll meet you in front by the cars."

Twenty minutes of double-time later Kirk came into view and met Ed and Dalton some fifty feet from the cabin front porch.

"Our bug listener may be tactical, meaning armed and dangerous, rather than seeking only intelligence," explained Dalton. Kirk's expression turned very serious.

"I thought I heard a muzzle blast. Did you hear it?"

"No. Nothing," replied Dalton

"You found and removed the bug?" Kirk hoped for progress securing the cabin.

"Yeah we found it and we've left it, assuming the

listener was remote and just gathering intelligence, but we have no idea who this is or how they knew of this cabin. There's a bigger picture here than we're seeing." Dalton sighed. "I was hoping you and Steve would find the listener and we'd get some information on the group shadowing us. If there was a rifle shot and Steve is non-responsive, we must assume he is lost to us. I expect some form of encounter with us tonight or tomorrow, don't you agree Kirk?"

"Yes, I'll set up in that tree which should give me a view of the cabin all night." Kirk pointed to a large tamarack in the distance.

"Good. Ed and I will alternate taking a watch inside the cabin until dawn. Is that okay with you?"

"Yeah, I'm going to get set up now. We'll communicate through my headset phone. Do you two have the equipment with you?"

"Yes, we just didn't expect to use yet." Ed grimaced. He really hadn't planned on needing it this early in the game.

Dalton explained to Susan and Jane about the concern of a nearby hostile, perhaps the one listening. The women tried to go to sleep, assured Ed or Dalton would stand guard and Kirk was set up outside to watch for an intruder. It was hard for everyone to ignore the magnitude of the information that Toro's disks might contain ... data which some other party was ready to kill for.

Kirk positioned himself about twenty-two feet up in the large tamarack tree about one hundred and twenty-five yards from the front porch. He was facing southwest with a clear view of the entire cabin and the surrounding woods. He was comfortable, having found a wide crotch upon which he could perch and lay back to catch short naps. By eight-thirty, the woods were dark and there was very little wind to create a background noise level. Kirk thought of his friend Steve, who he feared was lost, helped keep his senses sharp as the night chill rolled in. Kirk slipped into a semi-conscious state, waking every minute or two to look around. Time slipped by at a crawl.

Kirk woke with a sudden flinch, he had been deep asleep, and was startled by the full bright moon reflecting on his body and equipment. He surveyed the surroundings, seeing nothing he settled down a bit. He saw a small light glowing in the cabin; hopeful it meant Dalton or Ed was awake and alert.

Gilles stood leaning up against a large pine tree directly east of Kirk about one hundred and eighty-five yards away. He had been watching Kirk and the cabin for over two hours, and relishing the fact that he had managed to get into an attack position without the security specialist, Kirk, even knowing of his presence. Gilles listened constantly for talk over the communication headset he had taken from Steve's dead body. Then almost on cue, Kirk called into the cabin,

"Scout one checking in, come in."

Dalton whispered back, "All's quiet here, how's your situation?" Grateful to hear Dalton's voice, Kirk said,

"All is well, no hostiles seen."

Making small moves, Gilles screwed the silencer onto his Heckler–Koch assault rifle. He had let twenty minutes pass since the last communication from Kirk. All appeared quiet and he hoped the man named Dalton inside was also drowsy. Gilles adjusted his position against the large pine tree to shield the muffled muzzle blast from the cabin. He wanted every advantage in taking down the cabin inhabitants.

Gilles looked through the night vision scope and could clearly see Kirk, motionless and sitting in between the tree trunk and two large limbs extending out to make a comfortable resting platform. With no wind, no obstructions, and one hundred and eight-five yards the 223-caliber ball would exit the barrel at about 3,200 feet per second. The shocking power alone could render a man unconscious even if hit in a non-vital area. Gilles chose a high chest shot, believing that his target probably had a protective vest which would provide effective coverage over an area from waistline to a few inches below the chin. Crushing the windpipe, disabling speech and perhaps hitting a main artery in the lower neck would do the job just fine, he thought. As in a dozen prior kills, Gilles was methodical and patient, looking and waiting for the perfect moment to strike.

Having never failed an assassination assignment, Gilles remained confident and cool as he steadied the scope on Kirk's upper chest held his breath and in a seemingly endless process pulled the trigger back until it released the firing pin. An instant later a muffled shot left Gilles's rifle, no echo, no detectible noise, no warning. Kirk fell from the tree and hung some ten feet off the ground suspended by the security straps holding him in the tree. He dangled lifeless and made no sound over his headset. Gilles smiled at his own resourcefulness. To Gilles, it was like shooting ducks in a pond. There was no movement or noise from the cabin. Now was the time for him to approach the cabin.

Dalton had just taken a long sip of his not-so-warm coffee when he saw a faint flash of light — a muzzle flash he instinctively concluded. He focused looking out the window and saw the suspended form of Kirk dangling in the dim moonlight. Dalton's heart began to race; what were they up against here? He questioned, *Why all this firepower and where did they come from . . . who do they represent?* Dalton withdrew, slipped back to the couch and woke Ed. "We've got visitors, Kirk's been shot, get up real slow." The two women were still asleep, having given in to the stress of the last few days and comforted by all the firepower guarding them.

Ed and Dalton sat armed with pistols and now the 270 Winchester rifle stored in the cabin. Dalton surveyed the dimly lit woods although he saw nothing. Many minutes had passed, and Dalton wondered when the next shots would come — at dawn when light improved, or sooner. Suddenly the air lit-up, full of gunfire; a man coming up the front steps to the porch was firing back at Kirk, and Kirk, wounded but not yet dead, was firing from his slung position in the tree. Two rounds hit Kirk in the left leg, causing him to scream with pain. Gilles took a hit in the leg, fell to the ground, rolled and fired a dozen rounds back at Kirk and then aimed toward Dalton. The cabin was torn apart by the rapid onslaught of gunfire. A full twenty rounds hit the cabin, yet none found Dalton. Ed dove behind a large padded rocking chair and tried to get into position to fire at the shadowy shape of the man he saw on the porch. As he rose up to see, two of Gilles rapid-fire rounds caught Ed Kosko, one in the left shoulder, shattering the joint and causing massive bleeding. The other drove through the neck just missing the carotid artery although damaging the voice box. Ed dropped to the floor motionless.

Dalton stood up, leveled the 270 at the man on the ground not twenty-five feet away. He fired, causing the window glass to break in a violent burst; jerked on the bolt action and threw another round in the chamber. Gilles crouched on one knee and turned toward Dalton as he completed firing on Kirk. Searching through the scope of the 270 Dalton again saw the man now getting up and aiming at the cabin. Dalton fired again, missing, and Gilles spun around shooting his Heckler-Koch randomly toward Dalton, as he ran off into the dark woods. Kirk reached for his combat knife and cut himself down from the pine tree. Gilles first shot went right through Kirk's upper chest just below the collarbone, a painful, bleeding, however not lethal, wound. The two leg wounds were on the front of the upper left thigh missing major blood vessels. He would recover.

Jane and Susan were out of bed and screaming for Dalton and Ed. Meanwhile Ed was laying low on the floor, he had taken the one round high in the shoulder from Gilles, breaking the bone at the joint and leaving his left arm useless. Now Dalton really had his hands full. Two wounded men, a missing security man presumed dead, two terrified women and a sniper loose in the woods shooting at them. Ed lay still unconscious as Jane applied bandages and tried to control the neck and shoulder bleeding. Ed was in serious condition and unable to speak; Dalton prayed he would also survive. As he crawled along on the floor to check on Ed's wounds, a small bullet-ripped-open sofa pillow revealed an unmarked 4GB flash drive. Almost without thought, Dalton grabbed the drive, put it into his shirt pocket and continued on to Ed.

Gilles limped off to about a quarter mile from the cabin heading west. He stopped and examined his bloody right leg; he had been hit just above the knee and was now bleeding profusely. He fashioned a tourniquet and knotted it around the wound. It hurt horribly, and he wanted to scream in pain, but his training and the sensation of combat adrenaline stopped him. The pain was increasing, although the bleeding had slowed. He had to get a full bandage and wrap on the leg or it would stiffen him and he'd be stuck in the woods with his prey pursuing him. Twenty minutes later Gilles made it back to his hidden SUV where Ted and Jeff had taken up a defensive position nearby the SUV and were looking to assist Gilles after he radioed them of his encounter and injury. Not knowing if Dalton or others were pursuing them, Gilles and his unit frantically drove out of the woods. It was just before daylight and the woods were beginning to show a soft light through the misty air.

EIGHT

THE work day had reached an end, and the skeleton operating and maintenance crew had just arrived to take up their stations. The day was warm and the sky clear, a pleasant break from the hot and humid conditions over the summer. The plant had started making enriched uranium, at a slow pace, about a hundredth of a kilo a month, yet it was enough to make several bombs of considerable impact in a few months.

Behind the mixed rhetoric and "show-boating" constantly coming out of Iran, was a well-educated group of scientists, all trained in the west during the sixties and early seventies when the Shah was a strong U.S. ally and immigration visas were easily obtained for education. Most of these students were engineers, scientists, and physicians, all being trained to help take Iran into the twenty-first century as a prosperous, economically strong monarchy. The political mood had changed; the Shah was forced out of the country and died a short time later of cancer. The Shah's successors lost control as Ayatollah Khomeini and his vision of a theocracy took hold in the country. Political tensions grew between the Muslims seeking a theocracy run from the Qur'an and the mullahs, and those believing in a free will and capitalistic society where religious freedom is tolerated and not imposed on the population through their government. Now these elite researchers were committed to, and supported, the radical government leaders who wanted to see Israel removed and destroyed. Their research, they hoped, would assist make this all happen through powerful, new weapons technology.

Mohammad Hatta, a chief nuclear scientist, and Israeli born undercover agent, had infiltrated the group several years earlier. Twenty-four hours before Hatta's day of escape from Jefrah, he had left the plant an hour earlier, called his contacts in Tel Aviv, and stated the "five new packages would be shipped in a few days." This was Hatta's spy-speak for, *the nuclear weapons factory is nearly ready to increase production by five fold in the next few days,* a huge problem for all in the Middle East. It also meant a personal achievement for Hatta; he had positioned the bomb, now he could finally return home.

THE ISRAELI BETRAYAL

SITUATION ROOM, OPERATIONS CENTER, IEC, TEL AVIV, ISRAEL, EARLY AFTERNOON OF THE JEFRAH BOMB ATTACK

Dr. Weiss had taken the call from Hatta on a secure private line that was setup to appear like a distribution center, and after learning what he needed politely thanked him for the call. He had learned that the months of earlier investigations had paid off; Iran was developing weapons grade plutonium. Minutes after briefing the Prime Minister and the Defense Secretary, Weiss gave the approval to detonate the custom bomb, hidden only a few hours earlier, in a power station no more than five hundred meters from the central campus of the weapons plant.

Dr. Eli Weiss also oversaw the Israeli top secret project on cold fusion at the Israeli Energy Commission. Previously, they had done little more than confirm the scientific claims and research of other groups investigating the slow fusion technology. However, eleven weeks earlier, Israeli sources in the western U.S. learned of the unusual ore discovery by Mitsui Mining and that Enertek was evaluating the material. After the container ship entered Haifa shipyards, operatives under Dr. Weiss's direction retrieved the six drums containing the special ore. The mineral, which literally appeared to be of another world, was taken to the cold fusion lab. It was inserted into an array of experiments to determine its influence, if at all, on cold fusion — or slow fusion, as it was sometimes described in the technical literature.

Just sixteen days prior to the Jefrah explosion, Weiss's group had confirmed the kinetics displayed in horrific fashion at Jefrah and now at Enertek. Weiss's group was extremely lucky and astounded when a laser beam heated an acidic plasma of the refined ore, designed to trigger the fusion reaction, appeared to modulate the reaction. In addition, by adjusting the laser beam intensity and wavelength they could initiate, diminish, or intensify the cold fusion reaction.

It amounted to achieving precise control of the fusion reactions at far lower temperatures than previously reported. They had proven that an arrangement of refined ore, in laser light plasma, could be a precision controlled detonator for a fusion reaction. The critical components were easily adapted to fit in small suitcases already equipped to house a bomb. These new custom bombs however, displayed much greater force than similar sized non-nuclear bombs, and could be modulated to the destruction level desired.

Israel felt ready to embark on a period of lasting prosperity and growth, free from the terrors of the region and the politically sensitive financial support of the U.S. They could use this new technology to customize the destruction of hostile facilities, clandestinely eliminate weapons aimed at Israel, and also fuel its economy and much of the rest of the world without the need for oil or conventional nuclear plants. World prices for crude oil would plummet over the next several years as the use and acceptance of the technology expanded. Israel's enemies, largely Arab oil producers, would have their economies in perpetual depression, depriving them of the financial resources to carry out their intentions for Israel. Furthermore, the weaponry afforded by this technology would allow Israel to eliminate a surgical target without it being traced back to them. The detonations could be set to the size needed for each target and no radioactive traces would remain. It would all appear as though horrible neighbors had their deadly efforts backfire on them in the testing stages.

This discovery also held the final, ultimate answer to allow commercial development of a fusion economy, thus gradually eliminating the need for fossil fuel combustion for energy. It appeared as a God Send for Israel and Japan.

The evening of the blast, following his call to Eli Weiss, Mohammed Hatta sat anxious and proud in a small rented apartment only fifty miles from the Iranian border. He sat watching TV as the network news told them that an explosion had occurred at the Iranian Energy Research Laboratory. He fell silent in thankful prayer that the bomb detonated successfully and he had proved himself able to assist his beloved

RICHARD TREVAE

Israel destroy an enemy's lethal weapons facility. He also prayed for a safe escape from Iran the next morning. As Hatta fell off to sleep, pleased with the results he had achieved, and chanting a prayer phrase . . . Benjamin Glickman, Servant of God, Benjamin Glickman, Servant of God. His next several hours were not nearly as uplifting.

Elko, Montana

KIRK was in rough shape, though thankfully he had not gone into shock, as one might have expected, although he had lost a lot of blood. "Let's get a tourniquet on that leg," Dalton said. Kirk nodded in pain. Dalton used his belt as a sling, while Jane and Susan helped control the bleeding.

Ed had come in and out of consciousness after Jane had bandaged his destroyed left shoulder and the lower right side of his throat. While not a professional triage, the makeshift care slowed the bleeding. During a moment of clarity, Ed used his other hand and retrieved his phone, punched in a speed dial number, holding it out for Dalton. Dalton accepted the phone. "Sam this is Dalton, we've been attacked and we have wounded, get a chopper out to the cabin road soon. Track the GPS signal from Ed's phone to get here."

"Will do now," said the attentive masculine voice on the other end of the phone call.

Dalton turned to Ed. "We've got a big problem Ed; who knew of our plans to come here anyway?" Ed moved his head a fraction and blinked his eyes, indicating he too had no clue how they were discovered out at this remote cabin. He began to fade away again.

"Hang in their Ed, Sam's flying in now." Jane held Ed's head slightly elevated to assist his breathing, while Susan covered him in a blanket and helped maintain pressure on the bleeding throat wound.

"Let's check this." Dalton displayed the 4GB flash drive. Ed, now stabilized although near passing out and very weak, directed Dalton through the passwords to fire up his high-powered laptop. The computer lit up as the flash drive loaded. Several folders were displayed on the set-up screen. One called "Recompense" first caught Dalton's attention. Opening the file revealed downloaded emails providing Toro with instructions to obtain and deliver files on the Enertek lab program for cold fusion. The protocol for evaluation of various test scenarios displayed. In his haste Toro had never password protected the files after last opening them. Copies of earlier lab reports issued by Jane's research group had been copied to the disk over the last two months. The emails came from a sender with a screen name of "Seeker" at *yahoo.com*. Dalton turned the screen for Ed to see.

"We need to speak to the President — soon," whispered Ed.

"Yes, but rest now, the chopper is on its way."

Within twenty minutes, the special marine helicopter hovered over the cabin and landed. Kirk provided a direction indicating where Steve had gone. With Sam's help Dalton found Steve's body and carried him to the cabin. Ed, Kirk and Steve's dead body were lifted onto the chopper floor deck, strapped down and the wounded further triaged on the way to Seattle's Claremont Hospital. Dalton, Jane, and Susan drove out to the Elko mine site with a compliment of two marines behind and in front of their SUV as they traveled out of the woods.

Khamal remained motionless, blanketed in a grassy camouflage netting of cloth, twigs, leaves and grasses. He positioned himself at a slight elevation within a downfall of trees and brush affording a narrow view some three hundred-fifty yards from the cabin. Khamal knew enough through Hatta to realize the Elko mine discovery played a key role in the events in Iran. His original plan to gather information on the U.S. participants in the Jefrah explosion convinced him he needed to capture, interrogate, and dispose of Ed Kosko and Dalton. His efforts halted when he noticed Gilles Montrose taking up a position between him and the cabin holding Dalton's group including the two military men, Steve and Kirk. Khamal's listening and camera device, disguised as a pepper shaker, continued operating undetected providing a partial picture of the situation. On his *Blackberry*, Khamal played back the three hours of video surveillance and listened to the staged conversation. Only when Ed and Dalton moved outside and away from his the audio pick-up range, did Khamal suspect they knew they were being monitored. However, Dalton's group still had no idea who and how many parties were pursuing them.

In scanning the video in fast forward mode Khamal noticed Dalton making a call on his mobile phone, and although the speech failed to clearly record it appeared he could not reach his caller. Khamal did however manage to record the key strokes of the number. Moments later Khamal learned Dalton had tried to reach a woman . . . a Carolyn McCabe.

From less than two-hundred-fifty yards away, Khamal watched Gilles's movement through his rifle scope as he limped away. The cabin, now increasingly visible now in the morning light, was awash in blood and activity tending to the wounded. It appeared Khamal was not alone in pursuing his quarry. He thought about how to achieve his objectives before his "competition" finished the killing part of his mission.

He first had to get the information confirming the Iranian suspicions of an American and Israeli conspiracy to attack the Iranian Energy Research Laboratory. Motionless, Khamal remained a lethal observer, delaying his leave until darkness set in while he pondered his next actions.

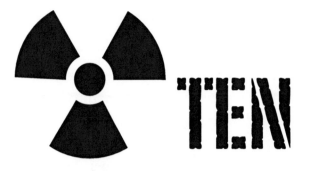

TEN

SANG Huchara sat restless in his leather desk chair high atop the forty-two story office complex housing Mitsui North American construction operations. A powerful thinker and strategist, his background as a metallurgist and then MBA from Chicago had moved him up through the ranks at Mitsui in less than ten years. During that time, he took over the president's role, grew revenues by 740% in just nine years, and became a major shareholder. The son of a Japanese diplomat, he had lived and worked all over the world, had high level business and government contacts throughout the middle east, USA, and Europe. He spoke five languages fluently and brokered construction contracts in the billions of dollars each year.

Now, at fifty-seven, he sat in charge of a nineteen billion dollar a year construction conglomerate, privately owned by him, a handful of key employees and a passive investment group located in Japan. It seemed time for him to slow down, although he never wanted to give up the immense power he wielded. He mulled over the startling events of the last few weeks; the ore discovery, the experiments at IEC, the explosion at Jefrah, Iran, and now the press coverage of a massive blast in Seattle at Enertek. He pondered if he and his partner government groups were about to shift the international global balance of power to Israel and Japan.

The plan had always been to get to the new discoveries first and invest heavily, gaining control of an organized, yet open market on future fuel/energy needs. Now, these events had all changed with the scope and power of this new technology. Sang pondered whether he, Weiss, and their respective governments could actually contain, manage, and control this new scientific discovery.

The secure satellite phone rang on his desk, the display said, *Weiss incoming call.* "Eli, I'm glad you called. What am I to conclude about the Iran news of a couple days ago?"

"I will be in Zurich in two days. We can meet there and I will bring you up to date on all issues. Though, suffice it to say, our contacts confirmed the Jefrah information. We took preventative action, which is now being reported worldwide as an internal accident."

"You mean to say—" Before Sang could finish his sentence, Eli interrupted him.

"I will explain it all to you on Friday in Zurich. Please be calm."

RICHARD TREVAE

Breathing rapidly, Sang replied, "Okay, yes, Zurich on Friday." Weiss hung up. Still holding the phone Huchara thought *Weiss made the technology work at Jefrah!*

ELEVEN

SEATTLE CLAREMONT HOSPITAL.

ED and Dalton were scheduled to meet right after the doctors reviewed Ed's injuries. They gave him instructions for hospital rest and to not resume normal activities. Not that a doctor's opinion would stop Ed Kosko from doing anything he wanted. After all, he had already taken up an entire quarter wing of the sixth floor of the hospital, secured it with twenty secret service officers, muzzled the press, and had a team of investigators ready for instructions coming from he or Dalton. Nevertheless, Ed was not "in place" to carry out his normal role.

"How's the shoulder today Ed?" Dalton asked cautiously.

"Damn thing hurts like hell, but I don't want a lot of pain killer as I can't think straight. Other than that I'm good as gold," muttered Ed.

"Yeah right Ed, though it sounds to me like you may be a pain elsewhere for the staff."

"Whatever. What do we know about our attackers? How did they know our location and how much do they know of this discovery?" Ed spoke with difficulty, as the wound and heavy bandages on his neck subdued his voice. "Toro clearly was not working alone. There is too much lethal activity around the people in his life for him to have been the only perpetrator."

"I figure he was trying to sell energy secrets to someone when he died attempting to retrieve them, just as the data was being generated from the experiments. That someone is probably behind the *seeker@yahoo.com* email address, and may well be a large crime group selling a promising technology."

"That's how I figure it too, but who are these folks and who do they represent and how did they know so much . . . damn it! At this point, I don't know who to trust and yet I have to appraise the President about my analysis on this problem. I can't do that from here." Ed sighed before continuing. "So, effective immediately you're taking over my role as acting Deputy Energy Secretary. Don't argue with me, I've already run this by the President. I will be recovering for weeks, they tell me. My voice hurts like hell when I speak, and I have to update the President almost daily. You're my most trusted confidant and, well, you're out in the middle of this already. Those other jokers from NSA or the CIA will just slow us down and bog up your efforts. You are my man for the immediate future. Okay?"

Dalton starred at Ed, in near disbelief. "All right, but don't think you're dragging me into the government payrolls; I enjoy my independence as your consultant."

"Agreed." Ed handed Dalton a letter he signed authorizing the temporary assignment.

"What can you, or I, tell the president what we suspect — foreign interests, an agency, or a group of the U.S. government?" asked Dalton.

"Caution," Ed offered in a very rough voice. "Besides I don't want the FBI, CIA, or other group outside my control messing this up until we know the players and targets. I'm going to stall for time and explain it as a random accident in my initial informal report. It goes out today. Then in a few days when we know more, I, that is, you, will tell the President in a direct face-to-face report what we know. You, my friend, have to take on the dirty investigative work behind the scenes, while I'm out of the spot light — got it?"

"Yeah, I got it Ed."

The earlier Iranian explosion seemed far too coincidental to be ignored by Dalton or Ed. So. Dalton had only five hours to pack a day's clothes and get to a dedicated department aircraft for the direct flight to Istanbul, Turkey. There he would meet with covert operatives working for Ed, now under Dalton's lead, for information. Dalton had his work cut out for him.

TWELVE

ISTANBUL, TURKEY — INTELLIGENCE OPERATIONS OFFICE

USING his "Special Consultant to the President" credentials, as well as Ed's letter, Dalton arranged to speak with Jack Tucker, the section chief in Istanbul overseeing Iranian counter-intelligence. Tucker operated from the nineteenth floor of an office building located near the hotel district overlooking the Bosporus. Besides the beautiful view, communications were easy from the twenty-story structure. It was built back in the 1970's as a hotel and now served as a second class retail and office structure. He had a staff of six operating usually outside the office building on assignments.

The 'NSA office' presented itself as a computer software developer so the presence of computers, printers, and all types of office equipment looked normal to the average onlooker. In reality, Tucker's office had some of the most powerful computers, satellite communications, and video and listening setups anywhere in Eastern Europe. The disguise worked well, and had for seven years, as Tucker's group kept a step ahead of the Iranians and Iraqis. They had provided key Intel for the

1991 Desert Storm war against Iraq after Saddam Hussein invaded Kuwait. Everyone tried to gain intelligence on the Iranians. They were the country most likely to be involved in Middle East conflicts or uprisings.

Steeped in a Muslim tradition of creating 'theocracies' throughout the region, Iran emerged as the one with the networks, resources, and technology to get it done. Recent political events in Iran had awakened a growing passive portion of the population, in their best earning years, well educated in the west and strongly opposed to a 'theocracy government' for Iran. Their most vocal spokespersons were now active, seeking western help and guidance on how to disrupt or remove the current leadership; and return to a more stable, progressive stance similar to the political landscape during the time of the Shah.

Jack Tucker was a good lead, as he had been tracking Mohammed Hatta and his actions at the IEC. They believed Hatta had in fact been either an agent or a sympathetic paid asset of the Israeli government, as his phone logs showed regular, although short calls to Israel for over two years. Dalton wondered about Hatta and if he played a role in the Jefrah explosion.

Why would a seemingly comfortable Iranian research scientist provide secrets and Intel to the Israeli's?

THIRTEEN

SANG Huchara arrived early, consumed with questions about the recent events and how deep he and his clandestine business associate, Eli Weiss, had involved their respective organizations. General Yong of North Korea was unable to attend on such short notice. It was tough enough getting out of North Korea with plenty of notice and a planned schedule, however with only a few days notice Yong had to decline. Besides, he was in the final stages of a plan taken from the Jefrah example that he and Japanese Secretary Kytoma were planning for North Korea.

Furthermore, Kytoma had a delegation scheduled in from Taiwan seeking further assurances that Japan remained willing to financially support a missile early warning system on the island. The absent KCG members would be brought up to speed by Weiss on the IEC's work following the Zurich meeting.

Eli Weiss had his priorities clear and focused; he oversaw the energy research of the IEC for sure, however overshadowing all was his goal to protect Israel from its antagonistic neighbors. He had the ear of the highest authorities in his government and was expected to make recommendations which, when solicited, were meant to help shape critical international policy. When Weiss learned of the imminent danger developing at Jefrah, and had discovered the ability to solve the problem with the custom bomb based on the Elko find, he acted.

Sang Huchara however, was less politically driven and remained more focused on the economic rewards for Japan, should they discover and control a major new energy source. As a mature, hardball player in the top two hundred engineering/construction businesses of the world, Huchara could reach across continents and commit billions to new projects and ventures. His Israeli connections, and his relationships with Eli Weiss, grew out of a successful bidding effort and completing the largest combined solar energy and liquefied natural gas (LNG) facilities serving Israel, valued at over $15.0 billion USD.

Weiss did not interact closely with the project team though he advised on certain elements throughout construction. His real importance arose when his organization, the IEC, awarded the contract to Mitsui. It followed that Sang Huchara and Dr. Eli Weiss became business partners and then friends during the four-year project duration.

RICHARD TREVAE

The KCG was born of those meetings and relationships. Huchara had already "signed on" with major Japanese investors and partners to find solutions to the Japanese dependency on foreign oil through new technologies. The KCG was created for this very purpose. The controlling members, with tacit approval of their governments, would ultimately determine the direction a new venture would take.

Sang knew how to run a business, yet not afraid to get rough and do what was needed, whatever was needed to get to "yes". However, that was just Sang's day job; more politically honed skills were needed to manage the interests within the Knowledge Consortium Group. Weiss seemed to have those skills, and Huchara hoped he had made the correct political calls.

Late again, Sang thought, and just as he checked his watch, in walked Eli Weiss, in a classic loose-fitting three-piece black pin stripped suit. He walked slowly compared to the sprint he displayed just a few years before. The lobby soon filled with people arriving, chatting, drinking tea and eating those scrumptious little chocolate balls wrapped in foil.

Extending his hand Eli said, "How's my favorite hand ball partner?" taking Sang back to a far earlier time when they spent many hours battling it out on a hard wood court.

"Well I'm good Eli, how's your game these days?"

"Very rusty, I'm afraid I need more time with a serious competitor like you."

The pleasantries ended, and after checking for curious passers-by, Sang got down to business. "What the hell is going on with the Waldron find and this Iranian thing?"

"Relax, my friend. We are totally safe and in control of an amazing new technology. Our dreams of the last six years are about to be realized." Eli Weiss's expression overflowed with confidence and pride. He for one never envisioned a breakthrough of this magnitude; a new safe source of unlimited energy, and a highly flexible and controllable weapon, easily deployed, clandestine and capable, through parameter modulations, of appearing like a dynamite explosion or one hundred Hiroshima bombs.

Each man ordered a small salad, red wine, dipping bread, olive oil, and a cup of mushroom soup. As the men began to explore the lunch before them, Eli explained about the rapid success, his IEC group had made. They had identified the properties, control parameters to the slow fusion reaction, catalyst influence, and energy yield that had arisen from the mineral find at the Elko mining site.

Sang asked if the Enertek explosion arising from experiments on the find had *gone bad*, or something else.

"Probably experiments that had gone very badly . . . for them," whispered Eli.

"Our simulations predict a violent explosion of the size and magnitude at Seattle if the parameters were not-optimized."

"Have you recovered the lab results your man, Toro, was trying to get us?"

"No, he was killed in the explosion. And because the area was secured immediately, I couldn't get my men into to recover anything. However, we are tracking the lab manager, Toro's, supervisor, who may have the data, and a team of Enertek people under the direction of a Dalton Crusoe — you know him?"

"Never met him, though he's very smart, formidable and works behind the scene, through the President's Energy Secretary I believe, usually on top secret, sensitive political matters. Keep an eye out for him."

"Just know that if he gets to this test data, and claims control over it, our position will be compromised. Do you get my meaning?" Eli paused.

Sang starred at Eli and slowly nodded his head in approval.

"This could backfire in epic proportions if the U.S. government makes all the connections and pressures our governments to cooperate. Right?" asked Sang.

"That is why we must stop the lab team from a hard analysis and investigation of the Seattle explosion. I can tell you the Israeli leadership will not reveal these findings, if ever, until our enemies are eliminated with this technology. They will not relinquish this opportunity to forever wipe out the threats to my homeland."

"Well that's scary Eli, going toe-to-toe with the U.S. on a technology they can claim is their own."

"They can only claim it's theirs if they can extend the research and protocols begun in Seattle now destroyed through their own mistakes in the explosion. Our efforts have already put us at least six months to a year ahead of the Americans, *if* they are denied access to the data leading up to the Enertek explosion." Speaking into his napkin Eli said, "The Iranian nuclear weapons facility was eliminated by this very technology and it appears to the world as a mistake by the Iranians. They will not complain of outside interference because they cannot trace the source or provider of the bomb. They will be kept busy trying to explain to the world why their innocent little energy lab blew up." Eli failed to control a brief smile.

Sang looked shaky and was feeling even more nervous. "When can I report the raw lab results at Enertek will be contained and those involved eliminated?" Eli questioned.

"My God man, you are really putting me, and us, out there at huge risk. I'll know more tonight after I speak with my man handling the people involved at Enertek," huffed Sang.

"Make it quick and make it final, Sang. All we have worked hard for is before us now. Keep me updated by secure phone lines only, okay?"

"Of course. You will provide an update to General Yong and Secretary Kytoma?"

Leaning in to add emphasis, Weiss stated, "Yes, of course, but the details will only be provided verbally. I will not risk an email being intercepted by the Americans at this stage."

The men shook hands, wished each other a good return trip and parted company. To the casual observer, it appeared as a classic meeting of two boring business-men. Sang Huchara learned enough about the actions taken by Weiss to make him very concerned about exposing the role the KCG played in the Iranian events if the technology ever became fully understood by the Americans. He had to get Gilles more involved.

Unknown to them, Sandy Corwin, an espionage operative working for Jack Tucker, had been recording the images and conversation from forty-five feet away. It amounted to the scoop of the millennium; she would send her report to Tucker and Dalton via an encrypted email file in ninety minutes. The video and understand-able words between Sang and Eli were a massive break-through in penetrating the KCG.

FOURTEEN

WASHINGTON D.C. — PRIVATE CONFERENCE ROOM AT THE NSA

VIEWING the Sandy Corwin video and voice recordings, Dalton could not believe the extent of involvement Huchara and Weiss had in the Enertek technology. Ed Kosko, operating from a communication-enhanced hospital room, opened his email from Dalton, downloaded the encrypted file and saved it in a password-protected file labeled "XR-211 Aftermath". Connected by conference phone and remote desktop webcam, Ed watched the amazing, clear audio and video of the meeting between Weiss and Huchara.

As the streaming video and voice recordings played out, Dalton knew he had guessed right in tapping the Mitsui phones in Vancouver, Elko, and Seattle. Of the two dozen curious calls that were obtained, the one between Sang Huchara and Dr. Eli Weiss on Wednesday mid-day was the most intriguing. Dalton questioned why an apparent world-class construction leader like Sang Huchara and Dr. Eli Weiss, an Israeli researcher, some-time professor, and confidant of the

Israeli political leaders have an all too emotional discussion with each other days after the Enertek explosion.

Ed then emailed President Conner and then voiced the message to Dalton. "Dalton, I'm arranging a private meeting between you and the President ASAP. I will be teleconferenced in from this hospital room. He needs to understand the data we've just obtained from Sandy. Be prepared to speculate what Weiss and friends are up too and recommend a course of action. Are you good with that?"Dalton thought carefully before replying. "I'll be ready to explain the facts as we know them and outline a probable agenda for dealing with Weiss and Huchara.""Great." Ed hung up ending the telephone connection. Dalton looked in a nearby mirror to see sweat streaming down from his forehead. He had some thinking to do.

Sandy had done her job well, and Ed offered grateful comments. Dalton reviewed the video and voice recordings several more times and began to formulate a presentation for the President of the United States. A private discussion with Dalton, Ed, and the President, now scheduled in eight hours, before the morning dawned, took over Dalton's thoughts for the evening.

FIFTEEN

ED looked tired and sore as he shuffled to his converted hospital room connecting him via satellite to the White House west wing with Dalton, already on line. Dressed in a hospital gown, soft slippers, and bandages everywhere, Ed looked a bit less formidable than when he was in his tailored suits and coordinated tie.

The president came to his office, smiled at Dalton shut the door and glanced at the screen image of Ed Kosko. Extending a hand to Dalton the president said, "I'm pleased to see you again, Dalton. I look forward to your briefing."

Dalton stood, shook the president's hand and waited for him to be seated.

"How's the shoulder, Ed? Looks like you've been making some upgrades to your room." asked President Conner. He looked at a thirty inch by five-foot wide high definition screen as he seated himself across from Dalton.

"It still hurts like hell, Mr. President, but I'm getting used to it. The docs tell me another three days and I'll be down to mild pain medication, then some reconstructive surgery on my shoulder and neck, followed by a light weight arm sling. And my voice is getting stronger — practically brand new, don't you think?" The large video screen made Ed look even worse than he sounded; his voice was rough and weak, and he was still bandaged heavily and healing from the gunshot wounds.

Dalton smiled recognizing Ed's standard MO. He never admitted pain, discouragement, or defeat in a conversation.

Meetings in the White House were "old hat" for Ed, though not for Dalton. In fact, except for two rather casual meetings, he had not interacted with the president one-on-one in over a year. Well, here he sat, in the Oval Office, as acting Secretary of Energy and about to render his opinions to the President of the United States on a possible theft of new U.S. technology that could alter energy and weaponry forever. Meanwhile, his boss sat in a wheel chair across the country, conferenced in through satellite video and sound feeds. Dalton's nerves were being exercised trying to maintain his composure and focus.

President Conner displayed a mixture of Jack Kennedy and Bush '41. He had the personality and interpersonal skills to be successful at virtually anything. In fact, he had enjoyed a very successful career as lawyer and then as a CEO in technology-related businesses prior to entering politics at the senate level twelve years earlier. He was an efficient decision maker. His analytical side saw the need to move quickly against known and perceived threats against the United States, particularly following 9/11, and as such, he strengthened the elite secret presidential "Deterrence Force," It was comprised of a core of eight men from the Seals, Green Beret, and Delta Force units reporting directly to him.

Now, at fifty-four and midway through his first term, he enjoyed a 63% approval rating, a good economy, and 13,600 on the Dow Jones Industrials, a 4.8% unemployment rate, and a relatively quiet world. A fast analytical thinker, supported by a small although close inner circle, he knew the impact of the Enertek trouble. Ed had effectively misdirected the press and other groups like the FBI and Seattle police while he made his case and gathered data. Now with the Corwin recordings, he had strong probable cause and the President could make the call for action.

Dalton narrated as the entire video and voice recording were played twice, including final remarks by Sandy Corwin, relating the time, place, weather, and other details about the extraordinary recording she made in Zurich. Trailing the video and voice recordings were all of Toro's flash drive files, now cataloged as to time and place showing how Mitsui, operating through Sang Huchara, had seduced Toro into some small scale intelligence espionage at Enertek. It was possible he never even knew the magnitude of his actions.

The President listened, very impressed with Dalton, his intelligence, speaking skills, temperament, and his quick mind cutting through complex issues. Kosko was right he thought. . . . *JD could fill in as Secretary and be immediately up to speed.*

After a long silence the President said, "Excellent work Ed and Dalton, what do you recommend as our next step?"

Ed gave a brief background and status summary, and asked Dalton to explain and interpret the extraordinary events of the last few days. Dalton began a compelling theory of how Mitsui and Dr. Weiss were involved with each other. He assumed the relationship began back in the solar/LNG energy project days in Israel and carried through until today. Both men enjoyed political and intelligence agency connections far in excess of their publicly known activities. Perhaps the ability to connect with one phone call to investors, companies and government units controlling billions of dollars allowed Eli and Sang to cross paths many times

Whatever the mechanism, these men saw the potential for political and economic power, kept their hands in the energy research fields, and were able to engage the highest powers in their respective governments, as hidden passive partners. Now that the incredible power this discovery portends for energy and weapons is known, the passive partners would step up and control future events.

Dalton continued. "From our perspective, the U.S. has some complications. First, this find was made on Canadian and Montana land, and notwithstanding our lease rights, Canada is likely to demand being a player at the table. Second, we suspect the Israelis have advanced the findings of only several weeks ago to levels beyond our current knowledge and likely disguised and used this new weaponry technology to carry out destruction at Jefrah Iran; their most feared neighbor's nuclear weapons plant. Third, the Japanese, who also have sworn enemies in North Korea, desperately need this technology to support their economy without being slaves to the Middle East oil producers. Last, whatever ultimate knowledge is gained through this discovery, Israel and very likely Japan, are ahead of the U.S. in understanding and deploying the technology. They may already have enough material, from Mitsui's management of the mining operation, to make a formidable weapons cache, and some level of long term energy generation."

Dalton paused a moment and concluded saying, "It appears to me, Mr. President, that physical possession of the unique ore contained at the Waldron range is critical to securing and ultimately controlling the technology arising from this discovery."

Clutching his hands in a tight fist under his chin, the President mulled over Dalton's dissertation. "Either of these countries would be tempted to deny their involvement in these horrible events at Enertek to employ this technology for their own purposes; some militaristic and some energy driven."

After reflecting, the President continued. "A worst case scenario would have them breaking the trust and support with the U.S. in the near future as part of a plan to emerge as the new millennium super powers dispensing unlimited energy where they chose and having the flexible weaponry of mass destruction to enforce their will. Not good." The President rose and began pacing.

Ed spoke up saying that he accessed the situation as heading in precisely the direction outlined by the President. "Based on the sniper and commando attacks on Dalton, myself, and the others with us at Elko, I believe Weiss and Huchara do not know, and therefore both Israel and Japan also do not know, that our research is static and stalled at the explosion period. They are trying to confirm if we have a true understanding of the magnitude of this discovery." Ed paused and rubbed his heavily bandaged shoulder. "If they conclude that we don't have the knowledge then they will likely hold tight, deny accusations of involvement at Seattle, and press forward to take quiet control of the deposits and technology as they become more emboldened."

"Exactly as I see it Ed," proclaimed the President. Pointing at Dalton, the President commanded, "Get whatever and whomever you and Ed need to first finalize the legal lease on the Montana and Canadian land. The leases covering these new ore deposits are critical to the interests of the U.S. and our national defense. Any problem with that?"

"No sir, I've had Enertek attorneys working on that part," announced Dalton with support from Ed.

"Final signing can be done today Mr. President, as these contracts are all in final format, signed by both Canadian and Montana authorities and simply await execution by us, through Enertek," continued Dalton.

"Good, obviously these leases must be assigned to the benefit of the U.S. Department of Energy, in exchange for the security, further research funding, testing and implementation of the energy technology component. Adequate consideration through patents or whatever will be provided to Enertek shareholders, of course. However, the weaponry issue has to be handled carefully through the Department of Defense, and the applied research done with a small controlled group we can absolutely trust. Clear?"

RICHARD TREVAE

Dalton nodded his agreement, as did Ed, unable to force out the words past his throbbing throat.

"Dalton we need a detailed plan to take us through this mess that began at Elko. Can you do that?"

With Ed withholding comment, and the President studying him, he replied, "I have an idea for a comprehensive plan sir, and it's bold. Would you like to hear it now?"

The President appeared visibly relieved. "Absolutely."

6-TEEN

ELKO MONTANA — WALDRON RANGE

OVER four days, a team of scientists, technicians and a detachment of forty marines set up camp near Elko, directly at the U.S. and Canadian border in Montana. Several million dollars of laboratory and analytical equipment arrived on site in "stand up facilities" for the research, communications, and defense of the area. To avoid the interest of Canadian officials, Mitsui's site security team were rounded up, replaced by plain clothed marines, and then confined and interrogated for knowledge of the explosion at Enertek.

Sang Huchara became uncomfortably suspicious after his field superintendent tipped him off, remarking that his crew was being replaced, and he didn't know why.

RICHARD TREVAE

ISRAEL — GOVERNMENT HEADQUARTERS — PRIME MINISTER'S OFFICE

With Defense Secretary Dyan at his side, Dr. Eli Weiss informed the Israeli Prime Minister, and six of his inner cabinet members, about the extraordinary discovery at Elko Montana. He explained that his IEC facilities and his research team had been able to evaluate the reactive mechanisms inherent in the technology. He informed them that they had confirmed and demonstrated the technology's powerful weaponry side in the dramatic Jefrah explosions, several days ago. Now, the entire world, perplexed and bewildered, could not point blame at Israel.

He went on to explain the clear potential applications from controlling a slow fusion reaction. Following more applied research a full understanding would evolve of the protocols to effortlessly produce safe power without dependence on oil.

Weiss paused and let the information sink in. The Prime Minister began to smile as he gazed at Weiss. "Eli, I can't express how much this means to our country. If all the potential that you say rests in this technology, then Israeli will become a leading world power. Our borders will never be challenged again and our economy will shift from military to energy based."

Applause and congratulations were generously bestowed on Dr. Weiss.

Weiss accepted the praise as humbly as he could pretend. He began again, "Enough raw ore has been shipped to Israel, which, when refined could provide catalyst for slow fusion power for the next thirty years in Israel or provide material for some thirty bombs each, capable of detonations ranging from the size at Jefrah to one hundred Hiroshima bombs."

The small gathering broke into excited chatter. The Prime Minister raised his hand, quieting the men, and said, "Eli, please continue."

"The research we need to fully develop all aspects of the technology is underway. I expect to be able to present an update in three to six months." Weiss beamed with pride and self confidence.

A cabinet member asked Secretary Dyan how Japan is involved going forward from this point.

Dyan stood as Weiss sat down still holding the smiling gaze of the Prime Minister.

"Three initial *Jefrah*' bombs had been made, one already used, one still in Israel, and one on a special boat to Japan. The bomb in route to Japan represented the first dividend of many expected by Sang and his fellow secret Japanese members."

Dyan further explained that Japan was not privy to all the research, although they were heavily invested in the activity through Mitsui. They also expected to be a partner, a full, equal, partner, in the energy aspect of the technology. The cabinet members pondered the remark.

Interrupting the Prime Minister pointed out, 'We will control the technology and how it is deployed, correct?"

Still sitting Weiss, answered, "Yes, this is our discovery, even though the American's have the raw ore."

"What if the Americans replicate our research and understand the potential. Couldn't they thwart our efforts to control its use?"

Weiss stood once more to answer. "I am certain the U.S. has not yet arrived at our knowledge level on the energy and weaponry uses of the technology. They may never reach a level of understanding where they can safely utilize the raw ore...without our cooperation. The Enertek explosion, while reported in the press as an accident involving fuel storage facilities, is likely an unfortunate, and unknown, mix of detonation parameters culminating in the blast. Their research is stalled and they may never learn the critical reaction parameters to unlock the power."

"So that could provide us an avenue to guarantee a longer supply of raw ore, correct?"

"Yes, that is our belief now. Despite the fact that Enertek will eventually learn we acquired the raw ore, shall we say by *'back channels'*, the power of what we now own, that is, the critical reaction parameters, will make certain Israel is a co-owner of the raw ore."

The elite group of Israeli leaders warmed to the logic Weiss explained. Weiss and Dyan however, both had concerns

While suspicious about the timing of the Jefrah blast, the Japanese Secretary Kytoma knew none of the details which had been communicated to Sang Huchara. Nevertheless, Weiss knew Kytoma wanted a bomb as well, for the same reasons as Israel: destroy a dangerous enemy's attack capability. Weiss indicated he planned to hold back operational information needed for programming the third bomb until he knew the extent of the American knowledge base on the technology. Elated and smug in their success, the Israeli leadership believed enough raw ore had been refined into catalyst to produce several more bombs in a few months.

As a result, a dangerous decision later took shape between Eli Weiss and Secretary Dyan. Destroy the remaining ore deposit at Waldron, making it appear, as in Jefrah, as an unfortunate laboratory mishap. This would leave Israel alone with both the only known viable supply of the ore and the resultant technology; an addictive thought for all who were burdened with concern for Israel's future. Weiss and Dyan starred at each other following the cabinet meeting.

"Are we agreed we will make this happen?" asked Weiss. The tension was high.

"Yes Eli, we must stop the Americans."Military and intelligence experts, working at the IEC directly under Weiss, went to work on a plan to eliminate the known ore supplies in the Waldron range and leave a false trail away from Israel and Japan. A tall order yet very compelling.

Things had to move fast and Eli needed to speak with Sang.

VANCOUVER

The time approached midnight, the restaurant had stopped serving and the bar was about to close. Gilles Montrose sipped his whiskey and water, trying not to move anything that had been recently stitched up or bandaged. He endured constant pain, even though he was alive and loaded with a morphine painkiller, which, when added to the booze, felt like a cheap high from his earlier days as a mercenary.

Sang Huchara stood still, twenty-five feet away from Gilles, and studied him for a few moments. Gilles looked thin, weak, and distressed. Sang approached him from behind. "When did you get here?"

"Two damn hours ago, where have you been?" growled Gilles without bothering to look at the questioner.

Ignoring the antagonistic question Sang asked if he had retrieved the XR-211 disk of final lab results. Gilles looked up, sipped his drink and said, "Never even saw it; are you sure it exists?"

"Yes, you idiot. Our listening devices confirmed Crusoe and the lab woman had disks containing the experiment results right up to the explosion."

"Well I couldn't find it in her car, home, or that damned cabin near Elko."

"What the hell happened?"

"They were prepared, armed security, helicopters, and two women, one of them the Holman woman and the other I guess was Toro's girl. Why she was there, I don't know, but they were looking for something."

"Do you think Toro hid a disk copy of the experiments there on a previous trip?"

"Yeah, I'd bet on it, he was too smart to expect he could hide it at his home or even on Enertek systems under a bogus file. It's there somewhere, or now with Crusoe and his men." Gilles took another long slug of his whiskey and water. "Anyway, I was damn lucky to get out alive. I took two rounds on that trip, one in the leg giving me this limp, and the other through the left side just above my belt. Lucky for me it was a minor flesh wound missing my liver by only an inch." It was unlike Gilles to seek sympathy.

"I did get their two security men and probably Crusoe or his boss - Ed whatever. I needed more men because your information was lousy; the cabin was not empty, or just one man there. They were ready for something," Gilles complained.

Sang thought pensively for a moment. "I want you to go back with two more men, you know them, Ted and Jeff, and monitor the mine and the cabin and wait for further instructions. Go in quiet, stay hidden, armed, and with comsat gear. Take out Crusoe, if he's still alive, and that Holman woman."

"This is going to cost you more than the $750,000 for my last little trip in the woods. And when do you want this to start?" probed Gilles smiling.

Looking as serious as he could, Sang said, "Early tomorrow. Can you do it?"

Gilles nodded in an assuring pose. He was not easily out maneuvered, even by an old pro like Sang Huchara. Showing a smirky smile Gilles finally said, "Tomorrow it is, after I confirm the remaining $2,250,000 USD for this job has gone into my Swiss account, you know the one."

"True enough, but you were to have retrieved the disks and eliminated the targets," Sang said with emphasis.

Gilles just looked up at Sang and said, "Yeah, well, this mission is a little more dangerous than you first explained." They appeared to be at a standoff, yet Sang knew he had to make the payment or lose Gilles from the mission. Without question, he could not afford to lose him now with so much at stake. Time passed, minutes seemed like hours and then Sang said, "Done, a deposit will be made by 6:00 a.m. your time. Jeff and Ted will meet you at the Mitsui hanger at 7:00a.m."

Gilles smiled and winked at Sang. "I'll be there."

7-TEEN

SEATTLE — ENERTEK LABORATORIES

JANE Holman seemed to be the logical leader for the next phase of research needed on the XR-211 project. Ed and Dalton had persuaded the President and his national security team that, with timing critical, and secrecy also extremely important, Jane should lead the new team of twelve hand selected researchers. All were cleared for the highest level of technical security undertaken at Enertek.

Jane had two major objectives to accomplish as soon as possible. One was to promptly investigate the reaction kinetics, and other parameters needed to define, and control, the weaponry aspect of the slow fusion process. The second was to create a bogus set of operating guidelines on the energy aspect of slow fusion, so it could be slipped clandestinely into the Mitsui/Israeli network. When employed in the Israeli research it would destroy their inventory of the crystalline ore find. It was developed as a bold, though necessary plan to avoid dangerous nations from obtaining and utilizing this technology against the world.

Two weeks passed, and the research Jane directed gave impressive results. The weaponry was rapidly dissected and defined, and the energy research followed close behind. Jane saw the implications for the world in her assignments and took to her work like a committed patriot and humanitarian. The world had allowed the Iranian explosion to drift into memory as a botched laboratory accident as the Israelis had hoped, and the Iranians drew no favor trying to cast aspirations onto their enemies. Thus far, the efforts through Khamal had not made the complete connection between the Elko discovery and the Jefrah explosion.

ELKO MONTANA — WALDRON RANGE

Dalton's team at Elko had successfully re-directed the basic Mitsui mining activity to a nearby range some three miles from the ore find, telling them seismic studies suggested more nickel further west. This came without much blowback from the field, as they were always being re-directed to a more attractive dig site.

The plain clothed marines secured the ore find area. Studies confirmed that it contained a limited concentration of ore representing about three acres of area and about twenty foot in depth, buried about one hundred feet below the surface. A manageable area and located about seventy percent on American soil. There was ore for over a couple of hundred years at current energy needs.

Dalton had created a plan, now approved by the President, which involved inserting bogus research procedures into Mitsui and Israeli hands. Jane had devised a research protocol, which would consume the raw ore in an unstoppable autocatalytic reaction, and then over several days, degrade the raw ore to a lifeless inorganic mineral. The trick would be to get the Israeli's to take the research at face value, and employ it on their refining operations to prepare the ore for use in slow fusion.

Susan Wallace was neither an intelligence spy, nor a combat-trained soldier, however she had access to Toro's life and that could be used to attract the Mitsui agents. After explaining the issues at hand, Susan finally agreed to assist in the plot. Dalton was confident she could fulfill her part. He introduced her to the research team as a companion, and confidant, of Toro's and an expert in data management and document encrypting. In reality, Susan knew nothing of the Enertek files, though it allowed all to view her as being thrust in the middle of the research.

THE ISRAELI BETRAYAL

THE LAST OUTPOST —
NEAR ELKO MONTANA ON THE CANADIAN BORDER

It had been two days since Gilles had spoken to Sang. He had set up in Canada some seven miles from Elko, along with Ted and Jeff. The three were pretending to be hunters from the east coast up for the early moose season. The Last Outpost, a dingy, dark, and noisy bar and restaurant, became their favorite haunt. They had stayed very quiet and tried to blend in over the last week or so, striking up meaningless conversations with the locals about hunting and fishing. Their large motorhome, outfitted for camping and hunting, offered a perfect cover parked outside the bar in the evening. Tucked back deep in the woods, it appeared as their modern campsite while out hunting. In reality, they stayed close to the hotel in their SUV, waiting for the right moment to steal the latest Enertek findings.

Sang had communicated with them twice, once as they settled in and then two days later, alerting them that a small shipment of generator parts and camp equipment was arriving by private air carrier that day. The package, not much larger than a large ice cooler and weighing about thirty-eight pounds, was actually a direct replica of the Jefrah bomb, disguised in a camouflage carrying case. Dr. Weiss's second bomb was about to find a home.

Several of the workers at Mitsui were local men who had been hired three to five years earlier when Enertek began their excavations at the Waldron range. One of them, Jake, was a drinker, a talker, and a pool player. He became Gilles's unwitting inside source for the goings-on at the mine.

Jake had already referred to Susan as a beauty he would like to date, though she was a bit younger and really outside his class. Nevertheless, he continued to fantasize over her during his drinking, and several times spoke of her looks, age, and job office area at the mine. He even knew of her temporary home at the Best Western condo suites.

Gilles reported to Sang that he soon would be ready to extract what data and files Susan surely handled each day. The Israeli's were pressing to know the American knowledge base concerning the slow fusion break-through and the Japanese were demanding some return for their sizable investments thus far. Gilles had to make his move soon.

After three days, Ted took up residence at the Best Western and monitored Susan's comings and goings for a few days. The routine was the same, leave for work at about 8:00a.m., work through lunch and head to the Best Western about 5:30 p.m. Occasionally, she would have dinner with Jane or others, and retire about 9:00 p.m. or so. Susan carried her powerful laptop to and from work each day, as instructed by Dalton, and she left it in her room when out for dinner. Two marines made to look like fishing buddies were always nearby Susan, though never directly associated with her, very inconspicuous although heavily armed and wired.

Gilles and Ted had been photographed and scanned through the FBI and CIA files. Gilles popped up instantly as a former mercenary, although with no known affiliation with Mitsui. Ted however came up clean and listed as a security specialist for Mitsui. This made the connection Dalton needed to be assured Mitsui was about to take the bait and steal the test data on Susan's computer.

Susan's hotel room phone rang. As soon as Susan picked up, Jane began speaking. "Hey, Susan, it's Jane. Are you ready for dinner? I'm starved."

"Yes," said Susan, with an eager tone in her voice. "I'll meet you in the restaurant in about five minutes."

"Great."

Gilles felt charged up, and pulled the earphone from his left ear and shut off his listening bug in Susan's suite. This would be the time to access the XR-211 files and the new research, or so he believed. Gilles called Ted, "You're clear to go; you have about thirty minutes max."

"I'm on it, and my headset is on. Call if she returns early."

Ted found the laptop sitting on Susan's small conference table in the living room area of the suite. Gently inserting a disk into the external drive, he then bypassed a simplistic password step and downloaded twenty-three files under XR-211, including the files leading up to the blast at Seattle, and the new bogus research in convincing formats for a scientist to accept. Eight minutes had gone by, and Ted had finished downloading the files. He replaced the laptop exactly as he found it and stole away.

EARLY THE NEXT DAY
OUTSIDE ELKO

Gilles sat smoking a cigarette in the sunny, chilly air while leaning against his Nissan SUV. The day had revealed a fall sky that seemed extra clear, crisp, and refreshing. He took the last drag on his cigarette and let the smoke slowly bleed out from his lungs and nose. Straightening up, he took in a deep, long breath and closed his eyes. It felt good to spend some less intense time than that of the recent past. Killing folks had never bothered Gilles, yet the intensity of the last two weeks had taken its toll. He had almost lost all the headstrong determination and steely dead nerves that had propelled him through his military and mercenary days twenty years ago. Now, he felt more vulnerable, less sure of his decisions, and drawn to a quiet life enjoying his millions.

As he held the long breath in his lungs, he could feel the deep pains from the wound in his leg and left side. Heavily bandaged even now, he welcomed the low impact duty, and the help of Ted and Jeff, so he could direct things from remote locations.

The small pontoon plane, a Beaver De Havilland, circled the small lake once, and Frank Montgomery called Gilles on the radiophone.

"Alpha Romeo Hotel Thirty-Four, making pass over Ellis Lake, Come in Ground Team."

"Ground Team here, at the north end of the lake."

"Roger, Ground Team. I see your vehicle, down in a moment."

Frank was an experienced bush pilot and made frequent private hauls in and out of Canadian air space. Usually he hauled in men, supplies, camping gear, and occasionally mail. This time, he hauled in two packages labeled lab equipment. One contained a small satellite link communicator, and the other a *twin sister* bomb to the Jefrah device. Tightly packed in a small skid like base, metal banded, vapor wrapped, and nailed tight, it was labeled *Lab Equipment 09835, Handle with Care.*

Frank just served as a convenient mule to get the materials Eli and Sang had intended for use at the mine.

Once beached, Gilles surveyed the surroundings of pure wilderness; the only roads were two miles away. Frank maneuvered the small plane to within four feet of the water's edge. Gilles stepped into the six inches of water and helped Frank unload the items to the SUV.

"You must be part of the mining operation up near Elko I suppose?" questioned Frank.

Careful to show no signs of secrecy Gilles said, "Yeah, I'm just doing the suits a favor to replace a busted lab monitor or something." Taking the manifest from Frank, he looked down at the paperwork. "Would have taken six days by truck, thanks a lot." Gilles quickly signed the manifest in an in-descript scribble, and Frank left on his way. Gilles was off to get his next instructions.

SUSAN'S ROOM AT THE BEST WESTERN

A marine watched closely from his room as Susan opened the door to her room. Susan smiled as the door opened easily and all appeared normal. As instructed by Dalton, Susan fired up the computer and checked all the files; a hidden program monitored all loads in and out of the hard drive.

In a single line, the screen flashed: XR-211 FILES DOWNLOADED TO EXTERNAL DRIVE 7:54 p.m.

Susan shook with uncontrollable fear and quickly surveyed the room and windows; all were locked and un-tampered. Trying with all her might to control her emotions and fear, she left the room, shut the door and called Dalton on his secure satellite phone line. "Someone was here, Dalton. They got in the computer and downloaded the files." She stopped just before the marine's room and looked around. "It happened while I had dinner with Jane, what do I do now?"

"Relax, this is exactly what we expected and wanted to happen. Come into work tomorrow just as you usually would, no change from your usual routine. And don't appear concerned, we are all probably being watched and examined to see what we might reveal."

Nervous yet calm, Susan said okay and headed back to her room. She closed and locked the door for the night. She slept in spurts, longing for Toro, and wondering why he had gotten involved in such a dangerous business.

8-TEEN

SEATTLE CLAREMONT HOSPITAL.

ED Kosko reviewed his report for the President on the happenings at Elko. At 11:10 p.m. Washington time his satellite cell phone rang. Dalton Crusoe's name flashed across the screen.

Ed didn't waste any time and got right to the point. "Anything new to report?"

"Yes, tonight Mitsui operatives took down the XR-211 files from Susan's laptop as we hoped and apparently they believe it's the real thing." Dalton sounded very confident.

"Everybody is okay and it's playing out as planned?"

"Yes, now we just need to know how successful the bogus files will be in destroying the Israeli ore."

Ed smiled at his protégé's success. "We have satellites positioned over the IEC lab night and day. We will see if Eli Weiss or Sang Huchara appears on the grounds. I'll call you tomorrow," concluded Dalton.

THE ISRAELI BETRAYAL

TEL AVIV, ISRAEL — IEC LABORATORIES

Dr. Eli Weiss went ecstatic over the captured American Enertek files. Gilles had delivered the disk to Sang, who had then zipped and emailed the files under encryption to Eli personally. Two of Weiss's top scientists following the XR-211 experiments and entrusted with the new information were carefully going over the differences between their work, that of the Enertek team prior to the explosion, and the most recent results taken from the mining site.

Anxious to get their raw crystalline ore into a refined state suitable for weaponry, the Weiss team re-formatted the processing equipment and wrote new batch operating instructions to incorporate the American findings into their development efforts.

Jane had been clever in her creation of the bogus lab results. She knew experienced and capable scientists were going to be studying every modification, permutation, and variance from their own work to check for the presence of new information. Jane grew compulsive in her attention to detail and deception in creating the new file; after all, she nearly died carrying out the initial protocol and those meant to receive this "new research" had corrupted Toro, and had sent assassins to kill her and everyone else now involved with his technology. Her creation was complete and seductive.

The Israeli team took the bait just as Jane hoped they

would. They were emboldened by their own pride, smug in their belief they had outsmarted the American Enertek team, and giddy in the riches this find would bring to them from a grateful Israeli government.

As the disk contents loaded data onto the Israeli servers, the process controllers began to re-direct and tweak the refining steps. The slow, yet inevitable, neutralization and de-activation of the raw ore began. In about forty-five hours, if the refining process continued, Israel would be without a source of raw material for their new technology of weaponry and energy.

Jane had also buried a stealth program to capture and re-task their satellite instructions to activate and eventually detonate a bomb under Israeli control. After uploading, the Israeli's could communicate with the bomb, although they could not detonate it as long as the stealth program remained active.

Gilles pulled his SUV off the road after the Beaver Dehaviland had taken off and disappeared against the cloudy sky. He turned on his satellite phone and called Sang Huchara.

"I have the "special package" in my truck. It just arrived by sea plane a few minutes ago. What's next?"

"Eli and I devised a plan to insert the second bomb

on the Elko site. Isn't there a storage area for parts and digging equipment deep on the floor of the open pit mine?"

Gilles found himself grinning. "Yeah, there is and it's close enough to everything to do the whole job."

"Good, proceed with the placement plan as discussed and call me when it's in place."

"Right." Gilles closed his phone cover ending the call. Disguised as machine parts and relabeled to match other supplies on the warehouse floor, the lethal device was programmed to explode on command from a satellite signal.

Gilles drove toward the mine to not only complete his assignment, but also extract revenge for Dalton wounding him at the cabin. Once the bomb got positioned, Eli and Sang would control the timing on the final step to detonate the bomb. Gilles kept thinking, *hopefully Crusoe and his team will be killed in the blast.*

Jeff and Ted positioned themselves three miles up Highway 132 leading to the small, single blinker town serving the mine in the Waldron range. Several trucks a day came down the road carrying parts and supplies of all kinds. Some stopped at the mine and made drops at the lab headquarters, others at the mine's field office. That day, a delivery truck known to the mine was on time at 10:32 a.m. as it approached their location.

Earlier that day, Ted had stalled the Nissan SUV, containing the disguised bomb in the middle of the right lane. He opened the hood and started a small fire to appear as though the engine was ablaze.

The big sixteen wheeler slowed as it rounded the turn and approached the stalled vehicle. As the driver pulled up, Ted waved him down appearing very stressed and helpless. The old trucker from the Calgary area stopped and stepped out. "What's the trouble young fella?"

"My engine's dead. Just stopped running about ten minutes ago."

"Well let's take a look," said the weathered truck driver, opening his cab door.

Three hundred forty yards away, up a forested slope the scope crosshairs found its target. Two steps out of the van and Jeff's 270 Winchester barked, ripping a hole through the center of the trucker's chest. He dropped in a slump, dead as he hit the ground.

Ted dragged the body off into the heavy brush and jumped in the cab. Jeff came down from the roadside hill and moved the Nissan out of the way and parallel to the truck. Ripping open the back latch on the trailer, Ted and Jeff loaded the bomb into the back and positioned it with six other similar boxes and crates.

Seconds later the big rig began moving, only five miles from the Elko site entrance.

4:00 P.M.
WALDRON RANGE — ELKO MINE SITE

Ted started his down shifting to slow the big sixteen wheeler as it approached the mine site entrance. Jeff had covered himself in the back of the sleeper cab just behind Ted. A UPS truck had stopped at the gate and was apparently in no hurry to enter, as the driver and guard exchanged meaningless chatter about the opening of the early black bear season in Western Canada. After a frustrating delay, the final UPS truck moved on through the security checkpoint, and Ted nudged the big rig forward.

"Good afternoon, what do you have for us today?" asked the guard. He personified one of those overweight, talkative types who loved to hear himself speak and fully capable to offer the final humorous quip in a conversation. Perfect thought Ted, *an absolute idiot guarding the entrance to the greatest mineral find of the century.*

Engaging in the banter, Ted said, "Well let's take a look, haven't really studied it myself, you know what I mean." Grabbing the truck manifest and handing it to the guard created a very assuring sign, nothing out of the norm, thought Ted as he performed his part.

"Six crates of machine parts and lab stuff, right?"

"Yeah, that sounds like what I'm usually driving down these mountain passes with." Ted sat emotionless with a slight grin on his face.

Flipping through the true manifest, though uninterested in checking the cargo hold personally, the guard handed the sheets back to Ted. Then he asked, "Know where to go?" Ted paused, looked down the road and sure enough, an answer was provided to the guard's own question. "Just follow this road down and around the first maintenance building on the mine floor and look for the deep well receiving dock on the left."

"Thanks buddy," Ted chirped as he started the rig into the fenced mine area without raising any suspicion from the pathetic security guard. Before getting to the dock, Jeff came out from cover and sat beside Ted as a load helper. Once at the dock, Ted stayed in the cab and Jeff directed a forklift driver to unload and stack the crates in the center of thirty other similar pieces of truck cargo.

The bomb was in place at Elko.

9-TEEN

ED arrived early for his meeting with the President. Ed was moving slowly, however he was unwilling to take his recovery lying down. He had a few more days before the planned corrective surgery that was now scheduled in the D.C. area. Then he would be bed ridden again for a week or two.

Kosko had a lot to say and wanted the President at his best, which usually meant in the morning. Hours earlier, Ed had received a full update from Dalton and was pleased with how well the team had performed under Dalton's leadership. Ed and Dalton performed like a well coordinated tag team for the President.

The issue now, or very soon, would be when the Israelis realized their supply of ore had been rendered useless because of the bogus processing technology Jane had provided. Japan would become very suspicious, as they had yet to examine the entire technology, and could only rely on the Weiss team to give them the facts. Perhaps the Israelis would make up a story about losing their raw material to a flawed operating process.

On the other hand, Weiss may claim the Americans discovered enough new information to challenge the Israelis on the efficacy of their research. One thing was certain, the weaponry aspect of the technology works. The Japanese had one bomb about the size of the Jefrah bomb, although they, like others, wanted the full potential of this technology at their command. Moreover, having the full potential of the technology is exactly why they were funding Weiss and Huchara.

During the meeting, Dalton informed the President on the events at Elko and how he felt the next few critical days would unfold with the Israelis. Ed interjected on occasion, although for the most part held back admiring Dalton as he smartly went through the complicated happenings and probable future events soon to unfold. The President thanked both men for their report and told them that he wanted Dalton to proceed with the initial phase of his plan. A plan built around bold actions and very enticing outcomes.

Unknown to Dalton's team, events were already in motion in Japan to model the Jefrah exercise against their dangerous neighbor, North Korea. Secretary Kytoma had pressed Weiss for their role, if at all, in the

Iranian explosion. After some feigned resistance, Weiss proudly explained the spectacular success the weapon afforded them in terms of deployment, modulation of intensity to exactly what the issue needed, and no more. The Secretary and Dr. Weiss then made a dangerous decision. Driven by the power and flexibility of the Elko technology, they decided to take out the North Korean Missile Research Complex (NKMRC) in Hyesan, soon to be completed, and claiming extensive capability to attack Japan. Kytoma reasoned that the same logic used by Israel to attack the Jefrah site of the IERC also stood available for Japan concerning the North Korean Missile Research Complex.

While nothing official had been alleged or acknowledged about Israel's involvement in the Jefrah explosion, the Japanese Head of Intelligence already concluded their bomb, sitting in secured storage aboard a reconnaissance ship off the Bay of Japan, was identical to that used in Iran. Secretary Kytoma had all the evidence he felt he needed to commit to the same clandestine and highly effective route Israel took. He made the decision and set plans in motion. Kytoma reasoned Japan's economy, wealth, and standard of living were a source of major irritation for the North Korean leadership, and they now possessed intermediate range, nuclear tipped missiles capable of reaching Japan. Growing doubt about the willingness of the USA to defend Japan against a hostile act or threatened aggression made a compelling case to take out the Korean leadership and major elements of their offensive capabilities, especially if they could do it under the guise of a nuclear accident in North Korea.

With the commitment of a mid -level North Korean military leader, General Yong, and secured through the payment of $6,300,000 over several years, Japan had a paid asset willing, and able, to assist in deploying a bomb near the North Korean site. In two days, the bomb would be loaded onto a cargo plane taking "machine goods" to Hong Kong where General Yong had arranged to direct its routing through China and then into North Korea by truck. The truck would be unloaded at the new military complex for advanced missile development, the NKMRC, and soon to be dedicated by the North Korean Prime Minister and his senior military staff. Member number four of the Knowledge Consortium Group, North Korean General Yong, stood ready to take action to change the future course for North Korea.

If all the timing issues could be handled, Japan would remove the North Korean threat to them and their neighbors for decades. General Yong's information had proven valuable and accurate in the past. Twice earlier, Yong had predicted the exact days North Korea would test a missile over the Sea of Japan, including the intended target location at sea. Each time he delivered information personally through encrypted email sent through the KCG to Secretary Kytoma. Now it became critical that the North Korean dedication meeting place and time were known so that the second bomb could be positioned.

General Yong hoped he could set the stage for a reunification of the North and South, followed by a casual retirement in the west for his services to the enemies of North Korea. His work for the Knowledge Consortium would be complete.

Dalton was still perplexed as to how the assassin knew about the cabin and that he, Jane, and the rest would be there. Four days after the attack, he and Jane left the mine at noon and drove to the blacktop road nearest the cabin. The weather became clear, beautiful, and crisp. It reached fifty-two degrees, with no wind and brilliant blue sky, and only a few scattered bilious clouds floating overhead. After about another twenty minutes of two-tracking, they arrived at the cabin. It didn't look as bad as it felt several days earlier when Gilles Montrose attacked, intent on retrieving the experiment data and eliminating all who knew of it.

Thankfully, Gilles's plans were frustrated by Dalton and the rest.

Gilles Montrose watched once more from a lookout some two hundred feet above the road as it made a wide arc to the point where the two-track worked its way back to the cabin.

Outsmarted you again, thought Gilles. He thought they would return to the cabin for data, the files, or just evidence gathering from the assault.

"Bird Perch to Falcons, come in," whispered Gilles into his voice mike.

"Falcons, here, we read you five by five," announced Ted, confirming the voice signal was strong.

"Party of two appears headed to nest, proceed to intercept, and detain, over."

"Roger that Bird Perch," muttered Ted.

Dalton was drawn to follow the blood trail the assassin must have left as he departed, limping out of the woods in a hurry. Rain had not been seen in the area for over two weeks and he hoped a blood trail might still be staining the leaves and underbrush. Dalton knew he had hit him with the 270, and it should have just about taken a leg off if it had hit squarely. However, no evidence of a leg appeared as they walked along moving away from the cabin as they re-traced the path taken by Gilles.

Ted and Jeff stood about one hundred-forty yards

apart, scanning the distance for movement. Dressed in dull black camo, they blended in with the cedar, pine, aspen, and the frequent rock outcroppings covering the area near the mine. Shadows broke through the woods followed by a splash of sunlight then back to shadows as the sun and trees moved in a slow rhythm. It instilled a calming sensation.

At over two hundred yards away, Ted intermittently caught the only visible movement as he scanned through his 60 x 20 binoculars, trying to pick up the motion of Dalton and Jane. A coyote ran across and then toward Ted and Jeff. It moved fast and gave rise to the idea it may have been startled and ran off. Moments later a dull red barn coat flashed across Ted's view, and sure enough, there stood Dalton, a Glock 40 in one hand and the 270 rifle slung over his shoulder.

Looking down, Dalton saw a spot of dried blood, still bright red and dispersed as though it had been sprayed from a can instead of squirting from a man's leg. Instinct made Dalton stop and carefully survey the distant wood line in search of a dead and decaying body. Nothing moved nor looked out of place to him. He moved forward in stealth mode, crouched over and in a combat ready position. As a precaution, he motioned for Jane to position herself behind him, back closer to the cabin and within a tight cluster of tall pines. From some thirty yards away, her heart raced as she watched Dalton follow the blood trail.

Meanwhile, Jeff had backed away, retreating to a thick tree line that gave cover to position himself to the side and behind Dalton. Jeff withdrew an arrow from the quiver strapped to his leg and silently knocked it onto the bowstring. He cocked the 70-pound compound crossbow to its full draw position and steadied it on Dalton's left shoulder blade some sixty yards away. Aimed like a rifle and scoped for up to a hundred yards, Jeff had killed many an animal, including the human kind, at this range.

Instead of taking up an assault Uzi and blazing away, Ted and Jeff decided to hunt in silence. A rifle shot could be heard for miles and they did not want to alert the marine security force at the mine to their presence. Jeff's 45-caliber silenced Glock strapped to his hip would not be accurate enough to assure a successful hit at sixty yards. Rather, they would try to capture Dalton or Jane for interrogation. Mitsui paid good money and the better the intel obtained, the better the bonus might be.

Dalton moved like a stalker, taking slow steps, easing his dropping foot to the ground in front of him on each deliberate move, and always scanning the woods in front of him for movement or shapes which did not belong there. Cautious and patient, putting all his weight on his left foot, and shifting forward he froze hearing, he thought, an unfamiliar sound . . . a faint click.

A fraction of a second later Dalton felt the arrow stab his jacket, carve through his shirt and into his flesh. Jeff had hit his mark, although not in a lethal spot. Dalton whirled in pain and anger to his left, and fell to the ground with his Glock 40 aimed five feet above the ground from his fully extended arm, while coursing the woods to his left. Jeff shortened his stance and disguised his image and outline in the brush and trees. Seeing no adversary approaching, Dalton quickly examined his bleeding side, which did not reveal severe damage, though nevertheless, it was a bleeding flesh wound.

Ted appeared from behind Jane, cupped his hand over her mouth and pressed a six-inch dull black military knife against her throat. Trembling in fear, she could only watch as Dalton looked for his adversary now some hundred yards away.

Dalton removed a handkerchief bandage from his jacket pocket and pressed it to his side, seven inches below his armpit. The pain was excruciating, though tolerable. Another second later and Dalton again heard another strange sound, *"curhoose"*, it resonated, and another arrow headed directly at his neck. Dalton fell fast to the ground and heard the arrow slam into a tree, five feet above the ground and six yards behind him.

RICHARD TREVAE

From a flat defensive position, on his belly, and cringing in pain, Dalton looked up and saw a man moving in a rapid staggered run away from his position. In four seconds, the man disappeared out of sight.

From the cover of fallen trees Jeff caught his breath and spoke through his headset to Ted, "I hit him but he's not down, can you take him out?"

"Negative at this time, got the companion in my arms, and under my knife. I don't want to reveal my position or allow her to warn him."

"Roger that, hold five," whispered Jeff.

Again surveying his surrounding terrain, Dalton stood up and back stepped slowly until he stood about fifty yards from the near fatal attack. Jane was nowhere to be seen. Ted had backtracked with her in hand toward the cabin. Suspecting he was dealing with more than one bad guy, Dalton withheld his desire to call out for Jane. He scowled mentally; *she must have been caught or worse.* His mind went into combat mode. Within seconds, Dalton ran into the deep woods, away from the cabin, and put the afternoon sun directly behind him.

Laying flat on the ground, he steadied the 270, fortunately against his uninjured shoulder. The pain eased to a warm, dull throbbing, and the bleeding slowed and started to clot. He could make it sometime in this condition, he reasoned. Controlling his breathing Dalton lay still for more than two minutes, when, as he hoped, a movement appeared 150 yards out stalking his escape from the trail to the cabin.

Jeff tried to follow a nearly non-existent blood trail from Dalton. The arrow had hit him; however, it went clean through and did not find a major blood vessel. Dalton maneuvered the 270 scope over the terrain searching about one hundred and twenty yards out. Moving from tree to tree for cover, Jeff searched the ground then the distance for signs of Dalton. He moved slowly, in stealth mode, like a hunter in search of his game, certain it lay on the ground bleeding out.

A fatal flaw for Jeff, as Dalton leveled the cross hairs of the 8-power scope on Jeff's neck. Without second thoughts or hesitation, Dalton squeezed the trigger and the 150-grain ball ripped open Jeff's neck and upper chest, he fell dead to the ground. Dalton partially covered his head and body with leaves and remained motionless. Hearing the shot, Jane shook uncontrollably as Ted covered her mouth and scanned the distance from very near the cabin. Ted feared the worst, made quick work of tying up Jane, tapping her mouth quiet as he took up his Uzi to check out the situation.

"Jeff, come in," whispered Ted.

A very low whisper returned, "Back in two, stay in place."

Unaware exactly what he heard, Ted pressed forward. Dalton lay still as Ted emerged from the forest.

RICHARD TREVAE

Moments later Ted froze in his tracks, for out some sixty yards in a pile of fallen limbs and leaves lay a motionless man in the dull red jacket he'd seen Dalton wear into the woods. *Jeff got him after all,* thought Ted as he approached with his weapon trained on the motionless body.

Now twenty feet away Ted set his Uzi down and proceeded to turn the man over. Jeff was dressed in Dalton's jacket and cap. As Ted grasped the red jacket, Dalton sprang and attacked from nearby where the piled leaves were covering him. Knocking Ted to the ground, Dalton delivered several quick, hard smashes to his face, cutting the lip and nose. Ted grabbed Dalton by the shoulders and threw him off. Ted jumped to his feet, pulled a knife and lunged at Dalton. Dodging the thrust Dalton hammered the man's back and neck hard with a powerful blow. Ted again fell to the ground and once more came up quickly moving toward Dalton.

Now in hand-to-hand combat, Dalton could feel the incredible strength of the man and his intensity. His karate skills were too elaborate for a street fighter like Ted; rather he relied on brute strength. Dalton knew he had to end this fight soon. Kicking at his groin dropped Ted to his knees groaning in pain. Dalton followed with a fast high turning kick to the jaw, knocking him back leaving him unconscious.

Within moments, Dalton had tied and bound Ted

with his own equipment. Seeing his adversary still unconscious, Dalton began to look for Jane. He did not want to shout, as he feared others may be nearby to assist the two attackers. Returning in the direction Ted had appeared, Dalton began to approach the cabin and found Jane bound, though all right. As he released her, she began trembling from fear; very happy to see Dalton alive, yet still uncontrollably crying. Once freed and walking toward the front porch of the cabin, she realized Dalton was obviously hurt and bleeding.

"My God, what happened to you?" gasped Jane, as she assisted Dalton into the cabin.

"Our friends are still around, probably looking for more data and files for their bosses," struggled Dalton.

"Are they still out there looking for us?"

"I doubt it; the first one took off fast, only to pursue me at the expense of his life."

"Was that the shot I heard?" asked Jane

Dalton nodded calmly. "Yes, he's dead, and I tricked the other one holding you to find me, or what he thought was me, and I have him bound about two hundred yards that way," Dalton gestured. "Are you all right?" He asked looking for blood on Jane.

"Who are these men and what do they want?" Jane demanded an answer.

"Well, they were probably hoping to eliminate me

and you, or capture us for some less than pleasant talk time," offered Dalton. "When they saw I was armed and not killed or taken down by the arrows, they must have decided to use their guns during their next assault."

Dalton sat as still as he could while Jane, behaving like a surgical nurse, removed his jacket and shirt, and began cleaning the pass-through route of the arrow on his left side.

Her hands were steady, warm, and gentle as she applied gauze and tape to the wound. He looked up at her and saw a strong woman, hurting and scared yet committed to help. Jane did not hide her fears well even when tending, much like a physician, to Dalton's wound.

"Thank you, that feels much better." Dalton looked down at the bandaging.

Jane folded her arms in a steely motion yet trembling, as she pondered their predicament and a sense of vulnerability from the unexpected attack.

"I just thought they wanted the experiment data, why would they want to kill us?" she asked looking back at Dalton with terror in her face."

Realizing the unvarnished truth was best, Dalton explained. "Jane, this is too big to be concerned about taking lives of a few folks who could stymie their plans. These guys and their bosses are determined and ruthless." Jane slumped in her chair and struggled to withhold tears. Dalton tried to assure her they would be alright, and kept an eye towards the forest.

Ted groaned, came to, and gnawed through the tape binding his hands, he then retrieved another knife hidden in his boot to cut the remaining tape and rope securing him. Grabbing his weapon still laying on the ground, he pulled up the lifeless body of Jeff to his shoulder and began moving out of the woods in quick steps to evade Dalton.

Ten minutes later with Jane in hand, Dalton retraced his route and learned of Ted's escape and the removal of Jeff's body. Still perplexed, Dalton had no real clues who these people were or their connection to Weiss and Huchara.

They quickly moved back to the cabin.

# TWENTY

JEFRAH, IRAN

THE Iranians were stuck. They could not plead their case to the world, for a real scrutiny of the devastation would reveal the true operations at the Iranian Energy Research Laboratory, a bomb making facilities along with a missile delivery system — not new energy studies. Their own scientists were coming around to the belief that a bomb had caused the explosion and not their operations at the IERL.

Khamal had learned through his persuasive techniques Hatta was the saboteur. Hatta's handlers were careful not to reveal the source of the breakthrough that led to the Iranian blast. As a result, Khamal only knew that Hatta had planted the bomb, obtained it from Israeli sources at the Israeli Energy Commission, and a U.S. operative was involved and the man's name was Dalton Crusoe. The Iranian Defense Minister became totally convinced U.S. and Israeli black ops group were involved and he grew determined to find someone to blame publicly.

Furthermore, the Iranian military received instructions to prepare plans for their own attack on Israel targeting the IEC, and the Iranian President wanted it to happen soon.

TEL AVIV, ISRAEL

Eli Weiss remained euphoric. His crack team of scientists had intercepted the American's discovery, rapidly furthered the applied research to a point where he felt they now had exclusive control of perhaps the newest and most valuable technology ever developed by mankind. The call he had just received from Gilles Montrose confirmed the bomb at Elko sat in place. Now it was time to bring the bomb, through its local detonation controller (LDC), to active status.

Weiss closed the door to the top-secret laboratory situation room. He addressed his team of seven loyal and well-compensated scientists. At the press of a key pad, after entering the proper access code, a wall of the conference room opened, the lights dimmed and revealed the secret operations center, within the situation room; a real-time link to the underground Israeli Defense Command Center. The IEC setup the fully equipped alternate command center to operate with floor-to-ceiling, wall-to-wall, visual satellite screens of

North America and the Chinese/North Korean border. The seven-member team took positions at their respective consoles without a sound and awaited further word from Dr. Weiss.

Without giving details, Weiss told them to commence the process of making the Elko bomb active and downloading software instructions to the LDC, which would establish the strength of the explosion. A GPS type-tracking beacon initiated the first stage of electronics taken active. The satellite imagery was state-of-the-art, and in large part funded and developed by the Japanese. Only the highest level U.S. security sites had better and faster technology. The satellite had just come into range three minutes earlier and could hold a signal and image for about twenty-five minutes. As the satellite focused in over northern Montana, it quickly picked up the homing beacon from the bomb in the mine area.

Further resolution revealed its location near the southeast section of the mining site and that a "ground zero" area of about four-tenths of a square mile would be required to assure destruction of the mine. After a few computer iterations on the detonation size, the instructions were sent down from the satellite to the receiver on the LDC, and it acknowledged:

```
Instructions   received   and   loaded>>>>
device is active.
```

Weiss then withdrew his encrypted satellite phone and dialed Gilles. Moments later a voice said, "Gilles here, what's our status?"

Weiss replied slowly saying, "Package is confirmed in position and active." And after a pause, he ordered, "Proceed to commence Fire-Fly operation at 0200 local time."

The immediate response came from Gilles. "Roger that and I will not seek contact until contacted — correct?"

"Contact will be initiated from here, command out." Weiss shut off his phone.

The satellite did not move in a geo-synchronized orbit, though it circled the earth every two hours and twenty-seven minutes. In about eleven hours, at 04:30 a.m. local Montana time, the LDC would trigger detonation.

20-ONE

ELKO, MONTANA

THREE days had passed since Jeff was killed and Ted was nearly captured in their encounter with Dalton and Jane. With no bodies to explain, Dalton kept the event quiet from the local marines and operational people remaining at the mine site. He had of course, updated Ed Kosko and President Conner, and despite urgings for more security support for Dalton and his team, he felt it best to not show an increased presence, but rather to continue the plan to draw-in the opposition to a trap.

Gilles and Ted sat on the airstrip five miles northwest of the mine and could see their handiwork at setting the forest on fire. Huge flames began spreading rapidly from the top of the ridgeline just above the mine down and across the entire area surrounding the mine. In a strange twist, Weiss's plan called for the pre-emptive fire to minimize loss of human life and also camouflage the following detonation. Gilles reasoned that Weiss felt fewer deaths would draw less attention to the blast, and help hide the attack. Nevertheless, Gilles hoped a certain Dalton Crusoe would remain to fight the fire and be killed in the ensuing bomb blast.

It was 03:40 a.m. when the evacuation alarms began to sound. The entire mine camp had to be evacuated before the fire hit the mine compound containing barracks, laboratories, and warehouses. Gilles and his team carefully designed their efforts to close the only road in and out of the mine camp with smoke and fire, and within the next hour or so, the mine would be empty and only the elite fire fighting crew, procured through the marines, would be there when the bomb detonated.

As anticipated Gilles's phone rang, it was Weiss. "Fire Fly is underway?"

"Yes, evacuation is starting," replied Gilles. "We are just about to fly out to Vancouver."

"Good, I'll communicate with our friend there tomorrow." Weiss hung up.

3:45 A.M.
ELKO MINE — WALDRON RANGE

Dalton felt like he had awoken in a nightmare. The air had become thick with smoke, and flames were coming down the hillsides toward the mining camp. Sirens were blaring out the evacuation alarm, and all the construction and non-critical staff were being transported out. Deep wells were operating at peak capacity for the first time in years as they fed the local firewater distribution circuit, however to no avail, as the flames were too large and the heat too intense.

Dalton looked around, still pulling his shirt over his shoulders as he ran outside. Jane and Susan were already outside, still in their nightwear, and looking very confused. They were talking to the night security manager.

"What's going on?" inquired Dalton

"Looks like a damn lighting storm lit off some pines on the northwest ridge, but I didn't hear or see incoming weather that would trigger this size a blaze."

"Can we contain this thing at this point?" Dalton yelled back to the manager.

"Not a chance, we'll be lucky to save the laboratories, but the barracks look like they will be lost for sure."

"Don't let the fire reach the labs; do whatever is needed to protect them, understood?" yelled Dalton.

Dalton looked cautiously around the site and questioned the predicament. *Could this be an act of sabotage, or just an act of nature? Far too convenient for it to be nature, with a clear day before sunset and no weather warnings.* His mind reeled with possibilities. *Could Sang and Weiss have staged this, and for what reason? Why would they want to affect this mine this way? How would fire ever stop the eventual re-opening of the mine?*

Then a terrifying thought hit Dalton. *Had they managed to plant a bomb at the mine in an attempt to destroy the crude ore for use as fusion fuel? Was the fire a diversion to cover a subsequent explosion?* His mind raced into hyper-speed thoughts.

NEAR HYESAN, NORTH KOREA

THE clandestine custom bomb in the machine parts box kept moving along the route General Yong had intended. The last leg of the trip by truck began from just inside the Chinese border with North Korea. Then it went three hundred and fifty miles south to the military complex soon to be dedicated by the Korean Prime Minister.

As the large truck and trailer groaned up the slow, ascending roads after just passing into North Korea, the weather was getting worse. Strong winds, cool temperatures, and a late fall kind of cloud cover, were all laid against a barren landscape devoid of human or animal signs. It was a horrible place and country to work in, much less live.

The driver grew weary after working for the eleventh day in a row for about fourteen hours per day. After this run, he would have two days off before starting all over again. General Yong had directed two personnel trucks to provide front and rear coverage as the truck rolled along to its destination. At 7:45 p.m. local time, the driver pulled into the construction gate at the military complex, backed his rig up to the unloading dock, and shut off his engine. Exhausted, he rubbed his eyes and fumbled to locate his paper work for unloading the half-full carrier.

The receiving clerk was not much of warehouse manager; in fact, he had been removed from driving the trucks because of three accidents in the last eighteen months in which vehicles and cargo were damaged. He had a tendency to drink, drive, and fall asleep at the wheel. The local commander at the construction site allowed him to stay on one last year while completing the final work. He was your classic paper shuffler, no clue, nor interest in the job, just putting in his time, and receiving his usually tardy monthly payment equal to about $15.00 USD. The sergeant leading the escort envoy stood by and watched the driver and clerk stumble through their routine; then they began the process of unloading the carrier.

Eleven larger wooden crates eventually emerged from the truck and were neatly stacked and segregated into storage areas for the building, equipment, communications, vehicles, weapons support and computer control components. The smallest box labeled weapons support contained the bomb tucked in perfect position. The sergeant overseeing the delivery of all the containers had no knowledge of the real contents, only that general

Yong had specifically assigned him to this "most important" matter to make certain all was in place for the Prime Minister.

The sergeant had done his job well and the bomb came into the military complex, a full three days before the dedication of the facility, amid much publicity by the Prime Minister and his generals. The sergeant radioed General Yong's headquarters and politely informed staff that the deliveries were completed and the driver left, returning to his post at the Chinese border.

General Yong felt anxious and proud at the same moment. He had just earned enough money to retire, as an ex-patriot, and longed to enjoy the west. Yong was very political and didn't care about the demands of the eccentric leader of North Korea. He was not in it just for himself, rather to someday lead a re-unification of both Koreas. However, he must disappear for a while from the entire Korean peninsula while the dust settled following the assassination attempt. He planned to make his escape to Japan after the explosion which he hoped would bring death to the Prime Minister and his top generals.

20-THREE

DALTON was not about to under estimate the possibility that a bomb might already be in place at the mine. He assembled the marine captain and the security team he oversaw, explained his fears and directed a six-man team to quickly scour the site for a bomb, most likely hidden or disguised as something innocuous or plain.

Dalton reasoned that if a bomb had been delivered it must have arrived in the last ten days. He began with a manifest summary of the shipments received in the recent past. Shipments arrived every day for hundreds of specific items brought onto the mine site. Six items delivered over the past five days were prime candidates to hide a bomb. They included machine parts, computer hardware, vehicles, and lubricant oils and greases. The marines began to track down and investigate the shipments. Twenty minutes into the search the marine captain called Dalton on the site phone system. "I think we've found something sir," barked the captain.

"What is it?"

"Well it is labeled machine parts, but the wooden crating is extra heavy for its size and I can't find a supplier label anywhere, so it may have been repackaged at some point."

"Take it to the concrete bunker protecting the north side of the excavation, immediately," Dalton commanded.

"On it sir," replied the captain.

The concrete bunker resembled a large three-sided retaining wall some twenty feet in height, eighty feet wide and protected the main roadway to the excavation bottom from eroding hillsides and rainfall run-off. It served as a good spot to examine the crate. The time in Montana showed 4:08 a.m.

The crate, still sitting on a skid, opened easily and revealed a myriad of pulleys, bits, weights, tooling, and motors. Underneath it laid a plywood false floor covering the lowest depth of the crate. Beneath the plywood false floor lay a metal brief case about two feet by eighteen inches and seven inches deep was the bomb.

At Dalton's request, Jane had already established a video-teleconference on site at the bunker when the examination of the bomb began. Ed Kosko, the President, his Head of the Joint Chiefs and two bomb experts from the defense department were all conferenced in. Jane led the explanation as Dalton directly oversaw the disassembly of the crate revealing the suitcase containing, what all felt could be, a bomb. Except for Ed, Jane, Dalton and the President the others simply thought this might be a tactical bomb planted by an environmental group — eco-terrorists. Questions continued as Dalton managed the field activities.

"Remove the side walls of the crate but do not tilt or jar the metal case." Dalton pointed at the marines wielding large axes and power saws.

The marine captain stood next to his team and called out every piece he wanted removed and how to do it. The process went slowly, for Dalton feared the device could detonate upon tampering or impact. Jane held a scanner near the silver case after the wooden crate sides were removed. "There is definite electrical activity inside this thing, but the sensors detect no known explosives."

"Let's get this area clear of all personnel as we send in a robot to investigate it contents," suggested Dalton.

The seasoned, senior bomb expert viewing the activity interrupted. "Wait! Dalton this thing may have a timer on it, or a movement trigger. We just don't know."

Jane agreed and insisted they carefully remove it from the area using a helicopter harness. The marines managed to fashion a series of military straps under the skid base and around the case itself. Plans were put in motion to fly the helicopter, lifting the device from harness cables, and drop it all into an abandoned empty

mine shaft only one-quarter mile from the open excavation at Waldron.

The old shaft, 600 feet deep, dating back to the late
1800's was not connected to the mine site containing
the rare ore. By 5:25a.m., a marine helicopter pilot had
the bomb in a harness hanging forty feet below the
chopper and lifting off from the bunker yard.

Dalton grew very anxious, as did Jane, watching the
lift off, slowly extending over one hundred feet of cable
into the air before the silver case and crate bed left the
ground. The helicopter gained speed and headed north
dangling the bomb below. The bomb did not detonate
by movement, which made Dalton speculate that perhaps it had an internal timer or controller.

The abandoned mine shaft made a good choice,
because as Jane and the other scientists concluded the
bomb looked like a small yield device, even if nuclear,
and an explosion 600 feet below ground would contain
the blast and protect human life. As Jane and Dalton
watched the chopper disappear over the northern ridgeline, they hoped and prayed the device would not detonate on impact, or in the air, taking with it the
helicopter and crew.

Moments later the chopper's big searchlights
found the shaft opening, and positioned the harness
and bomb about twenty feet above the entrance. After

releasing the bomb, the chopper roared turning hard climbing to the west and circling above the mine shaft.

As Dalton's watch approached 5:50 a.m. while the sky was still quite dark, Jane and he took a deep breath as the helicopter crew announced a successful bomb drop into the shaft and without triggering an explosion at the shaft entrance. Deep in the cold abandoned mine; the LDC continued to operate, broadcasting its location and awaiting instructions from the satellite.

20-FOUR

DR. Eli Weiss studied the clock on the wall and the satellite reconnaissance streaming into the large video screens on each of the walls in the operations center of the situation room. Weiss looked about, visually connecting with his situation room manager, and then around the room at the various screens displaying the area around Elko. The manager held Weiss's look for approval to detonate the bomb at the Waldron mine. Eli returned to the manager, looked directly at him and nodded, affirming the silent order to proceed.

Moments later the satellite imagery came into view. Seconds passed as the screens flashed, followed by grey and black movement as the clouds and landscape beneath reflected varying amounts of light back to the satellite. A bank of large clocks displayed the time in major world cities and a digital screen flashed the local Montana time as each second passed. The operations center grew silent as the detonation approached.

THE **ISRAELI BETRAYAL**

At 5:52 a.m. and 27 seconds, the IEC screens lit up in a brilliant yellow, orange, and white flurried display of activity. The room remained eerily silent. Those controlling the detonation could only image the sounds and destruction-taking place on the ground. In that instant, all felt Eli Weiss had secured his country's new role in the world as the only military and economic power with this new technology — or so they thought. The room fell motionless and somber as the satellite passed over and then out of view of the Waldron Range mine site. The easy use of this new destructive force affected some.

Dr. Eli Weiss reveled in the belief he had stolen the world's most elegant energy technology, completed the applied research to define and control it, and then eliminated the only other known reserves through an explosion that appeared as a horrible site accident. His mood reached ecstasy and he even had flashes of receiving the Nobel Prize for science and peace, when the entire world learned of his achievements. Weiss accepted the subdued congratulations of the entire team in the situation room.

RICHARD TREVAE

5:52 A.M.
ELKO, MONTANA

The sound seemed very unusual — not a typical bomb blast, more of a sharp sound burst followed by a low, long running roar from deep within the ground. Jane jumped into Dalton's arms and buried her face into his chest for protection. He held her tight, grateful to know they had reasoned out the problem. A faint, brief tremor was felt at the time, and the sky became a fireball some quarter mile from the primary excavation at the Waldron range dig. The sky stayed bright for several minutes as plumes from the mine advanced upward and spread over the Elko mine site.

Kosko, the president, and his demolitions team were fortunate to have discovered the bomb, removed it, and dropped it to detonate harmlessly in an abandoned mine shaft safe from the excavation and the new ore vein.

Studying the blast plume, Dalton wondered if the bomb had detonated by impact or some other mechanism — the question would not leave his thoughts.

Over the next few hours, the marines were able to contain and then stop the fire that had begun their eventful evening with only the loss of one warehouse and a barrack. Fortunately, neither the labs nor human life were lost.

By 6:20 a.m. Dalton ended his video teleconference with Ed and the President. He had brought them up to speed on the entire sequence of events during the early morning hours and created a story to release to the press, which blamed the blast on a fuel depot exploding after a "dry lighting" storm started the adjacent wooded hillsides ablaze. It sounded good and all felt it would fly. By noon that day, even the local folks in Elko and the mineworkers were of the belief that it occurred just as reported.

Both the Canadian and Montana local authorities were convinced the fuel depot explosion was the source of devastation. Only a brief mention without photos or film footage of the mine site appeared on the six o'clock news. Dalton had good reason to believe the Israelis and Japanese were unaware their plot to destroy the mine was foiled. Fortunately, the rapid evacuation of the area prior to the bomb search had all of the staff personnel located off the site.

As a further deterrence to more inquiries, Dalton ordered the indefinite shut down of mining operations and closure of the site until a full NSA investigation was completed. That would provide enough time to investigate the explosion source and secure the land in Montana and Canada from further attacks.

Five miles away, Gilles looked in his rear view mirror

RICHARD TREVAE

and saw the boiling plume of clouds over the mine site. Drawing a deep breath on a fresh Marlboro, feeling the pain from his leg wounds Gilles whispered a sinister *goodbye* to Mr. Dalton Crusoe.

20-FIVE

THE construction project was immense, at least by North Korean standards. Almost four thousand workers and construction specialists had worked as part of a seven-contractor symposium on the project for over three years. Only the last few crews on instrumentation, computer systems, and some limited mechanical work remained following the upcoming dedication. They were completing the "punch list items" noted in a final walkthrough by the resident managers of the complex. Mitsui had portions of the work, not much, yet enough for Yong to maintain easy access for personnel and equipment needed for his *personal* mission.

The Hyesan site occupied 1,320-acres in a barren, isolated, flat raised hill section of a northwestern mountain range, elevation 2,537 feet above sea level, in North Korea. It revealed a lightly forested, unimpressive topography, with gravel roads throughout the complex, no site lighting during evening hours to assist outsider intrusions, yet massive emergency lighting protecting against a remote, although feared, ground invasion by the south with American help. Seventeen buildings that were all connected through tunnels or above ground corridors made for a tight, controlled security at the facility.

The project developed into North Korea's most extravagant effort to show off its technical prowess to the world. In addition to the laboratories and test facilities, it contained fuel depots, missile final assembly buildings, and administrative offices for the military personnel overseeing the site security, and all the technicians, scientists, and engineers.

And at the eastern edge of the complex were four underground missile silos containing intermediate range weapons capable of delivering a nuclear warhead to Japan and, of course, South Korea.

The launch command center was midway between the research and administrative buildings and the buried silos. A huge radar and communications area soared skyward nearby to monitor and control the tests during missile launches from the complex.

General Yong selected the dedication event for detonating his bomb at the missile research facility following the morning arrival of the Prime Minister accompanied by his top staff. Yong figured about twenty-two high-ranking North Korean military, political, and scientific types would be attending. It felt like a dream-come-true for Sang Huchara and his high-level, very clandestine superiors in Japan.

Not only would they be able to eliminate a new, major facility publically touted by North Korea as their headquarters for weapons development, along with all the key leaders, and decisions makers. Moreover, the rogue Prime Minister would surely be killed in the blast. In addition, with luck, the world would again suspect internal problems as the cause of the explosion and not an outside entity.

General Yong, also expected to attend the dedication ceremony, struggled with how to escape the explosion and still have it appear as though he too died along with the others. He had hidden a personal military transport vehicle, a Korean version of a Jeep, for his escape. He decided to fake his own death, at the time of explosion, escape in his vehicle to the coast, some one hundred eighty kilometers away where a Japanese Navy team would transport him by a landing craft raft out to sea where a spy ship disguised as a fishing trawler would take him to a Japanese island.

From secure surroundings near Japan, Yong would remain in solitude until the press coverage and speculation arising from the devastation at Hyesan subsided. In time, he would convene with his associates in Vancouver and plan his next move. General Yong hoped to become the "darling" of the South Korean government and play a major role in uniting the Korean peninsula. Fantasies of becoming a respected political figure in a united Korea had long intrigued the general. He had friends in North Korea and many military types who would likely support his leadership of the north once the current regime left power and a new direction got underway.

At 7:45 a.m. local time, the dedication ceremony at the NKMRC was to follow a brief tour where the state controlled TV and news network would run video and sound of the Prime Minister and his staff walking through the complex, making meaningless idle chatter and pointing out the capabilities of the complex.

A press release would highlight the fact that North Korea now had the capacity to strike invaders from afar through missile technology, and that nuclear warhead capability would be achieved through ongoing work at the complex.

A buffet type late morning brunch was scheduled after the tour. The reception hall and conference center at the launch control center were set up to host the dedication. Yong had the bomb located a quarter-mile away in a parts warehouse crib associated with a missile fuel depot and maintenance area. It was hidden perfectly in the site and would inflict maximum damage. Near a source of highly flammable fuel, the fireball should spread and help cover the true source of the explosion.

Connections through the entire site via underground tunnels to the launch control center and several other buildings assured destruction.

The calculated blast would take out about half the complex including the critical launch control center and all the personnel attending the ceremony. If international news correspondents were present, which seemed unlikely, they would also be casualties of the blast.

Yong emailed a fellow North Korean general to deflect possible suspicions of his involvement in the Hyesan destruction. It also allowed him to alert his Japanese co-conspirators, as a blind copy, that the bomb attack was imminent.

```
To: Major General Kim:

I will not be able to meet you for
review of the new special security group
you plan to commission this week, as I
am committed to assist in the dedication
ceremonies at Hyesan, the new missile
research complex. I will call after the
formal dedication about 11:00 a.m. local
time.
    Regrets, General Yong
```

The recipients of the blind email account were Yong's

Japanese and South Korean contacts. The message was clear to them; add three hours to the time the email was sent and command the LDC to detonate the bomb.

The words *"I am committed"* signaled the bomb, personnel targets, and dedication program were present and underway as scheduled. Now all that remained was to draw in his victim, kill him through a deadly neurotoxin, and then substitute his body before the blast. The highly potent, fast acting poison added to tea became the choice Yong made after talking to his contacts about his escape. At 10:05 a.m., the plan went in motion.

He dismissed his staff of six to attend the walking tour with the press and military leaders, and then called back his executive officer, Sam, a man who had been serving Yong faithfully for five years. Sam was younger, although very close to the same size and weight of Yong. Ideally, thought Yong, enough destruction would prohibit a thorough coroner's evaluation of the body. Yong reasoned sacrificing his friend and colleague, while clearly an unpleasant decision, was necessary to complete his ruse, and successfully conceal his role in the day's events. Big issues require big sacrifices.

After a few questions about daily matters, Yong offered his faithful exo a hot tea, as a "celebration toast" and within a minute Sam slumped silently into a death coma. Watching his trusted exo slip into a paralyzing coma and convulsive seizure caused painful images for

Yong. As Sam slipped away, his gaze focused on the general and seemed to beg the question, "What have I done to deserve this?"

Yong pulled Sam into his office, sat him at his desk and put a dress jacket on him complete with ribbons, metals, and buttons identical to his own. Yong also removed the wallet inside Sam's rear pants pocket and added his own to help identify the corpse.

Touching Sam's hand the tearful Yong thought solemnly, *Goodbye my dear friend, I am sorry to betray you, but what you do not know is that you serve a noble purpose, aiding the reunification of Korea.*

Yong moved unseen through the myriad of tunnels and walkways connecting the buildings. As he prepared to leave in his "Korean Jeep", he thought back to his betrayal to Sam. He hoped he could someday forgive himself. Yong checked his watch . . . 10:12 a.m. and if all went as planned the detonation would happen at precisely 10:35 a.m.

20-SIX

THE crowd grew noisy and began congregating at the grand display of food, champagne, fruits, and desserts seldom seen in anything except official parties or military functions. The average peasant in North Korea lived every day in starvation and this tasteless display of indifference to the plight of his people offered a further justification for General Yong as he exited the complex by-passing a security gate with a "re-programmed" entry card from his South Korean and Japanese friends.

Maybe all this would lead to a reunification of the north to the south and his homeland Korea could join in the fruits of a successful, growing free economy in the south. At least Yong hoped this would be achieved, and further justify his actions of today. Driving his utility vehicle, Yong drove about eight kilometers from the base while heading southeast to the coast at exactly 10:17 a.m. local time.

THE ISRAELI BETRAYAL

TEL AVIV, ISRAEL —IEC COMMAND CENTER

Dr. Eli Weiss again found himself in the IEC locked in the operations room with his manager and six key technicians. As before, the team were busily positioning satellite data onto screens and downloading real time imagery over the Korean peninsula. Next to him were Sang Huchara, Secretary Kytoma, and the Japanese Deputy Director of Intelligence, watching as the satellites repeatedly scanned, focused, and then magnified to greater detail.

After the third focus cycle, the young technician said, "We are locked on to lat seventeen and long thirty-four, for the next thirteen minutes before losing images, sir."

By eight o'clock North Korean time, Weiss's group, as with the Jefrah detonation, had downloaded instructions to the LDC. The custom bomb, surreptitiously inserted into the enemy site, finished setting the timing and extent of the bomb blast. Per the information gained from Yong's email, the bomb would automatically detonate at 10:35 a.m. local time in Hyesan, North Korea.

20-SEVEN

CAROLYN McCabe had just finished her latest novel, a rich thriller set in exotic locals and featuring a romantic lead man who was continually superimposed in her mind as Dalton. Her clock table read 10:25 and she started growing tired. The open bedroom window to her two-bedroom 1,800 square foot condominium kept cooling the room. She liked the mild night breezes rather than air conditioning, and it made her very comfortable sleeping at night. She stood and stretched, and then walked to the kitchen and poured a glass of water.

Closing the hard back novel still in her hands, she stretched again and began to ponder where Dalton was, what he was doing, and when she would hear from him again. Their brief weekend getaway, cut short abruptly, stirred her imaginings. Staring out the window into the dark night air her world suddenly changed. A sharp blow to the back of her head dropped her to the floor. Her head in a fog, Carolyn briefly thought she saw a flurry of movement, through blurred flashes and footsteps near her feet.

Nearly unconscious, she could feel a man picking her up and throwing her on the bed. Helpless to react, she could see hazy images of a slim, strong man dressed in black, wearing a lightweight ski mask, proceeding to tie her hands and feet. Feeling it safer to play unconscious rather than fight at this moment, she feigned a limp lifeless body. After binding her arms and feet, the intruder taped her mouth shut, at which point her eyes instinctively opened wide and looked deep into the man's shadowy face. The room remained dark, showing only his eyes, intense, dark and foreboding. Carolyn's heart began to race, now conscious her panic emotions released a scream, muffled totally by the tape.

Aware of her conscious state, the intruder drew near and whispered. "Stay calm and quiet and this will all turn out okay." His voice was clear and calm, in control, disciplined with perhaps just a hint of a Middle Eastern accent.

Carolyn nodded in acknowledgement of the words. Frightened beyond anything she had ever encountered before, she remained motionless, and yet felt an odd sense of sincerity in the man's words. He did not seem to act like a local burglar or even a rapist, his actions were studied, deliberate, efficient, and without emotion. She wondered if her situation was related to the issues with Dalton. He had run off quickly, and with Ed Kosko calling him on a holiday weekend it had to be important, although the matter seemed straightforward — an explosion at a major government funded research site. Carefully turning her head, Carolyn could see the man scan the room, check various drawers, her purse, and a desk where she kept and paid bills. He remained silent while he dialed a number on his cell phone.

Barely audible sounds came from across the room, although he was clearly reporting to someone else involved in the attack and her capture. Carolyn's mind fractured, it began to scramble random thoughts. *What was all this about? Was she going to die? Why was she attacked?* Positioned behind her the man pressed a small patch to her neck; it felt warm and she sensed her heart rate slowing.

The man moved out of view and then the small reading light near her bed went dark, she could hear movement behind her and then the bedroom door closed. She could not keep her eyes open and drifted into a light sleep.

Khamal closed his phone having updated his Iranian contact, and began to scroll through Carolyn's phone for numbers.

After a moment, the phone screen stopped scrolling,

and displayed: *Jameson Dalton Crusoe (JD) 214.567.8909 Mobile*

A photo of a young handsome man appeared under the number.

Less than a minute later, he configured Carolyn's cell phone to also join his phone during each call she made or received, and store in his voicemail the conservation of the parties speaking. His task for the evening accomplished, he packed away his gear, left a listening bug near Carolyn's landline phone, and removed the tape binding Carolyn. He slipped away quietly into the night.

20-EIGHT

Tel Aviv, Israel. — IEC Command Center

DR. Weiss's technical teams were all at their posts in the IEC situation room, the walls flashing with images of the Korean peninsula. Some images were focusing in with extraordinary resolution over the North Korean Missile Research Complex. The room tingled with an electric energy in anticipation as 10:35 a.m. approached on the wall clock, set to local North Korean time. Weiss included the Japanese Defense Minister Kytoma, at his insistence, to witness the activity as it neared the detonation time. Japan was not about to remain a passive player in this major discovery which they had principally funded.

One satellite scanning west to east focused down to a highway leaving the missile complex revealing a vehicle moving at high speed from the complex. It was Yong, tracked through his satellite phone used to communicate with the other members of the KCG.

Weiss studied the speeding vehicle as it raised vast dust clouds negotiating tight turns on the narrow road. "Tighten up on the vehicle," Weiss demanded with concern. Responding as a well honed machine one operator enhanced the video capture of the transport as another overlaid real time data showing speed, direction, elevation, and weather conditions. Leaning to Kytoma, Weiss whispered, "We may be watching Yong's escape."

Both men smiled at each other enjoying the apparent success of their KCG member, General Yong.

Looking concerned Kytoma asked, "Will he be clear of the blast when the bomb detonates?"

Weiss's eyes never left the large wall screens. "Yes, he should be all right, but our view of his escape will likely be obscured by the blast cloud."

The operators held the tightened slide show on the race to escape the site. Only forty-five seconds remained until the detonation time. The vehicle, now clearly visible as a military personnel carrier moved out of range for Weiss's satellite coverage of Hyesan. Moments later the vehicle weaved violently on the road, spun around, rolling over, and then plunged down a steep embankment and burst into flames. Fixated on the missile site, Weiss and Kytoma could not believe their eyes. Again, Weiss ordered stronger resolution and replayed the prior twenty seconds.

"It looks like a tire blew out and sent the vehicle over the cliff near the road," announced a console operator. Looking attentively at Weiss the entire room awaited his instructions. Several seconds passed as the IEC staff absorbed the violent images, realizing the tragedy unfolding before them may have ended the life of the general. In quiet tones, Weiss looked at Kytoma and said, "He's certainly dead based on the fireball we are seeing."

Both Weiss and Kytoma knew what Yong would have them do. Complete the mission. Detonate the bomb and rid North Korea of the NKMRC and their terrible leadership. The fact that he may not have lived long enough to see the changes he helped bring about was beside the point. Others would step up to help the reunification of the North and South with the regime in disorder, without leadership and having lost their prized Missile Research Complex.

"Ten seconds till detonation, sir," announced another console operator.

Weiss studied the array of images showing the region, the coast, the entire Korean peninsula and the missile compound itself. "Return to main screen satellite imagery," announced Weiss. The fireball engulfing the toppled vehicle vanished and the missile complex re-appeared.

"Detonation minus five, four, three, two and. . . ." The room remained silent, except for the situation manager announcing the countdown, the screens showed no change, no fireball, no brilliant blast, and no explosion whatsoever. Technicians were busily checking settings and feeds. Seconds felt like hours as the console operator's screens flashed information.

Weiss commanded, "Check the feeds!"

"Feeds are confirmed, sir. What we are seeing is live."

"Replay the last ten seconds in slow motion, maximum resolution."

Moments later the screens cleared and displayed once more the seconds just before detonation, and again in a tenth real time the detonation moment passed with no change on the ground. Weiss sat speechless and very frustrated. Not only had they failed at detonating a third custom bomb, they apparently lost a key KCG member helping to rid the world of a radical, dangerous regime bent on destruction of Japan from achieving its will through nuclear weapons.

Kytoma looked at Weiss, his face strained from frustration. "What are you trying to do here Dr. Weiss?"

"Nothing, nothing, I don't understand, let me check into this," muttered a baffled Weiss.

Angry and embarrassed Weiss could not explain the detonation failure, under control through their satellite, after confirming uploading the size and timing of a detonation. Jane Holman's stealth program worked flawlessly, at least on this first test on the NKMRC.

Weiss and Kytoma moved to a sequestered corner of

the operations center and spoke quietly in stressed tones about the bomb's failure to detonate. Kytoma wanted assurances the technology worked and could be made to work again as it had for Jefrah and Elko. Kytoma was not going to accept that the technology worked for Israel's enemies and not for Japan's. Weiss got the message: Make this technology work for us or your funding may be in jeopardy. Moving to a console station with his laptop, Kytoma opened his encrypted email account, entered the group address for the KCG leaders, forgetting the vehicle explosion which may well have taken Yong's life. Angry and irritated he then emailed the following message:

```
TO: Knowledge Consortium Group,
Members@knowconsortgrp.org
FROM: Member Three


Planned events for the day were can-
celled abruptly due to technical fac-
tors yet unknown.

Investigations to Commence Immediately.
```

THE ISRAELI BETRAYAL

HYESAN, NORTH KOREA — MISSILE RESEARCH COMPLEX

The events of the dedication ceremony went on exactly as planned, and a great political statement made to the world about North Korea's ability to extend its military impact beyond its own borders.

The next morning following the dedication, security staff at the NKMRC found Yong's exo Sam. Moments later the perimeter security force called into to report finding General Yong's dead body, badly burned in a military pickup over a hillside eight kilometers from the compound's entrance. The tire failure became obvious as were the skid marks leading to the point where the vehicle left the road.

Hours later, the head of Security at the Missile Research Complex, Major Roh Kunghee sat at his desk looking at General Yong's identification credentials and his emails of the last twenty-four hours. Seeing the general's uniform apparently being worn by the exo Sam, he asked himself, *What or who killed Sam? Why is he in the general's clothes, carrying his ID, and why did the general seemingly leave this important event when he indicated he would attend?*

Juicy scenarios sprang forth in Kunghee's mind from a high-level assassination of the exo and the general, to a plan gone badly by Sam and conspirators to kill the general, to a cover up by someone, or the general, to mask an escape from the premises.But why? However, Major Kunghee did know he would miss his good friend General Yong.

Uncertain he had anything upon which to base his report, Kunghee simply reported Sam died of apparent natural causes and the general met with an unfortunate accident. Only time would tell if the report gave enough convincing evidence to prevent reopening the case by others who would not remain silent, as Major Roh Kunghee chose to do.

20-NINE

ELKO, MONTANA — WALDRON RANGE

DALTON had taken Jane back to the hotel near the mine and made preparations to return her and Susan to Seattle. Both had done their jobs, and done it well. The Israelis were slowly degrading the ore they acquired through Mitsui. The stealth software Jane inserted into the XR-211 files that Gilles's men downloaded from Susan's computer, compromised their operational protocols.

The marines had a tight control over the mining site; the locals were unaware of the details about the fire and deep well explosion of the bomb Dalton had found and disposed of in the old mine tunnel.

The Israelis were rejoicing in their clever subterfuge to acquire the ore and power through the applied research to get to the point where they had a basic and functional understanding of the technology. Dalton and his team felt the Israelis were behind the Iranian explosion, and it came off beautifully, a controlled explosion, minimal collateral damage, and no visible party to blame it on.

RICHARD TREVAE

Dalton escorted both Jane and Susan to the small airfield where a private jet fired-up preparing to take off for the eightyminute minute flight to Seattle. Both women hugged Dalton, and shared their appreciation for all his efforts to protect them and yet let them assist in the efforts to solve the mystery of the Enertek explosion. Also waiting at the airport was Marine Two, one of the White House choppers to take Dalton back to a small airfield where a Gulfstream G350 would fly him to the White House for a meeting with President Conner.

Ed Kosko would be brought up to speed later, following surgery scheduled for most of the day to reconstruct his wounded shoulder and repair extensive nerve damage. Despite his force of personality and determination, Kosko remained weak and the President knew it. Ed had already delegated most of his control over the Enertek matter to Dalton who felt it was time to take some offensive action.

Trips to the White House were never high on Dalton's list of fun times. Usually, he played a support role for Ed who ran all the early interference necessary to keep the meetings focused and brief. Dalton thought about how he would inform the President of his concerns and how to deal with them. After all, the game of cat-and-mouse between the Israeli's and the U.S. was live, and if Jane's embedded program kept doing its work, the Israelis would soon be out of raw material to process into a catalyst for bombs. On the other hand, the Israelis may have already processed enough material to produce several bombs and they could be deployed anywhere. U.S. and Israeli interests usually ran together, although there were notable exceptions, such as preemptive, covert, unilateral action against a Middle Eastern threat.

Dalton feared that the U.S. had only two options: either confirm it had destroyed the ore inventory taken by Huchara for Weiss's work, or confront the leaders in Israel and threaten to suspend financial and military support unless they turned over all information gained in their research. Without either of these two scenarios becoming reality, Israel would be unchallenged and emboldened to continue its efforts to eliminate their enemies clandestinely and claim a source of energy independent from oil. Both matters were seductively attractive to every Israeli.

The President's chief of staff emerged from the oval office and motioned to Dalton to join them. After the usual handshakes, photo moments, and offers of coffee, Dalton sat down and tried to collect his thoughts. The

President dismissed all the other people in the room, a surprise for Dalton.

Once alone, the President leaned forward and said, "JD what do you think really happened at the Elko mining site the other day?"

"Well Mr. President, we found the hidden bomb, and as you learned earlier in my brief email. We were able to remove it, heard and saw it detonate, and then secured the entire site with the marine contingent; no one was hurt."

"Do we know where it came from?"

"No sir, but we are working on it. Apparently a carrier was intercepted and the rig taken over that carried the bomb labeled as machine parts." Pausing to allow the President to ask a question if needed, Dalton then continued, "Also, we have not been able to locate the driver assigned to the rig."

"What do we know about the bomb itself?" posed the President.

"Again, I'm speculating a bit, sir, but I believe the Israelis or a front for them such as Huchara's group, could have transported the bomb, added it to the cargo of the intercepted rig and delivered it to the site anytime within the last two weeks."

Starring at Dalton intensely over his reader glasses the President stated, "You believe the Israelis intentionally meant to destroy the vein and thus deny us access to the special ore and stop our efforts to develop the technology?"

"Yes, exactly, sir, because the Israelis couldn't possibly know that we have recovered the raw data from the Enertek explosion and confirmed the mechanisms and exact parameters needed to establish and control an explosion."

"Yet in fact we have, right?" asked the President.

"Yes, sir. The team leader and a few others have interpreted the explosion data, and developed the operating protocol, apparently similar to the Israeli's, through their own research of the last month."

"So the raw ore and mine are safe and secure?"

"Yes, sir, Mr. President." Dalton stated his remark with assurance.

"Furthermore, sir, we were aware of operatives at the mine region apparently seeking to obtain the raw explosion data. We were able to anticipate their plans and we lured them to copy a version of the raw data with stealth operating protocols. If integrated into the Israeli processing plant, the stealth software will degrade and destroy the ore's capacity to initiate and control an explosion or a stable release of energy for peaceful purposes."

"What do you mean by stealth protocols?"

"These are subtle changes in the parameters and process settings which are needed to refine the ore into its active state to then produce the energy release. Jane Holman, the lab director overseeing the experiments at Enertek, has embedded into the stolen software sufficient false instructions, which, if allowed to proceed in the refining process, will destroy and render the ore neutral."

"We know the Israelis have the stealth protocols?"

"We believe so, sir," offered Dalton.

"Tell me what new information we have on the Iranian explosion."

"Our contact in the region, Jack Tucker, has been tracking events since the Iranian explosion and I plan to talk with him this afternoon."

"I know Jack," announced the President, "and he's here, at Langley for a week, briefing the agency. I am getting a briefing tomorrow. Let's see if I can get him here this afternoon."

Within moments, Jack Tucker came on the President's secure speakerphone in the oval office. His reporting for the day to a sub-group of CIA officials, all presently reporting to Ed Kosko, had just ended, and he said he could be at the White House in thirty-five minutes.

The president then recalled his chief of staff, and explained Dalton's role as overseeing the Enertek explosion investigation, although nothing more about the mineral find, or the events at Elko. Another aide to the president came in to take a lunch order, and the president instructed him to bring soup and sandwiches to the oval office as he and others would be working through lunch. Dalton felt awkward requesting a chicken salad sandwich be brought to the oval office for his lunch, however that is what President Conner suggested, so that's exactly what happened.

Just thirty-five minutes after his call, Jack Tucker appeared as promised and walked escorted into the White House to the Oval Office. Jack, Dalton, and the President exchanged pleasantries, refreshed each other on their activities, sat down without others present, and began to go over Jack's latest intelligence. Tucker's operatives using listening devices to learn of Iranian efforts to find a spy, and Mohammed Hatta's name was mentioned. Khamal, the interrogator and hired killer was also named, and Jack concluded that Hatta had been lost to the Israelis. What he knew and what he gave up to Khamal remained an unknown. Hatta had not been seen nor had his phone calls been intercepted in the last four days. Jack feared the worst. If Hatta knew current information about the bomb and its connection back to the Elko mine, then clearly the Iranians would surmise Israel and or the U.S. were behind their "explosion."

The President appeared very worried. He now knew this was not just a game between Israel and the U.S. trying to beat the other to the knowledge of the Enertek find, rather that Hatta's assumed *interrogation* by Khamal may well have tipped off the Iranians as to the power of this technology and they would try anything to obtain it. At this point, neither leaders in congress, nor the oversight committees, had been briefed on the entire matter. President Conner was not about to risk the opportunity to end this race to control a new technology without having all the cards played out. He hated slow congressional oversight, which meant meddling for political advantage, when he knew he and the country needed to act quickly.

"Problem is," said the President, showing frustration, "any help I seek outside this office is surely to leak and further fuel the Iranian suspicions."

The President strolled over to his desk and abruptly lifted his secure phone and called Colonel Ronet, a decorated marine, who now served as special liaison to the President for covert operations initiated by the President exclusively for national security purposes.

After one ring the President said, "Brad, can you come over to the oval office now? Great, see you shortly."

Colonel Brad Ronet was the ultimate, twenty-first century warrior. At forty-one, he had seen action in Iraq, Afghanistan, and Somalia. Fluent in Farsi and Spanish he was also fully knowledgeable in the latest weaponry, intelligence, and communications, extremely bright and decidedly loyal to the President, whoever the

President may be. He held the highest operative military authority when he carried out orders directly from the President. He commanded a top-secret military field unit, and was positioned innocently as a colonel, to avoid unwanted questions. The president's oval office gate-keeper, tapped his guarded door lightly, opened the portal and announced the arrival of Ronet.

"Colonel Ronet, I'd like you to meet Dalton Crusoe and Jack Tucker, we have something very important we need you for."

Over the next hour, Dalton detailed all the information, and events of the last sixteen days. Jack Tucker filled in with the intelligence he had obtained through his own staff and other Iranian Intel sources operating from Turkey.

Leading the discussion with steady approval prompting from the President, Dalton made the case for a secret small insertion team of military types, computer and communications experts, and bomb specialists to enter Israel and penetrate the close-knit inner circle of Dr. Weiss's team overseeing the research on the stolen Elko Mine ore. Colonel Ronet, a very quick study, was right on top of the situation.

"Gentlemen, I can have a six man team, under my command, and you two into Israel in thirty-six hours." Dalton and Tucker nodded their willing participation in the insertion team. Pausing briefly, Ronet continued. "My team will include a technology expert in weaponry based computer and communication systems, a native Israeli who speaks several languages and is medically trained, and three marines trained in Middle Eastern culture and close combat."

The room went quiet as all eyes, focused on the President. Formulating his thoughts the President stared out the window of the oval office across the White House lawn.

"Dalton, can you and this Enertek team leader, ahh, Jane Holman, secretly enter the IEC, plant listening and communication bugs, confirm the destruction of their ore is underway and depart without getting caught, or killed?"

Interrupting the question to Dalton, Ronet assured the President he could get his entire team in undetected and protect them while active in Israel.

Dalton looked at Ronet and asked, "Are you sure Colonel?"

"Yes, sir I guarantee it," Ronet proclaimed.

The President turned to Dalton. "Dalton, it's your call. I can't, in good faith, require you to do this, but we can't take a chance that the Israeli's have discovered or disabled the destruction program embedded by Jane, and without firsthand knowledge I will have to confront the Israeli Prime Minister on our suspicions, who may, for all we know, have deniability on this entire matter."

Feeling the knot in his stomach tightening, Dalton looked at each man in the room and said, "I'll get with

Jane and we can be ready to go in about thirty-six hours, as the Colonel offered."

The President nodded, and gave Ronet the approval to put the plan in motion.

"I'll meet you in Tel Aviv at the airport the morning you arrive, Dalton," said Jack Tucker.

"I'll have a plan, equipment list, and mission schedule for your review and input in three hours, Mr. Crusoe," said Ronet as he stiffened to make his exit.

"Best you call me Dalton, or better yet, JD, since our lives are now critically intertwined," said Dalton, with a sheepish grin, failing to cover his obvious nervousness.

"Gotcha JD." Ronet gleamed confidence. He was ready to get on with the mission.

THIRTY

DALTON stood looking out to catch a view of the Enertek jet bringing Jane Holman from Seattle to their departure point. With less than two days back at home and work, Jane was not easy to convince that she needed to join this "group of Rambo's", as she jokingly put it, on a suicide mission.

Nevertheless, the explosion at Enertek had left her without an office or lab for at least three months, and she was not about to take a chance her stealth program would not complete its mission. She reluctantly agreed to join the team. Dalton smiled with relief, for he had neither the competence nor inclination to verify the performance of Jane's new stealth software programming. A full three minutes ahead of schedule Jane arrived, dressed in khaki slacks, a silk blouse, and a light leather jacket, fitted at the waist and looking casual professional.

Trying to put on her game face, Jane inquired, "Do I get to carry a gun on this mission?"

Dalton smiled and gave her a hug. "I'll carry a gun for you. Please, don't worry."

"We're going in as some kind of scientific team on a grant from Cal Tech to share results on prolonged solid battery life, is that right?" Jane cocked her head and displayed skepticism.

"Yup, that's it." Dalton smiled like he had total confidence in their cover.

"Man, this is going to be boring as we try to make dialogue."

"That's what we want. Ronet and I believe if we maintain a low tech cover we will never be under the scrutiny of Weiss or his team, just another scientific group taking a three day holiday in Israel and visiting the lab, mixed in with a little gripping and grinning."

Settling in for the five and a half hour flight, Ronet introduced his team. They were all excellent men, with strong skill sets in all the needed areas, including hand-to-hand combat, if necessary. A detailed "High Priority Mission Packet – Operation Trojan Horse" was handed to each of the six team members as well as Dalton and Jane. Jack Tucker would receive his in Israel.

Jane could not believe the detail and resource information Ronet's team had assembled: mission summary, new identity documents for the mission, photos, building plans, escape routes, personnel assignments along their expected walking route, camera locations, time schedules, and critical mission events, where to place bugs, communications taps, and where system access via computer's could take place. The next four hours were spent going over every point in the plan and the actions if the mission were uncovered or abandoned by Dalton or Ronet, the two team leaders.

4:40 A.M. LOCAL TIME
HANGER 19, TEL AVIV INTERNATIONAL AIRPORT,

Ronet had arranged for the aircraft to arrive at hanger 19, a private terminal, if you will, for U.S. government officials, and certain NGO's such as academic groups and researchers. Typical Israeli security, some of the best on the planet, was assigned to assist U.S. military personnel at hanger 19. For the most part, the U.S. security staff simply had to supply the manifests, paperwork, and assurances all was right with the entrants to Israel. In this case, it allowed Dalton and Ronet to bring in weapons, communications, and surveillance equipment, and their business suited combat-trained marines for their protection.

Two heavily armored Chevrolet Yukon's came outfitted with phones, satellite links, email, and sophisticated GPS apparatus for their work on the mission. The entire team loaded up the two vehicles. Dalton and Jane rode in one along with two marines, and Ronet had the remaining team members in his vehicle who led the group to the IEC. Jane carried a small two-gigabyte card for accessing the IEC files and emails, and also for monitoring the progress of the stealth software she had developed to degrade and neutralize the ore processed by Dr. Weiss's group. Local security at the entrance to the IEC prevented anyone from carrying in weapons; however two synthetic 40 S&W Glocks had been stowed in the titanium briefcase carrying material and information brochures on Cal Tech and its applied research on solid battery life, all of which was not particularly proprietary and was supplied by Enertek from its internal research.

The point was that if examined, a local security type would not understand the documents though it would support the guise of a team visiting from Cal Tech. Beneath a false floor, and only three-quarters of an inch thick were the guns, four full clips, Comsat gear, microlights, and neurological agents on skin patches. An arsenal of answers waited, if needed, should there be problems.

Once through the IEC security, a chaperone named Tina offered to lead the visit and arrange for tours through the various parts of the sprawling facility. Jane engaged Tina and began a dialogue about the pleasantries of the day covering weather, local events, and family — anything to make her group seem normal and uncomplicated. It worked beautifully and Tina dropped them off at an information lounge while they awaited their first tour. Having arrived early, Dalton used the next forty minutes to go over the day's plan. During their first lab tour Dalton managed to secure a small unique connector, disguised as a cable clamp, to the server cable feeding an operating computer in the Quality Control Center, which was the nerve center for all the activities at the IEC. Once clamped to the cable, Jane could activate the connector and wirelessly access the network through the computer she would check her email on at the lunch hour portion of the visit.

Five separate areas of the IEC were included on the tour, including a chemical treatment unit, which had to be the ore refining equipment. Aware that this was likely the section refining the Elko mine ore, Dalton asked, "Have you ever tried to re-process spent solid battery core to a fully activated state again?"

Tina was good, though not very familiar with the technical on-goings at the IEC, so she responded, "I don't really know, but many types of chemical operations are performed here." One of the marines touring with Dalton and the group quickly raised his hand and captured ten rapid sequence photos on his camera disguised as a working pen. Tina never noticed his movements, as she stayed focused on answering Dalton's question.

Politely, checking her watch, Tina suggested, "Shall we now take your lunch break, and relax for about an hour? It's been three hours of walking, and you might enjoy some rest and also use the lounge to check email and calls."

Dalton jumped at the suggestion. "That sounds great Tina, thanks so much for help on our tour thus far."

"Fine, let's get you back to the visitor lounge."

Within minutes, lunch orders were taken, and all settled in to appear like busy little business types, checking their lives back home or at their work places. In fact, four laptops were brought along on Operation Trojan Horse and all were inter-connected, assisting in Jane's activities on the IEC network. Dalton found Dr. Eli Weiss's email accounts and down loaded them. Ronet remained alert while playing with his computer, while his two marines were busy capturing files on various research, programs, personnel, and security.

Jane motioned to Dalton, nodding toward her screen, and he then entered a command which allowed him to view Jane's screen, which continued capturing the output results on "Project Process 36199". The streaming data looked very familiar to Jane; it was the stealth protocol for neutralizing the ore she embedded into the stolen software at Elko. She recognized the data trend, which she had simulated as if the refining were progressing normally, yet actually, the ore was degrading.

With a few keystrokes, Jane wrote to the four laptops, *Substance reduced by 19% so far, no disruption in scheduled processing.* Jane deleted her update moments after sending it to all her team members. Dalton looked up and glanced at Ronet and Jane. With a nod of his head, he confirmed the stealth program was still embedded, and working without detection.

Ronet got up from his overstuffed chair and strolled by Dalton. Interpreting this as a need to speak, Dalton stood and slowly walked over to the window, overlooking the Israeli hill country to the south and the Mediterranean to the southwest in the distance. The IEC sat on a modest knoll just out of town and nicely positioned to offer wonderful views of the area and still close enough to central Tel Aviv to be near other government offices and officials.

In a very low voice, Ronet said, "Sayd, the Israeli medical officer on our team just informed me he cracked into and translated the daily operating report for Dr. Weiss's scientists overseeing the Elko ore processing. He claims the report indicates that if yields hold as projected the refined ore should yield five additional bombs of similar size to the original three."

"What did you say?"

"I said we believe Weiss is processing material for five

more bombs," whispered Ronet as he looked about the vast visitor lounge.

"No I mean about the original three. Are you sure he translated correctly, three original bombs?"

"That's right, why?"

"We know, or think we know, of two bombs produced and used, but nothing has been mentioned or seen about a third," noted Dalton. "Remember the corridor leading from the labs to the central office core?"

Ronet nodded yes, and waited for Dalton's next words.

"Beyond that, according to our intelligence packet, is the situation room, and based on the electrical, communications, and security leading to *that* room, it must be the central command for monitoring and control of the bombs. We need to get in there and download some files. It's got to give us a boatload of intel about their use of the technology." Rubbing his neck, pacing, and starring at Dalton, Ronet looked frustrated.

"Shit, Dalton, we don't have a chance of getting in there on this mission. It's certainly not on our itinerary as a Cal Tech team, and a request would likely trigger unwanted questions," warned Ronet.

"I've got an idea that may just provide us secure access." Dalton smiled.

Giving full attention to Dalton, Ronet said, "Let's hear it JD."

30-ONE

BY 4:45 p.m., the tour had finished. Tina had expressed her pleasure in being their guide and if they desired further dialogue from the scientists or staff they met, just let her know and she would arrange another session.

Dalton kept his thoughts private as the afternoon tour continued. Meanwhile, Jane's interception of the network server was still downloading archived files and current communications between staff, outside email contacts, operational events at the IEC, and the process monitoring on the ore re-processing. Her hidden connector continued storing, although not transmitting, accumulated data for Jane's computer while they toured. She had shut off and closed her laptop to be with her at all times in her carry bag.

Upon leaving the IEC for the day, the team headed back to the Hilton. Dalton turned on his Blackberry, punched in a seven-digit code and pressed send. A status screen indicated the *"clamp"* which had allowed them to enter the IEC server network and download substantial data was full. Twenty minutes later the cable data clamp Jane had used uploaded its captured data to a flash drive connected through Dalton's phone, and then began to warm and disintegrate the microchip internals. Turning to the entire team, Dalton said "The clamp is now dead; I think we did the job."

Jane beamed with joy, for she was nervous all day, and concerned they would be discovered in the course of their clandestine activities. She began to relax.

Now at the hotel, the day seemed almost like it had been like another work day. Dalton handed his Blackberry to Jane who then retrieved the last of the extensive data taken from the IEC server network.

Scrolling through the new files Jane noticed the words "North Korea", which stuck out as out of place. After commenting on it to Dalton, he then said, "Let me see."

Several files opened up concerning email to and from a group called the Knowledge Consortium Group. Unimportant to Dalton at first glance, he then saw Weiss's name, and then General Yong's name. An email popped up:

Kytoma emailed the following message:

RICHARD TREVAE

TO: Knowledge Consortium Group,
Members@knowconsortgrp.org
FROM: Member Three

Planned events for the day were
cancelled abruptly due to technical
factors yet unknown.

Dalton saw other files from Weiss dated the same day. With the Israeli team member able to translate, he recites a memo stating: *The LDC software failed to respond based on satellite views over Hyesan. Programming review to commence immediately.*

"Does that mean anything, Dalton?"

Dalton dropped back in his chair, silent for a moment; he chose to withhold his true instincts, at least for now.

"No, ahh no not at this time," Dalton offered as though distracted elsewhere.

"Listen, Dalton, what is this idea you spoke of earlier with such interest?" inquired Ronet.

Still lost in his own thoughts Dalton hesitated and then said boldly, "We need to get into the IEC command center tonight."

"What?" Jane snapped. "Why?"

"I need to confirm the existence and location of a possible third original bomb now."

Before Jane or Ronet could respond, Dalton asked if Jane could locate the security grid covering the command center, and hidden passwords.

With a worried, yet excited look on her face, Jane scowled. "Maybe, just a minute." Ten minutes later, and during a brief summary by Dalton as to his concerns about a third bomb, from earlier production, Jane came through. "Yes, I know how to write software capable of intercepting commands given through passwords." Jane beamed at her resourcefulness.

"Twenty-two times today, passwords were used to enter various rooms. The operations center is room 376, and six entries were made there during the day." Jane continued. "One password command was entered electronically, not through a keypad, and while the password is still unknown, the encrypted command is downloaded here and has seven characters. Does that do you any good?"

"Can you up load the command password, in encrypted form, to my Blackberry, Jane?" asked Dalton.

"Ahh, yeah I think so, let's try it."

Ten seconds later Dalton saw flashes displaying seven asterisks on his Blackberry - the password to the operations room for the Command Center!

"Colonel, you and I, along with one of your marines, need to enter the Command Center tonight and access the computers located within the room, since they are apparently isolated in some fashion from the network server or we might see some record of it."

Jane, can you prepare a disk to download from those Command Center computers in the Situation Room?"

"Actually, I've already got one ready to go, as long as you are in the Command Center and the Situation Room is run from those computers."

Ronet stood. "I'll ready our equipment and team, back in thirty."

LATER THAT EVENING AT THE IEC

Security was always a top priority in Israel, and the IEC was no exception. Dalton, Ronet, and Israeli born marine lieutenant Spielman waited outside the IEC all dressed in black climbing gear with backpacks full of ropes, hooks, tools, and weaponry. Communication headsets were on and checked for signal. Everything was set to go except when and how to get in. Ronet and Dalton had spent hours trying to find a safe route in and out. All that seemed to make sense was to take out one or more of the security men on site at midnight, the standard shift time, and use their thumbprints to enter the operations room and Command Center.

At 11:59:07 p.m., the employee door opened and

four security guards came out. Two continued to the parking lots, two remained and lit up cigarettes. As the two who left reached their vehicles in the remote staff lot, Ronet and Spielman darted them with a tranquilizer from close range. Both guards dropped immediately after being stung with the strong neurotoxin, which temporarily renders the victim without muscle function, although would still be barely conscious. Ronet then took a right thumb print impression from each and dragged the limp bodies next to the main building, hiding them in the landscaping. They would sleep over the next six hours in a drowsy stupor.

After a four-minute cigarette break, the two remaining security guards entered the building and walked to their assigned areas. Moments behind them Dalton, Ronet, and Spielman entered the building apparently unseen by the two remaining guards who had not yet returned to see their monitor screen tracking entries. As the new entries were so close to the time of departure by the two guards lying in the grass, Dalton and Ronet felt they were covered on their entrance to the IEC. No alarms were heard and the guards were chatting and laughing as they strolled back to their stations.

Tucker and Ronet had done a good job in short order collecting data on the facility, for every camera, secured door, and password entry was noted and compromised by the intel Dalton carried. Arriving at the Command

Center Dalton held his Blackberry, called up the captured encrypted password, and watched the screen over the next few seconds text one asterisk after another. Following the seventh asterisk, the screen flashed once more and a noticeable click was heard. The substantial handle freed itself and the door opened to the Command Center, positioned in the center of the Situation Room, on a raised platform with minimal dedicated task lighting. The room appeared empty. A faint sound from the dozens of computer cooling fans simulated a white-noise sensation. Power lights were blinking in a staggered slow rhythm from every machine. Even in the dark, without personnel at the consoles, the area looked sophisticated and technical, with very little lighting on in the Command Center.

They continued moving down a narrow hallway toward the double doors at the end of the operations room. Each was marked "Security Clearance 4 Only".

Got that one handled, thanks Eli, Dalton thought to himself. Again, the Blackberry emitted the password and opened the left side of the double doors. The room was black except for occasional task lighting at a dozen workstations all blinking on and off as they collected, monitored, and manipulated data from all over the world. Three sides of the room were covered in large wall screens serviced by a recessed floor containing the work consoles for Weiss's elite group of operators.

Dalton crouched by a computer in the middle of the room and inserted his data capture disk. Within minutes, the computer flashed and whirled while processing the download commands. Ronet and Spielman stood watch as Dalton did the data collection.

Down the hall, the security central control had not detected the entry to the building as the break taken by the guards hid the entry of Dalton, Ronet, and his marine. Yet a movement sensor began flashing in the command control center. In the past, even a fax machine receiving a transmission from another time zone could trigger an alarm light. This alarm was coming from the Situation Room.

The man monitoring the screen reacted with suspicion. Maybe this was a fax coming in, it's happened many times before and the sudden movement of paper through the machine had triggered alarms. Once, even the air conditioning blew sheets of paper off a nearby desk and fluttered about the room for a moment setting off an alarm. Tired and bored the guard rose from his console chair.

"I'll check out this movement alarm light and hit the bathroom on my return, back in ten, okay??" The other guard, equally tired and bored waved his hand in acknowledgement without saying a word.

Ronet heard the guard coming from his footsteps against the hard surface tile floors throughout the complex. Alerting Dalton and Spielman through his head Comsat, all three took defensive hidden positions. Ronet and Spielman hid behind the open door as it swung open, Dalton remained motionless crouched down in the work cubicle he used while downloading data from its computer.

Not prepared for a true intruder, the guard opened the door without caution, stepped in and looked about. Seeing no one at first, he moved to a light switch, his handgun still holstered and strapped in place. Like two synchronized stealth lions, Ronet grabbed the guard around the neck, covering his mouth and Spielman applied a neurotoxin patch directly over the guard's carotid artery. Within three seconds, the guard fell limp and Ronet eased him to the floor and laid him next to the wall. He would awake in about thirty minutes, with a huge headache, and very little memory of the last hour, hopefully not recalling his encounter with Dalton's team. "Room is secure, but we must be out in two," whispered Ronet.

"I'm almost complete with the download," responded Dalton.

The computer finally flashed 'Download complete — disk full". Dalton removed the memory card and motioned he was ready to move to Ronet.

Dalton looked at the guard lying on the floor and called for Spielman to assist him to move the body to the center of the walkway and position a wastebasket on its side directly at the guard's feet. Spielman directed a small beam flashlight on the guard's neck to make sure the patch dissolved as expected to leave no visible trace of the neurotoxin exposure. It was gone, and hopefully when he was found, or awoke, it would appear as a clumsy fall leaving the guard unconscious for a short while. Ronet remained on watch for more activity by the remaining guard, as Dalton and Spielman finished their work and prepared to leave.

Twenty seconds later, the three were at the main entrance door, directed the encoded password on Dalton's Blackberry, and the door lock snapped open. The remaining guard in the security control center saw the alert that the entrance door had opened and then closed.

Without concern, he thought *another cigarette break? He probably faked the movement alarm to have another.*

Dalton, Ronet, and Spielman had masterfully planned and executed the retrieval of key information about the Israeli program on refining the Elko mine ore and their clandestine bomb making. The information Weiss's group obtained would change the balance of power in the world if the U.S. did not stop the Knowledge Consortium Group. The night's activities were a very good start towards taking down the KCG.

30-TWO

DALTON had gotten only three hours sleep, for after Jane had uploaded the IEC data to NSA computers and applied some powerful de-encryption software, he stayed up planning his briefing to the President.

As he slugged down another cup of black coffee, Dalton greeted Ronet and Tucker as they came into the conference room. A white house assistant had set up the link with the Oval Office at 6:30 a.m. Washington time and the President had just arrived, appearing on the wall-sized screen before them.

"Good morning, Dalton. I gather you had a successful mission yesterday as I had no urgent calls and heard no talk of killing spies?" The small attempt at humor did not go unnoticed.

Dalton appreciated the demeanor of the President in this situation. Everyone involved knew the risks were huge and unforeseen events could have blown the mission and led to some very difficult negotiations to settle matters down. Yet, without a prompt, the President put all at ease with his introductory question set in a humorous comment.

"That is correct, Mr. President. It was, well, frighteningly smooth, thanks in no small part to Colonel Ronet and his support team on intelligence."

"Good, what else do we know?"

"Well, sir, I've been able to verify through emails and memorandum that the Israeli's are ahead of us in their development efforts on the entire potential of the energy and warfare aspects of this technology. Jane Holman is now reviewing the Israeli work and overlaying it onto our own research to bring us up to the latest knowledge.

"It appears as though our stealth program is degrading their supply of ore and at the rate of progress observed, the material being processed should be rendered neutral and without activity in about fifty hours."

The President interrupted. "JD, do we know if their entire supply of ore is being processed now?"

Dalton paused as Jack Tucker handed him another packet of material.

"We don't know, sir, but we doubt it based on the equipment sizes used in the refining process."

"We have to verify that somehow guys."

"Yes, of course, we are working on securing that knowledge as soon as possible."

"We have another major concern Mr. President,"

announced Ronet. Looking to Dalton, Ronet nodded for Dalton to explain the concern. "We believe the Israelis, along with Japanese participants in this Knowledge Consortium, have assembled another, that is a third bomb, and have it positioned somewhere in North Korea."

"What? How could they have done that?"

"Through the help of General Yong we believe, who, we now learn, was killed in an apparent car accident two days ago outside the North Korean Missile Research Facility near Hyesan."

"Jack, have we heard anything over the intel networks about the North Koreans claiming knowledge of this bomb?"

"Nothing, sir, not a word, nor anything about the general, although the dedication of the facility was a *great success*, with lots of chest pounding about the new capabilities they now have to repel a U.S. or Japanese attack."

Dalton continued to explain what they learned from the IEC files and emails. Yong, Kytoma, Huchara, and Weiss were the leaders of this international, well financed, politically connected group, with contract operatives capable of manifesting themselves into small armies, covert assassins, governmental officials, private bankers, and business leaders.

THE ISRAELI BETRAYAL

Their presence, while nearly invisible to the general public through the legitimate components of their activities, was a global force to be reckoned with when presented a technology as attractive as the Elko mine discovery.

Yong, by all accounts is now dead, believed killed in an auto accident. The North Koreans apparently had not learned of his role with the Knowledge Consortium Group, or his connection with the Japanese. They clearly had not suffered the bomb detonation Yong and his associates were planning at the new Missile Research Facility. Nevertheless, it was certain a third bomb had been assembled, positioned in North Korea, and sat ready to be detonated. Dalton surmised that Weiss's email to the Knowledge Consortium indicating, "the day's events were cancelled due to as yet unforeseen problems" was compelling evidence that the detonation was planned on the same day at the heavily attended dedication ceremony for the Missile Research Facility.

The President looked overwhelmed with the depth and seriousness of the information just given him. "Jack, do we know how far up in Japan's government this plan may have gone?"

"It's very hard to say, Mr. President. Kytoma is a top deputy to the Japanese prime minister, although he also came from vast family wealth in Japan connected with the electronics and real estate industries. He may well have been a personal friend of Huchara; they are about the same age, and could easily have traveled the same business circles before Kytoma took on a political life some twelve years ago."

"My God man, these guys have gone power crazy over this technology and are setting themselves and their countries up to become the new future world economies," bemoaned the President.

"That's exactly how we see it, Mr. President," barked out Ronet.

Dalton then said, "I have a proposal, Mr. President." All eyes turned to Dalton. "I believe the detonation planned for Hyesan did not materialize because of the stealth programming we inserted into the stolen files taken days ago at the Elko mine. According to Jane, the same systems controlling the refining process also control the parameters setting the bomb's force, timing, and detonation triggers, which once downloaded into the bomb's LDC, can then be commanded by satellite signal to explode. Assuming the software programming had not been detected, removed, or altered, then the remaining Elko ore and the third bomb have all been disabled through the stealth software."

"Yes, I follow, but what does that do for us regarding the retrieval of the third bomb?" questioned the President.

"Well sir, I believe we can delete the software that

defeated the original bomb instructions and replace it with the correct software to activate and detonate the bomb — in place."

"Yes, that would achieve several nice results wouldn't it? But can you actually do this, a modification of software without physically being there to do it?"

"We are working on it, sir, and with your approval I'd like to have Colonel Ronet lead a team to implement such a plan."

A long period of silence followed Dalton's request. The President knew this was tantamount to a declaration of war against the North Koreans, yet he eventually would have to take up the issue of their missile facility and the frequent threats to take out Japan on several occasions. If he allowed such a program to be carried out, the North Koreans would not know where the bomb came from, or who was responsible for its use. The west could assert the facility blew up through actions of the North Koreans themselves engaging in their own attempts to develop nuclear tipped missiles. Many top politicians in the North Korean government could be "desired collateral damage" if the timing were carefully planned with official schedules.

The matter suddenly grew from proportions manageable by the President and a few very close advisors, to one in which the joint chiefs and certain congressional leaders should be advised of the situation. The problem was time was not available for a full discussion and debate on this issue. Moreover, the President never felt comfortable keeping confidential a matter of this enormous significance. Besides, the Israelis might soon discover the stealth software, correct the programming steps themselves, and proceed as the originally intended. Then there were the North Koreans themselves, and their investigations into the death of General Yong. His association with Weiss, Kytoma, and Huchara might become known and that could lead to the bomb discovery and retaliation against Israel and Japan. So far the decision had become the true seminal moment for President Jerome Conner in his first term of office.

The President looked up at the video camera and said, "Proceed to develop a plan, and have it for me by tomorrow at 3:00 p.m., understood?"

Dalton and Ronet responded in sync with, "Yes, sir."

# 30-THREE

Tel Aviv — IEC Situation Room

IT had been at least twenty minutes since his guard partner strolled off for his last cigarette, and Jonas was pissed. He knew things were slow on the late shift, however this was not acceptable. His anger grew worse as he rounded the last corner to the situation room, his pace quickening now just gearing up for a fight, or at least a strong verbal beating. Hyam, his fellow guard on duty this evening, was a good guy, although he didn't seem to take his job very seriously and tonight was a perfect example.

Just outside the door to the Situation Room, stood Hyam, looking a bit dazed and confused.

"Where the hell have you been? Did you really need a cigarette that badly?"

"What, what are you talking about? I fell, I guess, as I went in the Situation Room, and went unconscious for a bit."

"Oh bull shit you liar! You went to have a cigarette!" Jonas grew more enraged.

"Ahh, no I didn't really. I fell, look in here."

Hyam directed Jonas to the Situation Room entry

door, opened it and showed him the waste can, still sitting in the walkway.

"See, I tripped over that as I came in to check on things . . . I think." Hyam rubbed his forehead and the back of his neck then looked at Jonas to see if anything he said was believed.

Jonas calmed down a bit after seeing the scene now before him. "Well, so you never went to have a cigarette after all?"

"No, damn it, I didn't."

"All right, all right, let me see your head, where does it hurt?"

"Everywhere, I think." Hyam whined as Jonas twisted his head toward the light.

"What do you mean? Are you bleeding, or swollen up there?"

Jonas examined Hyam's head and found no bruise, injury, cut, or visible mark. He looked again once more seeing nothing.

Jonas was a veteran of six years on security at the IEC. He had spent four years earlier in the Israeli military police and had seen many types of injuries, several from falls, and yet none he could recall left a victim unconscious for ten minutes or so, without a huge wound of some kind. Trained to be suspicious of events which were too convenient, he looked around the area. With his nine millimeter, stainless steel Desert Eagle automatic pistol in his grip he moved about the entire room, yet finding nothing unusual. His suspicions worsened as he searched the room for other evidence or clues as to Hyam's "fall".

Back at the security center monitors, Jonas checked to door entry log and found two entries to the Situation Room not eight minutes apart. One was clearly Hyam's, but the other had no logical explanation. Then Jonas noticed the timing of the movement alarm Hyam claimed had occurred. It immediately followed the first room entry.

"An intruder?" Jonas remarked involuntarily.

"Where?" blurted out Hyam still acting a bit drugged.

"In the room with you, I'll bet." Jonas smiled.

"Look the main entrance doors also opened twice more after our one time at break to escort out the earlier crew. Someone was here, I'll bet." Jonas glared as his pulse quickened. "I'm going to put this into our report, and have you examined for injuries."

"When?" begged Hyam.

"Now. I'm calling in a replacement for you in an hour."

"Damn, this is going to look bad for me either way, right?" groaned Hyam.

"Well, look at it this way, you're not dead and the place didn't blow up."

"Wonderful."

30-FOUR

OUTSIDE WASHINGTON D.C.

KHAMAL had been working on his high-powered laptop for almost an hour. He had *Googled* Crusoe, then Dalton Crusoe, then focused in on a Jameson Dalton Crusoe and located his man. Complete with address, work location, various email addresses, and his photo taken for the Department of Energy while working as a technology consultant to the department, headed by Secretary of Energy Edmond Kosko, Khamal was getting to know his target. Several clicks later, the academic history, and various political functions revealed Dalton's name, many times without significant detail on his role or involvement.

Khamal's success in his profession was unprecedented, even rivaling the reports about the Jackal decades earlier. Khamal's clients were sophisticated, well financed, patient, and singularly focused on the task at hand. In the twelve years that Khamal operated as a well-paid assassin and terrorist, he had accumulated over $35,000,000 USD in "fees" and had completed seven kills, several eventually interpreted as either accidents or suicides. Only available via email, he had become an expert in communications technology and the ways to cloak his true identity. Even his trusted banker in Geneva knew only that he claimed to be an "international consultant" on very high retainers.

Born a Jordanian, Khamal had severed ties with his homeland at sixteen when a car bomber killed his parents on holiday in Jerusalem. Since then, he completed his education in London and worked for a few years in the financial world, where the first test of his terrorist skills successfully eliminated a Palestinian officer who directed the attack that unintentionally killed his parents. Without a core nationalistic agenda or religious beliefs, Khamal could work either side of a hypersensitive political issue. As a result, he had worked for the Saudi's, Serbs, Sudanese, Russians, and now the Iranians. He never failed to complete an assignment, never been detained nor questioned about the events he may have orchestrated. He stood above others, essentially in a league of his own.

Getting to Jameson Dalton Crusoe, persuasively extracting the energy technology derived from the Elko find, and eliminating each party involved with the Iranian lab explosion remained the objective for his $10,000,000 USD fee. When Khamal informed his Iranian handlers that the explosion at their Iranian

RICHARD TREVAE

Energy Research Laboratory (IERL) was very likely a plot of the Americans and Israelis, the pressure to get answers quickly increased. His determination swelled to not fail, and face the wrath of the Iranians.

TEL AVIV — DR. ELI WEISS'S OFFICE

THE air felt almost electrified, filled with a static charge. Weiss had called in the head of security at the IEC and was interrogating him ruthlessly. Also in the office were the two top scientists overseeing the special project "36199" which represented the refining process for the Elko mine ore.

Weiss went ballistic having seen the message in the Overnight Security Report. He believed someone had obtained entry to the IEC without detection and may have corrupted or taken vital information. Moreover, the lab results on Hyam revealed traces of a rare neurotoxin, which left him unconscious and immobilized for up to thirty minutes, without recollection of prior events. The euphoria over his success in Iran and apparent success in Montana at the Elko mine now dissipated, as the stark reality that outsiders may know of their clandestine operations on the ore turned catalyst. However *who* remained a question. The U.S., Iranians, perhaps even the North Koreans if they had discovered the bomb in their country or were able to interrogate General Yong prior to his *"car accident"*.

Weiss ordered a complete scan of all computer activity and each keystroke made on dozens of machines over the last twenty-four hours at the IEC. All non-credentialed personnel awaited entry until he could establish what did or did not happen the prior evening. Even Jonas and Hyam were ordered to submit to lie detector tests to see if their collective stories held up. Each passed without a hint of lying to the machine. Weiss had a new *partner* in this energy find and he now was just starting to accept it. He sent an encrypted email to the Knowledge Consortium Group explaining the recent events and his concerns that an infiltrator may have accessed the IEC. His once frequent fantasies about receiving a Nobel Prize over his work now looked like a childish dream.

PENNSYLVANIA — NEAR THE WHARTON BUSINESS SCHOOL.

Arriving at Langley, the team Dalton and Ronet used at the IEC all reflected on having successfully obtained critical intelligence on the Israeli research program. It was a great success, at least from their perspective. While obtaining much needed data, there were no human losses, and no serious combat encounters, except for the security guard, and he was hardly a combat event. Jane's program continued to run undiscovered and they had downloaded enough files to learn what else the Israeli's were up to. Ronet and Dalton made a terrific team and had become trusted friends; he felt he would team with Brad again if the President called him to the front of another crisis like this one.

Powering up his phone now back on land, Dalton saw flashing a voice mail from Carolyn McCabe. *Ahh, he thought, time to celebrate with another, longer weekend rendezvous.* Entering his voice mail, he scrolled down to Carolyn's call and pressed listen.

"Dalton, this is Carolyn. I'm sorry to bother you darling, but I was broken into last night and tied up while a man roamed through my condo. I'm all right; please call me when you can."

Dalton heart began to race, and he quickly checked the date and time of the voice mail, *Three days and eleven hours ago, damn, he thought.*

Dalton went into a mixture of shock and shame. How could he have not picked up this message? He had put his phone on silence and low vibrate ever since he entered Israel and had forgotten to reset it after they left.

Carolyn answered her phone recognizing Dalton's ID on the screen. "Hello darling, are you back in Washington?"

"Yes, I'm at Langley, whatever happened?"

"Late at evening a man was hiding in my apartment,

hit me hard so I went unconscious for a moment, tied me, and. . . ." She paused and attempted to compose herself. "Then he just calmly looked through my things, made a call, and left."

"Did he hurt you?"

"No, not really; well other than the blow to the head, which hurt but that was it."

Dalton flushed, stirring with anger at the plight Carolyn endured. "Did he say anything to you at all?"

"He said 'be still and all this will turn out all right.'"

"You mean he took nothing, didn't physically harm you in any way?" Dalton hesitated to even voice the menacing question.

"Yes."

Dalton closed his eyes and thought for a moment. "Thank God you're all right. Do you figure he was a common thief, or what?"

"No he was refined, intelligent, in control, and perhaps middle eastern. I really don't know, I had poor lighting, few lines of sight, and he spoke very little."

Dalton felt relieved, though perplexed. What in hell did this guy want if not a rapist, burglar, or drug addict? Then it occurred to him; perhaps someone connected to Sang Huchara is trying to get to me.

"Carolyn, I'll come over in the next few hours, and we'll spend some time together, okay?"

"Yes, I'd love that, please hurry, I love you."

THE ISRAELI BETRAYAL

Dalton arrived earlier than expected, though he could not stop worrying about Carolyn. Had she been harmed in ways she could not reveal over the phone or because they were too painful? He thought whatever the issues, he would stand by her and support her through the bad memories, frightening dreams, and emotional rehabilitation. Once he parked his car, he found himself running to her condo unit and pressing the doorbell button frantically.

When the door opened, Carolyn threw herself into Dalton's arms and began to sob. He kicked the door shut and just held her for fifteen minutes, very little was said. Finally Dalton spoke. "Have you had counseling help over this?"

Wiping her eyes, she struggled to speak. "Well, the police investigators had a trauma specialist who came over and she was a blessing." She burst into another tearful cry. "I thought he was going to rape and then kill me!"

"But he didn't honey, and I'm so sorry I wasn't here to help you."

"It's all right, really. I thought about you throughout the entire incident, it kept me sane."

They sat and made popcorn, kindled a fire, and had soft music playing. Slowly, Carolyn calmed down and was able to explain the encounter from a distant perspective, without feeling vulnerable anymore. Her instincts about the intruder were remarkable, Dalton thought. It seemed very possible this guy was looking for information related to the Enertek explosion and felt Carolyn might know or have something of use.

Likely an asset of Mitsui and the KCG, reasoned Dalton. *Damn* he thought, *I will uncover this prick and tear him apart.*

He stayed the night and had breakfast with Carolyn in the morning before returning to Washington. Carolyn appeared to be her normal self again, and Dalton felt relieved. The conversation flowed easily while Dalton kept a watchful eye on his girl to be certain she was moving beyond the attack.

30-SIX

FORMOSA STRAITS, TAIWAN

GENERAL. Yong was still sore from the car accident that nearly took his life. He had managed to escape the car before it burst into flames moments after it plunged over the small bumper separating the narrow dirt road from the river gorge beneath. Yong's keys and military cell phone were all that remained of the scorched truck and its remaining inhabitant, the general's older civilian brother. Yong planned to escape the country with his brother as the bomb destroyed the NKMRC. His brother's oldest son, a truck driver, luckily happened on the accident and found Yong, hid him until a Mitsui intelligence team, disguised as a fishing trawler crew took him to Taiwan.

Recovering in Taiwan in worker housing on a Mitsui airport project and under the security and care of his Japanese collaborators, Yong remained hidden and quiet while the news of his death sunk in and fell from view of top leaders in North Korea. He was sick at the death of his brother and that he couldn't even attend his funeral. Nevertheless, as his brother's son took him to the Japanese trawler, he explained why he must leave. The son, a bright young man, stifled his grief and simply told Yong to get strong, return with his friends to free the North of this wicked regime.

Yong knew the bomb was in position and programmed to detonate after instructions were downloaded from the satellite to the LDC. He had informed the Israeli command center at the IEC that all was ready, and he had faked his death by killing his most trusted, loyal senior officer and left him in his place. Somehow, the death of his EXO was accepted as natural and the uniform and documents left to identify him as General Yong were ignored, or removed during the investigation. Fortunately, Yong reasoned, the top government officials were pulled off track by the apparent accidental death of Yong in his car. The death of the EXO was almost an afterthought by the investigating team, reasoned Yong. Maybe he was just lucky or perhaps he had unseen secret help. Nevertheless, it was now imperative he make his status known to the other members of the KCG and devise a new way to finally detonate the bomb.

Just after the failed detonation, Eli Weiss sent an email to all members, including Yong. At the time Weiss sent his email, minutes after the scheduled detonation, Yong remained on the contact list for the KCG, as Weiss had no information on Yong's apparent demise. Consequently, three days after the planned detonation Yong managed to check emails and saw the email from Weiss. No explanation appeared for the detonation failure. Yong grew incensed, for he had done all the dangerous work, delivered the bomb, positioned it, readied it for operation, confirmed the time of detonation, and then nothing. He thought, *Had the North Korean's found it, had it tried to detonate and failed somehow, or was it still sitting undiscovered and awaiting new instructions?*

Yong opened his email again, read Weiss's newest message about a possible intruder to the IEC searching for information on the ore processing still ongoing, and then located the earlier message from Weiss. More concerned than ever, Yong now knew he had to meet with the other members and complete their original plan. He emailed Weiss alone in hopes he could explain the failed detonation and connect with the other KCG member.

```
Message from member Four to others. Also
failed to enjoy events planned for last
week,   seeking   further   explanation.
Recovering well in Saigo from my acci-
dent. Please email with status!
```

Yong still had friends and allies in North Korea who supported his plans for a reunited Korea, and wanted to desperately remove, or eliminate the current leadership. One such friend headed the internal security for the NKMRC and oversaw all internal investigations. Yong knew he could be counted on for the next attempt at regime change. The Japanese protecting Yong were all soldiers on the Mitsui payroll and operated on instructions of Gilles Montrose through Sang Huchara. Yong simply needed to convince the other KCG members that he remained ready and capable to re-start the mission. It was his destiny, he was certain.

30-SEVEN

OUTSIDE LANGLEY, VIRGINIA

DALTON, Ronet, and Tucker were busy organizing staff to review, classify, and summarize the data collected on the evening search and find mission at the IEC. Jane Holman, along with Jack Tucker, oversaw all the raw data as it came up on huge computer screens scrolling through endless files. Not long into the exercise Jane and Jack came to Dalton with some interesting emails. They were the stored emails between the KCG.

Finally, Dalton could see all four members involved, and their hidden supporting governments involved in the entire operation. Sang Huchara was a major player with construction sites all over the world, set up as information gathering points, clandestine operations centers, and storage sites for supplies, weaponry, aircraft, and staging of personnel.

Without connecting all the dots for Jane, he sent her back to Seattle. It was imperative she continued what she had begun at Enertek — incorporate the IEC work and lead a full research team, with highest security clearance, to complete the remaining research to refine the ore into a viable catalyst for slow fusion.

Dalton paged through the endless emails. Then, there it lay, the proof Weiss and Huchara had organized and set in motion the plan to detonate a bomb at the Elko mine site and destroy the buried vein of ore. They actually felt they could beat the U.S. to an understanding of the full potential of the technology, both as an energy source and as weapon system; create sufficient specialized bombs for implantation into known enemy countries and eliminate those threats, without ever being seen as directly involved. Dalton was astounded at the audacity and boldness of the plan. Clearly, the group was connected to, though far outside the oversight of, the top leaders in Japan and Israel. Ronet checked in on Dalton's lengthy review of the captured files and emails. "Find anything to help us nail there guys JD?"

"Get a load of this. Nine emails between Weiss and other KCG members on their plans and progress to develop and use the weaponry side of the technology against Iran and then the North Koreans. However, the wildest scheme was the attempt to destroy the raw ore at Elko. Weiss, an Israeli top government official, ordered an attack on American soil; the hillside fire and bomb hidden at the mine site. This couldn't have been authorized at the highest levels in Israel." Dalton and

Ronet gained a new appreciation how deep and pervasive the KCG operations were.

Dalton began to formulate an aggressive new strategy, and with the President's approval, he could *play* the game, control the technology, and remove the threats to national security. Using the cover afforded by Weiss's forced cooperation at the IEC Dalton decided on an *end game*. Ronet loved the idea and that it wasn't going to be debated in Congressional oversight committees. Dalton flew on the next shuttle to the White House with Ronet and Tucker in tow.

OUTSIDE THE OVAL OFFICE

Ronet and Tucker were tired, as was Dalton. They had spent all of the previous day returning from Israel, settling in at a sequestered conference center and briefing room near Langley, and dissecting the vast data stolen from the IEC. During the hour trip to the White House, Dalton explained his ideas to them. After outlining his plan, the marine in Ronet wanted to take up arms and stand opposed in war with Israel, or more specifically Dr. Eli Weiss. Tucker wanted to expose the entire sad story of our ally trying to sabotage efforts undertaken by a U.S. firm, with government support, on a new technology which could change the economic balance in the world. Finally, calmer heads prevailed, and Dalton, then Tucker, and eventually Ronet came to appreciate the bold ideas Dalton proposed. Now all they needed was an equally bold President to approve the plan.

The President's personal aide opened the oval office door and politely summoned the three inside. The room always took Dalton back, for even though he had been in there a dozen times, he never had the burden of leading and selling a plan or idea to the President. Rather, he was always a knowledgeable team member, able to reason out the strategy, justification, and implementation of a presented plan — not one of his own. However, this time it felt different, he was knee deep in the detail and there was no time to waste deliberating over the subtle ramifications of a course of action.

The President rose to greet the men. "JD have you heard the latest news on Ed's surgery to repair his shoulder and neck muscles?" The President asked with a serious tone.

"No, sir, I haven't how's he doing?"

"Not all that well, I'm afraid. He's had a stroke."

Dalton looked frozen in shock. How could this be? He was doing fine several days ago, barking out orders from his bed, and still participating as though he was not hurt or in a hospital.

"Complications with surgery I'm told. He's now in a coma, though they are hopeful he will snap out of it soon."

Ronet and Tucker were solemn, as they too had dealt with Kosko and knew he was a good man, in an exceptional role assisting the President. The room fell silent for a moment.

"Now let's hear your thoughts on how to finish this crazy business we've been drawn into," announced the President.

Dalton began with his summary of the quick *in-and-out* Ronet engineered so Dalton, Jane, and others could access and download critical incriminating information on the actions of Weiss and the Knowledge Consortium Group. He left no details out and gave significant credit to Ronet, Spielman, and Tucker for their excellent intelligence and planning of the excursion. He explained he had deployed Jane back to Enertek to lead a large lab group dedicated to quickly completing the remaining research to document the properties and functionality of the ore, and the critical refining steps to convert it into a viable catalyst for use in bombs or slow fusion energy.

The President remained focused throughout the fifty-minute explanation of Dalton's plan. His gaze never left Dalton's face. The initial phase of the plan involved Dalton, Ronet, and Tucker arriving at the IEC moments before the Secretary of State would call Weiss urging he take a short meeting, at the request of the President, with the three about an important energy matter. Caught by surprise and counting on invoking the President's name regarding the accommodation, Dalton felt Weiss would have no choice except to receive them as important visitors. The remaining details of the plan were delivered convincingly by Dalton, upon which the President said, "I'm extremely impressed. What a plan. Let me review it a few moments alone."

Turning to Ronet and Tucker, Dalton received a flurry of non-verbal compliments and approvals. After less than a minute appearing to study the White House lawn the President said, "The plan is on. You have approval to proceed under my authority."

Thirty-six hours later, Dalton, Ronet, and Tucker approached the IEC outside Tel Aviv. Dalton's cell phone rang and the caller confirmed the President's secretaries had just called and requested the Weiss meeting. Dalton carried a personal signed letter from the President authorizing him to conduct Operation Return Strike, the operational code name for Dalton's plan approved by the President.

THE ISRAELI BETRAYAL

Once face-to-face with Weiss, Dalton began to reveal the findings about the ore in Elko, and that they had obtained significant files and data detailing the involvement of Weiss, Huchara, Yong, and Secretary Kytoma in acts against the United States of America and its interests. Weiss sat quiet and un-phased for a time. Dalton calmly stated "We know of your actions to position and detonate a bomb in the Iranian Energy Laboratory, apparently successfully, several weeks earlier." Weiss began to show signs of stress.

Next, Dalton revealed that his group, along with President Conner, knew of their failed attempt to destroy the Elko find with an implanted bomb. Weiss's face tightened as he heard for the first time the precious ore had not been destroyed by his bomb attack. Dalton then further revealed he knew, and the President knew, a third bomb was positioned in North Korea at their newly dedicated Missile Research Complex; that General Yong was the key asset in the effort and that he was killed in a car accident following the failed detonation. Dalton paused to allow the head of the IEC to compose himself.

Within ten minutes of their arrival, Dalton had turned Weiss's world upside down. After the initial rush of receiving a team dispatched by the President of the United States, Weiss's world darkened. The smallish man, balding and with very little body-toning showing from beneath his ill-fitting suit, began to tremble. He started perspiring profusely, breathing rapidly, and failing to control a nervous tick flickering at his left eyelid.

Breathless, Weiss softly asked, "Did you invade my laboratories recently?"

"You're damn right we did," blurted out Ronet, almost leaving his chair to make the point.

"By what authority do you enter my country and steal our research?"

Reaching out to restrain Ronet, Dalton said, "By the personal approval and authority of the President of the United States, we came to retrieve *our* technology and stop your efforts to control *our* discovery."

Swallowing hard, and wiping his forehead, Weiss mouthed, "Assuming this is true, what do you want of me?"

"You're full and complete cooperation to finish our research, dismantle the laboratory undertaking your research, return of all stolen materials, and a teardown of the Knowledge Consortium Group."

Holding Dalton's stare for a long minute Weiss finally whispered, "And what am I to expect in return for this cooperation?" The air in the room loomed heavy with the tension of the moment. Dalton moved his eyes from Weiss to Tucker.

"Immunity from extradition to the states for criminal acts against the U.S. — a closed file on your involvement in all these criminal acts, an opportunity to have Israel become a test country for use of this new technology for energy development, and a written thank you from President Conner on your assistance in our research," declared Tucker after getting the nod from Dalton to announce the *"hook"* to Weiss.

"I must talk to my leadership to consider this proposal."

"No you don't!" declared Dalton. Weiss winched at Dalton's determination.

"You have clearly been conducting this entire effort with tacit approval of Secretary Hyriam Dyan, a member of your country's leadership. You can make the choice now to continue with us in control of future events, or we will cease this entire attempt to save your country, and you, from an embarrassing public display of political sabotage against your strongest ally." Dalton paused as he leaned in to make his point. "What will it be Dr. Weiss?"

Weiss dropped his head into his quivering hands, and quietly nodded his approval. Tucker presented a letter agreement covering all the points already signed by President Jerome Conner. Weiss signed the letter, visibly shaken.

Tucker called on his cell phone and advised President Conner the agreement was presented and signed by Weiss as expected. Dalton explained to Weiss that he personally would be overseeing and approving all operational decisions, staff assignments, and communications emanating from the IEC. Dalton expected to be stationed at the IEC, as a "guest" for a few days, and others would be joining him as "supervisors" for all activity arising from the situation room. Basically, Dalton and company were taking quiet control of all activity in the refining process laboratory, the situation room and communications; all still apparently under the direction of Weiss.

Weiss listened carefully to Dalton and took a sip of the bottled water sitting on his desk. Still shaking, he said, "What do you intend to do with the other members of the Knowledge Consortium?"

"Shut them down . . . permanently. By the way, your ore now in the refining process is being destroyed, and will be rendered inert in just a few more hours."

Weiss looked like he had been stuck by lightning and could not even get the words out to express his shock, fear and frustration at the way things were turning out.

Dalton gave a half smile and called Jane Holman to update her.

 **30-EIGHT**

TEL AVIV — HILTON REGENCY HOTEL.

DALTON began to set up an entire communications and coordination center on the top floor of the Hilton in Tel Aviv. Advertised as a conference of telecommunication executives, the Dalton team was inconspicuous to the casual observer. Sleeping quarters were on the north end and two large conference rooms, meeting rooms, a small kitchen, and several lounge areas finished off the south end. It was a perfect spot, only some fifteen minutes from the IEC and twenty minutes from Hanger 19 at the airport.

With the help of Ronet and Tucker, they had established a fully armed, plain clothes security group and two dedicated satellites for surveillance. A third satellite provided a communications link back to the White House Situation Room, a direct line to the President, email, internet, faxes, and hard phone lines to the U.S. embassy in Israel and Jack Tucker's office in Istanbul Turkey. The world lay at his fingertips, or so it felt to Dalton.

It was awkward to him, since this was the first such

operation he had taken without the support and direct involvement of his good friend Ed Kosko. Reporting directly to the President, and using his small personal "black ops" unit so to speak, afforded Dalton unprecedented power and mobility to take control of and settle the mess the Knowledge Consortium Group had created. The President had made several tough choices leading up to approving Dalton's plan and then making certain the "buck stopped with him" assuring him that no other government official was engaged in the decision-making.

It was a huge act of faith, Dalton thought. He felt Kosko had been able to convince the President that he was the man to manage and solve this problem fast and in the best possible outcome for the parties involved. It would have been easier for the President to send his Secretaries of State and Defense, make strong supported accusations against Israel, demand the removal and extradition of Weiss for criminal prosecution, and withhold military and financial support for Israel. This approach however, would have weakened the entire region while the U.S. exacted its punishment and humiliation upon Israel.

Then, of course, there was Japan and its funding and participation, not by the government directly but from high-ranking cabinet personnel, and an international businessman running Mitsui Mining Limited in an attempt to sabotage U.S. research interests and its security. None of the scenarios looked wise to the President. Dalton's approach, however, was covert, a fast implementation, and might just end up being a strong net positive for the U.S. image and power throughout the world.

The next few days were critical to achieving the outcome Dalton had conveyed to the President, Tucker, and Ronet.

30-NINE

SEA OF JAPAN, DOGO ISLAND — NEAR SAIGO AIRFIELD

GENERAL Yong sat nervously pacing the floor, waiting for some response to his email to Weiss. He thought about calling, yet feared he could be intercepted and his position discovered. It had been three and a half days since the failed detonation attempt at Hyesan. He felt he needed to connect with Weiss and Huchara.

Back in the IEC, Dalton read Yong's unopened email to Weiss. He then reflected. *Yong is alive and managed to fake his own death even though the original plan failed to materialize. He wants to get back in the game and finish the mission.*

Dalton created a draft response email and saved it for discussion with Weiss later. Tucker's communications unit had penetrated the email accounts of Weiss and Yong and embedded a command to copy all emails amongst the senders and recipients to a "receive only" email account at Tucker's office in Istanbul. With a direct communications link to Istanbul from the Tel Aviv operations room at the Hilton, Tucker remained connected in real time to the Knowledge Consortium Group.

Dalton began to see a way Yong could fit into the overall plan he had presented to the President. He had to confer with Ronet on his ideas.

OUTSIDE TEL AVIV — IEC FACILITY

Weiss was walking the complex, forcing a smile and showing the inner workings of the IEC to Ronet, Spielman, and two other marines presented as educators from the U.S. Dalton sat at Weiss's desk chair reading, for the third time, the twelve-hour-old email from General Yong to the KCG. Dalton felt he could use the break in communications between the KCG and Yong in the next phase of his plan.

Since Yong's email had not yet been opened before Dalton took over Weiss's office and no reply emails arrived from other KCG members, Weiss was *not* aware of Yong's survival and escape from North Korea.

Ronet had to move quickly if Dalton would be able

to use Yong in the next step of the plan. A high-speed transport stealth aircraft, a modified F-117, was brought over the Mediterranean from Italy and parked outside Hanger 19. It could accommodate up to ten personnel and cargo, beyond the two-crew members.

Dalton left Tucker in charge of continuing control of the IEC through Weiss, and took Ronet, four marines, including Spielman, and a new Local Detonator Controller. It had to replace the one on the Hyesan bomb after Jane's software jammed up the electronics so badly it would not respond to satellite commands. It appeared dead, and so was the bomb unless someone could design a way to detonate it from a new trigger.

Dalton's greatest fear was that the North Koreans had already, or would soon, locate the bomb and design an alternate detonator which could be timed to initiate the explosion some 700 miles from Hyesan over Tokyo. If they had enough time and figured out how to re-con-figure the bomb's parameters for more intensity, they could create a weapon the approximate size of the one used at Hiroshima. The North Korean's had already announced they were ready to begin missile testing over the Sea of Japan and were making the Japanese very nervous. The recent dedication of the complex only served to move them closer to a launch. Despite the warnings from the rest of the world, their crazy little military dictator was going to flex his muscle.

THE ISRAELI BETRAYAL

Yong received the email Dalton had created under Dr. Weiss's signature. Dalton figured a little sarcasm might make the message appears more in line with Weiss's style.

```
We are delighted to know your accidental
death was a bit pre-mature. A team sent
by Member One will meet you in Saigo
tomorrow at 2100 hours local time with
further details and instructions. Please
keep low profile until then.

Member Two
```

Sang Huchara was forwarded this same email, though with the additional note.

```
Please arrange for transport by con-
struction barge to North Korean coast
and provide vehicle to carry member
three, and two assistants to Hyesan
along with security and technical per-
sonnel numbering six. Must arrive at
Hyesan by 11:00 local time two days from
now. Maintain radio and email silence
unless absolutely necessary.
```

RICHARD TREVAE

Within an hour, Sang Huchara had
responded. Message received and understood, arrangements made to meet schedule requirements.

Dalton, Ronet, and friends were set to arrive at Saigo, at 09:30 a.m. at the north of the airstrip and drive a Mitsui construction truck to the old abandoned maintenance building a mile down the airstrip were Yong and a few guards were hold up. Only a half dozen aircraft a day made it to the little island, and they were either military making practice runs, or occasional contractor aircraft delivering personnel or equipment for staging to South Korea or Japan. The F-117 came in low, slow, and quiet about 09:22a.m., arriving as planned and parked at the north end of the field.

As promised, Huchara had his local contractor group ready to transport the nine by construction barge over the Sea of Japan, some 310 miles, and arrive at a small port used by Mitsui for its construction efforts. Twenty other contractors, inspector, and engineer types were also on the barge, and all maintained their own distance from Dalton's group, so no potentially compromising interaction occurred.

Once on the mainland, the Mitsui personnel moved off to four different construction sites and Yong, his two security guards, and the six in Dalton's team began the three-hour trip to the Missile Research Complex in Hyesan. The road vehicle looked more like an old tour bus with individual seats, a central aisle, and storage for gear, supplies, and equipment beneath the floor deck. Spielman took on the task of appearing like the Israeli point man for Dr. Weiss, quickly introducing himself to Yong who spoke some broken English, and was comfortable with the accent and look of Spielman that he was part of Weiss's team at the IEC. The rest of Dalton's team were described as security, communications, and weapons experts who would remove the original LDC and install the new one which could then be activated by satellite commands as originally planned. They remained very passive and quiet, pretending to tinker with small electronic gadgets needed for the mission.

As the personnel vehicle carrying Dalton, his crew and Yong's group approached the main entry gate, Yong called on a secure cell phone his friend and confidant, Major Kunghee, Head of Site Security at the NKMRC. The major was taken aback by a call from a friend he assumed had died. Yong quickly explained how he survived the crash and that he needed access and protection while on the site. Performing as the faithful friend Yong knew Kunghee to be, the major assured him he had cleared the route Yong requested and that he would meet the general there in one hour. He ordered the guard unit manning the entrance to process the vehicle through to the main equipment storage crib at building three, the location of the embedded bomb.

As the guard approached the transport, Dalton and Ronet both instinctively gripped the handles of their Glock 40's. Prepared to take him out and drag him into the vehicle, Dalton listened carefully to the discussion between their marine driver and the guard, all in Korean. It was brief and without a hint of concern by the guard. He returned to his station and opened the large swinging gate. Dalton and Ronet looked at each other, breathed a sigh of relief, and released their grip on their weapons.

Once inside the storage crib, a 50,000 square foot metal building, without general heating except for an occasional steam heater to avoid freezing internal water lines, Yong took the team to the location of the bomb container. Innocently disguised as repair parts for pump and compressors installed throughout the complex; it measured about four feet wide, six feet long and three feet high. Enclosed in rough wood framing, metal strapping and banding, the package was still in pristine shape, never opened or moved from its original position. Ronet and two marines took up watch positions and communicated through headsets and earpieces. Yong looked confused when suddenly Dalton began speaking, giving orders, making assignments, and taking charge of the activities at hand.

Dalton looked to General Yong, and motioned for

him and Spielman to join him a short distance from the bomb.

"General my name is Dalton Crusoe; I am an American, working directly under the orders of the President of the United States. We have come here with the express intention of helping you complete your original mission for the KCG."

Even though the general did not speak English all that well, he heard and clearly understood Dalton's words. He stood stunned and speechless, for a moment, and then rattled off some emotional words in Korean. Finally collecting his composure, he asked, "You're not working through Dr. Weiss?"

"Well, for now let's say Dr. Weiss is working for us." Dalton put forth a serious look as he delivered the answer. Yong seemed to accept the explanation yet did not understand exactly what Dalton meant.

Just then, the large overhead door servicing the front of the building began to open. Walking in was Major Kunghee, who was fully dressed in his military uniform, armed, and looking about for the General. Ronet and a marine jumped the major, knocking him to the ground. Kunghee reached for his nine-millimeter handgun, just as Ronet's marine pressed his Glock 40 against the major's temple. The major froze and raised his hands above his head. Ronet stood him up, removed the major's weapon from his side holster and walked him over to Dalton and Yong who watched the entire thirty-second encounter.

"He's with me, my friend, Major Kunghee, its okay," yelled Yong.

In Korean and some broken English Yong explained who Dalton and his team were, their purpose and about the bomb. Now Major Kunghee began to banter on in Korean trying to accuse the General of setting him up. Yong assured him the original plan would have certainly have destroyed his office and the security office. "No I had that problem covered," blurted out Yong. "Recall on the day of the dedication I ordered you to security servicing the airfield some three miles away. You would not have been killed in the explosion if it had gone as planned." Yong appeared very sincere.

Kunghee looked squarely at Yong and nodded, remembering the day and his location. He apologized to the General with a deep bow acknowledging he had not betrayed his friend.

Dalton then sat the General down with Kunghee and told them about the plan to equip the bomb with a new LDC so it could again be activated by satellite commands at the proper time. He indicated both men would be given sanctuary in the west and following this mission at Hyesan, neither man would be prosecuted for the actions of the KCG against American interests.

General Yong assured Dalton that only he had been

a member of the Knowledge Consortium and not the Major. Dalton acknowledged the General's statement as correct and understood. Kunghee had a million questions yet chose to follow the safer path and lend support as Yong interacted openly with Dalton.

The two marines and Spielman were almost finished installing the replacement LDC and were ready to test it. Dalton had set up a small Satcom antenna and coded in a dedicated satellite for use on this mission. Moments later the activation light on the LDC began to flash. Dalton oversaw this procedure by Spielman and gave him the approval to lock in the satellite's identity for future commands. Spielman punched in the code provided by Dalton and twelve seconds later the light remained green and stopped flashing.

The Satcom screen read *"LDC Activated-Awaiting Detonation Sequence."*

Tucker starred fixated on the large screen in the IEC situation room and saw remote camera scans on the crib storage building, the perimeter and the bomb container. Also showing were the command instructions and satellite connection programming occurring real time as the satellite and the LDC communicated with each other. On another wall, a satellite image of the Korean peninsula passed slowly by and an inset image of the Hyesan site was displayed with such detail as vehicle movement, steam emissions from the complex's power plant, and intermittent cloud cover.

RICHARD TREVAE

Dalton's plan was coming together fast; now they had to time the detonation to an event at the Missile Research Complex which would draw the top North Korean leaders to the site. It was clear the North Korean's were striving to launch a missile from the complex to demonstrate, following their grand dedication ceremony, that they were now a more formidable neighbor. Missiles were installed and ready for deployment in four buried silos on the complex. Fueling and targeting instructions were all that remained before a launch could be initiated.

Yong began to understand the full extent of Dalton's plan as he listened to the chatter between the IEC, and the team before him working on the bomb and its LDC. He realized Dalton's team arrived as a welcome rescue for him, and his friend Major Kunghee. Dalton's team intended to resurrect the original failed plan, crafted by the KCG, give it new life and carry it off as designed. He and the major would escape to the west.

If the bulk of North Korea's leadership and top military personnel were killed, the possibility for a new Korea, re-united with the south, could become a reality. Even the rogue actions of the KCG, led by Weiss and Huchara for the most part, would be exonerated for this action against the corrupt and failed North Korean regime. A bigger more important issue was at stake — the reunification of Korea, and removal of a dangerous, nuclear-missile-armed, hostile neighbor to Japan.

THE **ISRAELI BETRAYAL**

As the weight of their situation settled in on Yong, he had an idea which would facilitate Dalton's plan; recall the top governmental and military leadership over a false emergency of some kind and time the detonation to their arrival. Yong approached Dalton, and said in his best-broken English "I have an idea that helps your plan, Mr. Crusoe, would you like me to explain it?"

"Absolutely, let's hear it."

Yong's plan combined as a perfect component to Dalton's grand plan. He proposed that Major Kunghee who was not implicated with conspiracies against the current regime, dispatch a memo sighting new information. It would state that, General Yong might have been targeted for murder because he had discovered a plan by on-site contractors and engineers to take over the NKMRC complex during a test of backup power and deliver an internet broadcast to the world about the offensive war capabilities nature of the complex. Bogus records could be created to draw sufficient concern by all the top leadership to reconvene at the site and oversee a "cleaning house" and interrogation of key suspects in the conspiracy.

Dalton liked it, as did Kunghee. Both men began to detail the steps to create and pull off the ruse. Dalton summoned Ronet and set up a Satcom conference with Tucker. After all the strategy and timing had been worked out, Dalton gave the approval to proceed to

RICHARD TREVAE

carry out the deception as outlined by Yong. The newly fitted LDC rested in place and awaited instructions to detonate. Now they just needed the invited audience on site.

Major Kunghee's memo went out at 1730 the day Dalton's team arrived at Hyesan. They had left the complex site and were driving to a rendezvous point midway to the coast, where a low flying attack helicopter would arrive and remove Dalton's team, Yong, and Kunghee at or just before the anticipated detonation.

Within hours of sending Kunghee's memo, the word spread throughout the inner sanctums of the North Korean command and major government officials about the "conspiracy." Certain military types were dispatched immediately to the site intended to arrive within twelve hours of the memo. The Prime Minister, his Defense Secretary, a close security detail, and several top generals were all arriving within twenty-four hours. The complex was ordered on high alert and a status report was to be presented by Kunghee at 1400 local time two days out. Major Kunghee emailed his staff to expect him back from offsite meetings the morning of the status report briefing to the arriving visitors. The major hoped this would provide cover for his absence over the next two days.

Having departed the complex about 1740 local time, Dalton's team completed the installation and programming of the new LDC and set up monitoring cameras in the crib storage building to monitor from the IEC for intrusions or activity at the bomb location. Tucker's technicians were overseeing the Israeli staff actually at the consoles in the situation room receiving all the intelligence Dalton's team had been sending. External security to the room was staffed by Tucker's people; and Weiss played his role well keeping his staff cooperating without a hint he had been compromised.

When Dalton called in to Tucker stating they were leaving the NKMRC, everything was packed up, stowed, and hidden as though they were electrical and mechanical contractors simply finishing their day and going to off-site accommodations. They left the site without incident, sandwiched in amongst a half dozen contractors, engineers, and laborers on foot. Tucker studied the monitoring cameras showing the crib storage area; the bomb was hidden, fully programmed, awaiting the destruct code.

FORTY

JANE Holman had begun to feel a bit more normal after the events of the last twenty-two days sank into memories. She kept her mind off of the terrifying events at Enertek, the Elko mine, and the cabin belonging to Susan Wallace. Ironically, the work to isolate and demolish the laboratories destroyed on the Labor Day weekend kept her involved and active.

Then, a few days later, she gained responsibility over four other labs, eighteen more scientists, and lab staff to expedite the remaining research and functionality tests on the rare Elko mine ore. Kosko's request to quickly complete the applied research on the ore was fully supported by the president with funds, security, and staff.

The Israeli research was good and covered a lot of ground that Jane's group would not have arrived at for months. She set up a program that started where the Israeli work stopped, back tested to confirm their most recent results and then moved on to the next set of experiments. She felt that a full understanding of the weaponry and energy sides of the technology were close. Nevertheless, extreme care was taken to avoid another accidental explosion at Enertek. Jane emerged as the logical choice, and through Dalton, using Presidential authority and Ed Kosko's earlier endorsement to the executive committee; she got all she asked for in terms of equipment, staff, and money.

Just days into the second generation research with her new team of crack scientists Jane began seeing impressive progress. The raw Elko ore did, in fact, appear to result from a meteor impact thousands of years before in which the mineral contents of the meteor reacted with the nickel and cobalt compounds already buried in the Waldron Range, transforming the mixture of elements into the mildly radioactive lithium material found at Elko. To reproduce this reaction in a lab would be impossible with present day technology and equipment. The temperatures needed, while far short of conventional fusion reactions, were still outside current equipment standards. This clearly meant that, unless another large meteor hit a similar Waldron vein somewhere, no more "Elko ore" capable of being refined into the active catalyst for slow fusion would be found on earth.

The understanding of the refining process and modulation parameters to control and size the detonations were enhanced every day. Six patents were in the process of being filed as the research continued that would cement Jane, her team, and Enertek to the discovery and the technology that arose from the find. The government, through the Department of Energy, would control all uses and applications for the weaponry uses of the technology. The energy side of the technology, as expected, became clearer through the understandings achieved through the weaponry side research. This new energy source would also be controlled through the Department of Energy then licensed out to users in the power and energy business around the world.

Dalton was being heralded as the top man to oversee and secure the technology as it became commercially available and safe for the average person. This was not exactly Dalton's forte, as he considered the possibility to lead the commercialization of a new technology worldwide. Rather, he felt most comfortable in a project, or mission role, where the challenges were varied and unique each day. Nevertheless, as the President and his closest advisors deftly steered the conventional wisdom as to how, where, and when this discovery should be managed, the name Dalton Crusoe kept popping up.

Jane also developed a new respect for Dalton. She kept reliving the several moments when, had he not been there, protected her, and made her feel safe, she might well have been killed. She realized this seemingly normal, yet exceptional, guy had literally saved her life, fought off attackers, and protected a new technolo-

THE **ISRAELI BETRAYAL**

gy from being stolen from the U.S. and used by evil forces, all in less than a month. Against all her survival instincts, he encouraged her to help in the now successful dismantling of the stolen Israeli research on slow fusion. She truly owed Dalton for all the confidence and support he had shown toward her.

VANCOUVER, CANADA

Sang Huchara was not happy. He had always let Dr. Weiss take the lead on most matters of technology and research, however not on tactical matters, that was his expertise. Why would Weiss direct that he provide boats, vehicles, and staff in a remote location without more discussion, reflection, and debate? He should have been the most influential voice, not Weiss. Perplexed and somewhat worried he called Gilles Montrose.

"Where are you now?"

"North end of Vancouver island, enjoying a fine young French woman. Why?"

"Finish your pleasure time and meet me tomorrow early at the Country Club, say around 8:00 a.m."

"I'll be there at 9:00 a.m."

Sang Huchara hung up the phone and began to think the worst.

RICHARD TREVAE

It had been several days of no contact with anyone involved with the Knowledge Consortium, a bit unusual particularly, with all the attention to the Elko mine matter, and all the work going on at the IEC. Before the last email about General Yong, the only update on activities was the unexplained failure to achieve the North Korean explosion. Now three days later, Yong pops up alive and is ready to return under cover and complete the mission. Then Huchara is asked, make that ordered, by Weiss to commit personnel, equipment, cargo barges, and transport vehicles into North Korea. It just didn't feel right to Sang Huchara, and his many years in business handling tough construction issues made him suspicious he lacked all of the data. He thought to call Dr. Weiss directly, although he also knew that was not the best way to preserve their anonymity.

He withdrew his Blackberry, which he seldom text messaged on, and sent Weiss a message. *Sense all is not as it seems. Can we meet? Member One.* He then sent the text to Weiss's phone.

Weiss saw the message alert and excused himself to the restroom where he read it. Minutes later, Weiss replied. *Fully compromised. Not in control. Do not call/email.*

Sang read the message a second time, then a third, then recited it out loud to himself a fourth time. *What the hell is going on?* he wondered.

THE ISRAELI BETRAYAL

No one else had seemed to notice problems other than those in the two earlier Weiss emails. Fearful others he might contact concerning their operations were also compromised; Sang controlled his desire to start calling all his information sources. He would send Gilles to Israel in the morning on a fact-finding mission.

40-ONE

THE wind began to pick up and the sky slowly started getting darker. It felt colder than the 48 degrees registered on the transport vehicle dashboard. Now at 1810 local time, Dalton's team awaited the Apache troop transport helicopter. It ran fast and quiet, and as low as 200 feet above ground level to avoid radar. This one was modified carry up to twelve troops with full combat gear up to 300 miles out and back. Still carrying 50-caliber machine guns on either side, it no longer had the four heat seeking air-to-air or air-to-ground missiles. Ronet called in the chopper to bring them all out once Dalton confirmed the LDC was engaged and controlled by the satellite link through the IEC situation room.

Dalton checked his watch, seven minutes until pick up. Ronet and his three marines set up a tight perimeter around the vehicle and the small landing area tucked in between three small ridgelines extending off the main mountain range.

Dalton's headset suddenly came alive with radio talk from the incoming helicopter.

"Bird to Ronet, come in please."

Colonel Ronet pressed the talk button on his head set and responded. "Ronet to Bird, we are good to go at RP-A, team of nine plus one."

"Roger that, expect ETA in four, say again four minutes."

As Dalton scanned the sky to the southwest looking to spot the chopper, Ronet whispered into the headsets of all six in the Dalton team. "Lights coming over the hills to north could be vehicles, stay alert."

Twenty seconds later they heard engines of three military trucks that came around the ridgelines heading directly for Dalton's team. Ronet ordered all to seek cover. Expecting a shoot out any moment, the vehicles stopped in front of the transport bus, and Major Kunghee stood out in front of the first vehicle in its headlights and began yelling out orders of some kind, and waived his arms wildly. Yong, his security men, and all of Dalton's team sat crouched behind brush and trees not forty yards away, weapons drawn and cocked. Dalton whispered into the headsets. "Hold your positions, and let this play out."

Ronet then whispered into the radio channel to the chopper. "Hold five, hostiles present; circle south till I call all clear."

The chopper pilot, an experienced naval officer, abruptly turned the helicopter south, dropped to fifty feet above the ground and then held its position hovering just above the ground, with only a low muffled thump, thump, thump coming from the engine. Kunghee continued to play his angry, madman role for the attention of the sergeant leading the three truck caravan.

"Move out now or prepare yourself for a firing squad, you imbecile," shouted Kunghee one last time, pointing to the east.

After the wild verbal retorts by Kunghee, the three-truck caravan began moving south again, apparently none the wiser as to what they had come across.

Yong jumped to his feet and began laughing as he patted Kunghee several times on the back. He then explained to Ronet and Dalton that the major scolded the truck troop for contaminating an accident scene where General Yong may have died, and that he appreciated if they would get the hell out of here before they did anymore damage. The irony was so thick that all had a great laugh at the courage and quick thinking of Major Kunghee. Moments later the helicopter arrived and flew the ten men out of North Korea and to a U.S. destroyer fifteen miles off the coast. Ronet and Dalton again proved they were a formidable team.

40-TWO

TEL AVIV — HILTON REGENCY

DALTON sat positioned directly in front of a large computer screen set up for video conferencing with the White House. Jack Tucker and Colonel Ronet were present and sitting beside Dalton. Within a few minutes, Dalton would be updating the President on Operation Return Strike. It had all gone extremely well, up to this point, and he was pleased to soon report that while changes were required mid-course in North Korea, it all worked when Major Kunghee committed to aid the general and then later misdirected the truck convoy just prior to the helicopter escape out of North Korea.

Over the last twenty-eight hours the bomb had not been moved or detected, the LDC was active and awaiting instructions, and the camera surveillance around the crib storage buildings revealed more and more vehicles arriving. Streaming satellite imagery confirmed at least a dozen top ranking military officers had arrived, and only a few hours ago the aircraft carrying the North Korean leader was landing. A total of fourteen people departed the plane; they all took a transport the few miles over to the NKMRC, near where the bomb was positioned. The targets had arrived and now the decision to eliminate them and their threats to Japan and the western world was at hand. Dalton was very nervous, although composed when President Conner came on live to the conferencing screen.

"Good afternoon gentlemen," offered the President.

"Good morning, sir," responded Dalton on behalf of the team, and acknowledged the time difference.

"What is our status Dalton?"

"Our surveillance on the ground and from satellite imagery has confirmed substantial numbers of military and political personnel have entered the Missile Research Complex within the last day or so."

"Has there been an effort to locate Major Kunghee ahead of his planned briefing?"

"No sir, and the Major, on my direction, called his office on a secure cell and informed his staff he was to arrive within the next forty-five minutes, or about twenty minutes from this moment."

"Very well, are you prepared to proceed with the final step of your plan Dalton? Is there anything yet to be done before we take the final step?"

Dalton let his mind settle on the president's questions for a moment. His answer, if yes, would beg the next step — detonation of the bomb. If his answer were anything but yes, hours or days might be lost resolving the last concerns. Dalton thought hard. There were no reasons or issues why they should not proceed. In a final mental check, Dalton convinced himself again the plan was ready and the ethics were right. "Yes, sir with your approval, I will set the final step in motion."

It had only been a few days, however the President had spent some serious time considering if he should proceed to carry through on Dalton's plan. The timing and circumstances were perfect; General Yong joined as a willing and credible asset to assist in the transition that would surely follow a toppling of the current regime, based sadly and solely on a "military first" policy of governing his country. Beyond that, the threat of the North Korean Missile Research Complex posed real threats to Japan and other neighbors of North Korea. A few senior Presidential advisors had been brought into the loop, in confidence, on the events that unfolded since the Elko find. The unanimous decision approved the use of the technology, planted by Japan and Israel under the cover and setup provided by Yong and the KCG. Pausing for a moment, the President spoke with strength. "You have my approval. Proceed and keep me informed as news comes in on the North Korean reaction."

Dalton swallowed hard. It was now crunch time and there was no turning back. All had come together as he had outlined to the President days earlier, and if this last action, the timed detonation, is viewed by the North Koreans and the world as an accident, then a great good will have been done. Despite all the euphoric logic, Dalton still had to grapple with the taking of human life when not directly defending his own or that of a loved one. Coming full circle in his reflections he reasoned that someone, some nation, had to take a firm stand against evil, and if there was ever an evil worth removing it was the North Korean leadership. This approach just shortened the time it would take compared to years of pursuit by an international tribunal such as those rounding up Nazis, or Stalin, or the genocidist, Milosevic.

Dalton looked around at Ronet and Tucker and then ordered, "Initiate the LDC to detonate in ten minutes."

The team manager in the IEC with Weiss standing by directed the console technicians to enter the instructions to the LDC. Lights flashed and moments later, the screen displayed, "*LDC Activated >>>> Loading Detonation Sequence.*"

As the time approached, the satellite imagery focused to high resolution over Hyesan. The day appeared clear, with very little cloud cover, the local temperature steadied at fifty-two degrees, and the wind blew westerly at eight miles per hour. Extra equipment had been set up in Weiss's command center of the situation room to

direct the IEC satellite feeds to an NSA satellite showing the same images for the President in Washington
DC.

Precisely on schedule at 8:25 p.m. local Hyesan time,
the detonation took place. The screen went bright yellow then white and blank for a few seconds, and then
revealed a huge fireball directly over the North Korean
Missile Research Complex. Moments later, several secondary explosions, resulting from fuel depots, and rock-
et propellant storage blew up and added to the spectacle
on the large screen. Minutes passed before the satellite
images began to break up and eventually went blank. In
about twelve hours, another NSA satellite would pass
overhead and record the extent of devastation as the
fresh morning light allowed a detailed clear picture of
the blast site.

The IEC's operation room became very quiet now,
with each technician tending to his work as though this
was Weiss's show along with Secretary Kytoma's to rel-
ish and soak up. Dalton also sat quietly reflecting on the
last month, his mind drifting on how much he wanted
to spend some time with Carolyn, who still knew virtually nothing of the harrowing events of the last few
weeks. He reasoned she didn't need to hear all the
details of his mission, it would simply worry her.

Secretary Dyan was called to the U.S. Embassy in
Israel by the Secretary of State and given the full story

on the Knowledge Consortium Group's activities. Nothing was left out: the attempt to steal the slow fusion technology from the U.S.; destroy the supply of raw ore in the Elko mine region; undermined U.S. interests, and attempted assassinations of all involved in developing the technology. At first Dyan tried posturing himself to deny all the claims against him and Weiss, however before he could start his charade, U.S. officials, spearheaded by Tucker, offered them the evidence — emails, taped conversations, video surveillance, and the signed letter from Weiss. Dyan went limp, much like Weiss had done, and simply listened to the demands presented him.

First, Dr. Eli Weiss was to be arrested, removed from all scientific roles in Israel, not allowed to leave Israel, and cooperate fully with follow up investigations of his or Israel's role in the events arising out of the Elko incident.

Secondly, Dyan was to make a full report to the Israeli Prime Minister and stipulate he'd issue a formal, written, although private, apology to President Jerome Conner for their actions and those through The Knowledge Consortium Group, which endangered U.S. citizens, and were intended to undermine U.S. strategic interests. Furthermore, the U.S. would no longer recognize him as their Defense Minister; he would immediately resign and be replaced.

Thirdly, in exchange for these conditions being met,

the U.S. would share this peaceful energy technology in a demonstration project in Israel.

Within days, the Israeli Prime Minister delivered the requested documents and confirmation of the personnel changes in a face-to-face meeting with President Conner. The visit was officially described as an opportunity for the President to meet the new Israeli Defense Minister.

40-THREE

KHAMAL disliked meeting in the Arab countries, all Arab countries, and particularly in Tehran. It was too busy, too confining with their ever-changing mixture of secular and theocracy proponents, and too radical toward their nuclear ambitions. Not that he cared one bit as to how they chose to run their country; he just did not want to have to endure it.

Khamal had become comfortable in the south of France, Monaco in particular, and also the Spanish island of Mallorca. He had the money to do what he wanted, and with his western education and strong verbal skills, he blended in easily. Nevertheless, he owed the Iranian regime a progress report for their significant down payment and they demanded he deliver it in person.

He did not like that either, for exposing himself personally meant one more individual could betray him, and then he's have to kill the person. Nevertheless, Khamal tried to stack the odds in his favor, as he typically wore a disguise, used a different accent from his normal voice and never gave written reports; rather he used emails, or photos to make his mission accomplishments known.

In his update, Khamal explained what he found out from his surveillance and espionage thus far. He knew the events all arose from the Elko mine discovery, that Sang Huchara and Eli Weiss had been the primary co-conspirators to steal the raw ore and further the research and refine it into the modulated custom bomb that had destroyed their facility at Jefrah.

The Iranians also assumed the Israelis had destroyed the Elko mine site and its vein of unique ore, and working with the Japanese contacts of Sang Huchara, likely detonated a similar bomb at Hyesan North Korea. In the course of all this, Crusoe was perceived as overseeing the secret operations on behalf of the Americans at the Israeli IEC facility. Khamal reasoned that either Dalton Crusoe was the man orchestrating all the bomb attacks, or he had compromised Weiss somehow to penetrate their security. In effect, claimed Khamal, the U.S. was the steering force and ultimate authority for what happened at Jefrah and now Hyesan.

The Iranians were never so humiliated or angry, as the Israelis, with apparent U.S. help, successfully destroyed their prize research facility. A facility, the Iranians reminded Khamal, that was producing material for several first generation nuclear weapons and a missile delivery system validating their threat to "wipe Israel off the face of the earth." They wanted revenge, though without hard evidence to bring to the world attention, they could not convince anyone that they had not suffered at their own hand.

Nevertheless, with Khamal's help they could, they hoped, deliver death to the individual perpetrators. The Iranian President had a personal desire to make the assassinations very public, although Khamal would have nothing to do with it. His style allowed him to remain hidden and isolated from formal attempts to solve the deaths. He preferred to have a coroner report the cause of death as natural, and therefore no investigation for a killer would follow. Nevertheless, the Iranians wanted fast action and confirmation that the assassinations were accomplished. Khamal was put on notice to make good on his assignment.

A four-week time schedule was eventually agreed to by Khamal to eliminate Sang Huchara, Dr. Eli Weiss, and Jameson Dalton Crusoe using whatever method got the job done with certainty and conviction. The Iranians were confident they had the best assassin in the world for the job. Khamal was reminded that he told them "he never failed at a mission."

40-FOUR

FRENCH ST. MARTIN — 150 MILES EAST OF PUERTO RICO

CAROLYN McCabe had traveled a bit, mostly within the U.S. except also to England and Italy for academic outreach programs with participating universities. Never, however, had she taken a trip with Dalton to such an exotic and romantic spot as the Caribbean island of St. Martin.

Half-Dutch and half French, it offered a thirty-seven square mile island of gorgeous beaches, wonderful shopping, and food. Nevertheless, her real interests laid in the romantic sunsets and warm evenings she dreamed about with her man. Settling in was easy after the twenty minute ride from the airport to La Samana, their resort for four days, prior to another five days on a bare-boating trip through the leeward Antilles; Carolyn and Dalton were getting ready to enjoy their time together.

"Good after noon, Mr. and Mrs. Crusoe," announced the front desk manager, as they entered the open lobby after exiting their taxi.

"Yes, good afternoon to you, sir," replied Carolyn

faster than Dalton could correct him. She liked the assumption of marriage, even if it wasn't true just yet. She smiled while gazing at Dalton enjoying the moment.

"We have you in our beachfront units connected directly off the lobby to the south," said the manager pointing to the direction of their room. "I believe we are having you for four nights?"

"Yes," Dalton replied, distracted for a moment by the glow on Carolyn's face.

"Here are your keys, sir, and ma'am. Please enjoy yourselves and call me with any special requests. Your luggage has been taken to your room directly, so please enjoy a refreshing cocktail on our patio."

Dalton nodded approvingly and moved to the large patio, covered with a thatched high roof, and presenting an extraordinary view of Baie Longue and the Caribbean. Carolyn found a small table with chairs and sat down. "This is it, I'm never leaving."

Dalton was very pleased to see Carolyn truly relaxing and putting the intruder episode behind her. It had been a couple of weeks since the encounter and still no real explanation. Dalton still feared his activities arising from the Elko find were behind the incident.

After a late lunch, they went to change into bathing suits and walk the beach, full five miles of beautiful, pinkish white sand, in a long graceful crescent shape making up the bay. Rock outcroppings appeared near the shore every hundred yards or so, and the waves were rolling in from a quarter-mile out, building, rolling over, and crashing into a violent white froth that then flowed over their feet as they walked.

Carolyn looked radiant and very sexy as she strolled along beside him, topless like many of the Europeans frequenting the island every year. Her sensuality heightened in this distant, exotic setting, and she was going to enjoy it to the fullest. Having Dalton at her side, holding her hand as they walked, and offering an occasional kiss made the afternoon very special. Hours later, alone together a mile down the beach, lying on a blanket, watching a colorful sunset, she pulled Dalton to her and they made love on the beach. It seemed a dream come true for her; a much-needed continuation of the Labor Day weekend trip, so abruptly cut short. Dalton felt more relaxed than he had been in several weeks.

40-FIVE

St. Maarten — Phillipsburg Airport

THE flight from Tel Aviv to Lisbon arrived on time, even though the final leg was delayed about an hour. Khamal had changed his appearance to look like a man of fifty-five with gray hair, a small beard cropped near the chin, and thick dark rim glasses that made him virtually unrecognizable to a probing Interpol or Israeli security worker.

Khamal's plane arrived late to St. Maarten; the airport was nearly empty, and so security was modest. Dressed in jeans and a flowered shirt, with plenty of gold jewelry hanging on his wrists and neck, he looked like your typical gem merchant in the Caribbean supplying trinkets to the travelers. His checked luggage was never opened nor questioned. For the Dutch St. Maarten police, the main concern was drugs coming to the island, and after a German Sheppard sniffed Khamal and his bags without reacting, he passed through security without incident. He hailed a taxi to take him on the thirty-minute ride to the French side of the island, Marigot Bay, St. Martin.

THE ISRAELI BETRAYAL

Arriving at La Habitation Resort near Marigot, the French capital, Khamal thought, *I'll fit in here very nicely, it feels and looks like the south of France or Mallorca. I speak French fluently and can enjoy some great food during my trip to kill Dalton Crusoe.*

The magnificent weather began the next morning — nearly full sun, scattered white puffy clouds, and a pleasant eighty-one degrees carried on a mild breeze. Sipping on his gratis pina colada that he had left to stay cold in the refrigerator the night before, he began to review the subtle details of his plan to kill Dalton Crusoe.

Khamal had monitored seventeen calls coming into Carolyn's cell phone since his visit to her condo, where he configured her phone to copy incoming calls to his voice mail. One such call made his efforts all worthwhile, for he learned of Dalton's plans to take Carolyn to St. Martin and spend a few relaxing days on the island prior to bare-boating through Drake's Passage for another five days. *Quite a vacation,* he thought, *too bad I will make it your last!*

RICHARD TREVAE

Thirty-six hours earlier, Khamal had taken his first of three final steps toward completing his mission for the Iranians. Weiss was dead and sometime in the following day or so, a neighbor or friend found the disgraced former head of Israel's secret energy facility in his bed having suffered an apparent heart attack. The injection high on the back of Weiss's neck, near the hairline, delivered paralysis and death within five minutes and then the chemical agent degraded to nearly undetectable levels.

The next morning, Khamal began reading a Tel Aviv morning paper he picked up at a newsstand on his way to breakfast. A headline, below the paper fold stated, "Dr. Eli Weiss, long time Israeli researcher and IEC chief died unexpectedly in his sleep earlier this week. The coroner's initial findings suggest a massive stroke. He was sixty-seven-years-old."

The article went on to describe the major events of his life, his former wife he lost several years earlier, and a daughter studying at Jerusalem University. Comments from colleagues were flowing in with praise for the Israeli patriot.

Khamal displayed a controlled grin as he considered his resourcefulness. He had entered Weiss's home earlier that afternoon appearing like a business acquaintance arriving for a meeting. He overcame the lock and hid until just after dark to make his move when Weiss returned home. The small and somewhat frail Weiss offered no match for the agile and muscular Khamal who administered the lethal neurotoxin leading to a massive stroke. He laid Weiss in his bed, atop the bedding, still in the pants and shirt he'd worn during the day, to suggest he had laid down for a nap. The assignment took no more than five minutes once Weiss returned home, and then Khamal vanished out the door, disposing of his gloves and killing needle as he drove to his hotel room for the night.

Objective accomplished for the Iranians. Two more to follow, Khamal thought.

Carolyn and Dalton had perfect weather. The hurricane season was still ongoing, however the storms were infrequent this year and only two major tropical depressions had come through the Caribbean over the late summer. Both had headed toward Cuba and missed St. Martin, leaving the island in full operation for the active months of November through April. Several days of bright sun, billowy scattered clouds and temperatures in the low eighties made both of them forget Pennsylvania, Washington DC, and Enertek.

Dalton did check, a few minutes a day online, the condition of Ed Kosko, who remained in the coma following shoulder surgery, and the new studies at Enertek under Jane Holman. The doctors still felt optimistic Ed would awaken and recover soon. Jane reported the research, starting from where the Israeli's left off, or more precisely were removed, was moving along satisfactorily. The President encouraged Dalton to "get away from all this for a while", though he had the cell number to his Blackberry and would call, email, or text him personally if he needed to communicate with him. Colonel Ronet also remained on full alert for anything that needed further operational attention.

Carolyn had not been to St. Martin before and was enchanted with the quaint Marigot harbor at the north end of Simpson Bay lagoon. With only about three acres comprising the actual harbor, it was small and held no more than thirty sailboats and a few fishing boats at a time. Surrounded by open-air vacation condos, restaurants, shopping, and bars, the harbor district became a hub of activity almost all year round.

Prior to arriving at the harbor to begin their bare boating time, they had taken a rented Jeep Wrangler, peeled off the canvas top, and toured the island for four hours. Carolyn became dazzled by all the quaint shops and jewelry stores in downtown Phillipsburg, the Dutch capital on the southern side on the island. They walked along the shoreline, where all the large cruise ships dock, and felt like the island was reserved for them alone, as only one large cruise ship was anchored in the harbor in sharp contrast to the six or seven that frequently appeared in the prime season that was just two months away.

Dalton had selected a forty-six foot C&C two masted sailboat for their bare boating portion. With only a captain, first mate, and a cook, the couple could sail for days from small island-to-island, helping crew the boat, making landfall anywhere they chose, or just swimming in the open water.

Khamal pretended to be Dalton and asked to meet the captain hours before the scheduled sailing departure to inspect the boat. In a perfect Western Europe adaptation of English, Khamal said, "I've changed my mind and want to captain the boat himself, but I need the crew to assist. Is that okay with you?"

The French-speaking captain, Jacque Mastil, answered, "Well that's fine, have you handled one of these before?"

"Yes, many times. I sail one bigger than this from Mallorca to Monaco several times a summer," replied Khamal in perfect French. A broad smile from his French speaking customer impressed the captain.

RICHARD TREVAE

"Well I'll credit you a portion of my fee for the five days as captain," offered the suntanned and weathered Frenchman.

"Absolutely not," insisted Khamal. "In fact, I want you to have another 1,000 Euros for the sudden change in plans." He handed him a large envelop of Euros.

The captain didn't know what to say except "Merci, merci."

The young first mate and the cook, who only spoke a mixture of Caribbean Creole and a low class Parisian version of French, nodded in respect as they were introduced to Khamal posing as Mr. Crusoe. Before the captain could utter the name Crusoe, Khamal stepped forward held out his hand to the young crewmen and said, "Please call me Jacque, just like your captain, it's my nickname."

Holding on to the fat envelop of Euros the captain laughed loudly saying, "Yes, Jacque, Yes, yes, this is good." Looking at the envelope again, he said, "The boys will remember that for sure."

More laughter followed and Khamal smiled broadly while shaking their hands. The boys were dismissed to tend to the rigging. Khamal indicated he would have a business associate and his fiancé joining him for the first part of the trip, and they cherished their privacy. The captain restated the comments and then spoke to the crew who smiled and chuckled with understanding.

They moved quickly to load the boat with provisions for the five-day voyage. So far, Khamal's deception had worked just as he had planned.

Once alone on the boat Khamal began loading his special equipment buried secretly in his checked luggage — a 25-caliber Beretta with three full eight shot clips, a combat knife, several needles, vials of neurotoxin agents, communications gear, grey tape, and nylon rope. Dalton and his beautiful girl friend were arriving in three hours, and he was ready.

40-SIX

VANCOUVER ISLAND, CANADA

SANG Huchara was getting very uncomfortable. It was 9:15 a.m. and Gilles had not yet appeared. Gulping down his third cup of coffee, he reached for his cell phone to call when walking in, looking worn and tired, strolled Gilles Montrose.

"Do you ever get anywhere on time?" growled Sang.

"Come on, give me a break. I'm still limping and in pain over your last little assignment; I needed some rest."

"An assignment you still have yet to complete, my friend," reminded Sang.

"It will happen, don't worry."

"Well I am worried. I text messaged Weiss yesterday afternoon and he responds with some gibberish about being compromised, not in control, and not to contact. Something has changed."

Still tenderly moving his wounded leg, Gilles sat down and looked for a waitress. In a gesture of apology for his tardiness Gilles offered, "I still have friends in

Israel in my line of work; I could call a few and see if they've heard anything recently."

"All right, make the calls, but don't reveal too much interest in Dr. Weiss or the IEC. Just try to learn if he's been seen or heard from in the last twenty-four hours or so, okay?"

"Call me on your secure phone no later than tomorrow."

"Right, can we get some food now? I'm starving."

Montrose still kept in contact with old friends he had worked with on various missions. One man, Hank Benesh, was an Israeli that had actually saved Gilles's life once in Lebanon on a raid into Palestinian territory attempting to take out a fearless terrorist and his team of suicide bombers. Gilles and his team successfully entered the territory under cover of night, located the target, and caught him in crossfire of bullets as he came out of a safe house. His security force returned massive fire and took out two from Gilles group of eight as they were bogged down and trapped. A napalm fire grenade thrown into Gilles's area temporarily blinded him and left him with a mild concussion. Unable to defend him or mount an attack, he literally held on to Benesh who called in close air cover, knocked out the remaining terrorist cell, and took the team safely back to Israel.

Moments like those create life long bonds of trust

and confidence. So, even though they occasionally found themselves supporting opposing groups, their friendship and trust continued. Benesh was a good guy and very connected. He worked as a consultant to the Head of Police Security for the Israeli cabinet, and knew the inner workings of the government quite well.

LATE THE NEXT DAY

Benesh dug into the reports and files on Weiss, including his recent death. While nothing official had come down as to the predicament Weiss found himself in concerning the Elko find, rumors were rampant that he was assassinated by enemies of Israel. Gilles hung up the phone following his conversation with Hank, lit a cigarette and shook his head.

How in hell did someone orchestrate the removal and likely death of Dr. Weiss, and have it all appear like routine events? Surely, Crusoe and that bunch could not have done this. After all, they were still sorting out the explosion and fire at Elko without a clue as to what really happened.

The fact that Crusoe was prepared for the last attempt on his life, and had killed Jeff, came as no surprise to Gilles. Now Weiss was removed from his position at the IEC, found dead the next day, and the

Defense Secretary Dyan had resigned. He called Sang Huchara and relayed the news that his friend Hank had just read in the morning newspaper in Tel Aviv.

As Sang listened his heart began to pound, his face reddened and he began sweating profusely. "Are you sure of this Gilles, really sure?" begged Sang.

"Yeah, go to some Tel Aviv papers online and check it out. Of course, it all reads like normal, unfortunate events to the casual reader, but I'd bet something or someone is behind all this."

Huchara paused momentarily and thought about the risk to all within the Knowledge Consortium with Weiss gone. Had all his work stopped and IEC team been interrogated, maybe giving up the details about the Elko mine discovery? He had some serious questions to dig into. Deciding to lay low and sort things out Sang said, "Gilles go to your Montreal cabin, hide out for a couple of weeks, talk to no one and I'll come up to meet with you the end of this month with a new plan, okay?"

"Fine, it works for me, but I will finish Crusoe when we are back in action. I owe him for this hurting leg."

"Right, I'll call you by secure cell when I know I'm coming to Montreal."

Sang Huchara sat for the next three hours thinking about his future and his next steps.

40-SEVEN

CAROLYN walked to the boat after Dalton had dropped her and several bags of luggage at the dock near the sailboats. He then went to park the rental Jeep some quarter-mile away in long-term parking.

"Mrs. Crusoe, I presume?" inquired Khamal in much accented English. He attempted to make it sound like sloppy French that was heard throughout the island. He offered a friendly hand and broad smile to assist her onto the sailboat.

"Why, well yes, of course, that's me. Mr. Crusoe is coming now from the parking lot," said Carolyn flattered again by the marriage reference. She stepped onto the boat and thought; *this is going to be wonderful.*

Khamal ordered the two deck hands to assist with the luggage and escort Carolyn onto the boat. Dalton then arrived, offering his hand to Khamal, and asked, "Are we ready to sail Captain Mastil?"

"Yes, sir we should be underway in ten minutes or so," offered Khamal in his disguised accent and a broad smile. "Please make yourself comfortable."

Dalton found Carolyn, already packing away their clothes, and then she lunged at him for a hug and a kiss. "This is going to be a great sail, don't you think?"

"I believe you're right, though if you keep this up, we'll never get up unpacked and back on deck to enjoy it."

She slugged him in the arm, smiling broadly. Once down below in their cabin, Carolyn felt like she was nesting, directing Dalton as to where his and her clothes would be stowed, where they would have drinks and snacks, and which side of the bed she would like. As Dalton put on a bathing suit and a tee shirt, Carolyn said, "The captain seems nice, almost familiar in some way."

Khamal shone, playing a created character in a play he had written and controlled. He was convinced Carolyn had not connected him at all with their encounter a few weeks earlier. He wondered if Dalton even knew of the existence of a Khamal, the assassin. In two days, the crew would be given evening shore leave for an overnight stay in Charlotte Amalie on St. Thomas and Khamal would make his move to fulfill the second objective of his agreement with the Iranians.

40-EIGHT

Day Two of the Sail.
Two Miles West of St. Martin

THE sky had cleared of the heavy morning clouds early, and by 9:30 a.m. the rich blue sky, mirroring the Caribbean waters, was overtaking every view on the horizon. Dalton and Carolyn got up about 9:00 a.m. and had a light breakfast of scrambled eggs, salty bacon, and chocolate filled croissants sitting on the aft deck looking back at their hotel on Baie Longue. The coffee, made strong, black, and warm, assisted in removing the slight chill Carolyn felt as the morning sun worked its way up in the sky. A pleasant seventy-one degrees together with a three-knot trailing wind made the ride refreshing and smooth. The plan was to make Drake's Passage by 6:00 p.m. and St. Thomas by dusk . . . the helping wind aiding in their 11 knot pace.

Dolphins appeared in the small wake swirling behind the boat and jumped across the sea ripples like playful kids. A squadron of three brown pelicans flew to the north just off the stern of the boat, and then dove in a hundred yards away, all surfacing again with fish in their beaks. They gathered in a small circle and devoured the small fish they caught. Other sailboats were nearby, though not too close. All were adorned in bright sails and fully billowed spinnakers as the mild breeze carried each of them to the southwest. A few large powered cruisers were harbored in small bays and crescent harbors on the west side of St. Martin still anchored from the night before.

Both tucked into a large hammock, Carolyn and Dalton dug into their own reading material. Carolyn had a fiction piece set in the early 1900's on the French island of Martinique about a wealthy industrialist who had to escape the states with his mistress, as his financial partners discovered he had plundered their investments. It kept her content as she burrowed into Dalton's left side and felt his strong chest radiating heat to her.

Dalton rested reading a biography on Lord John Maynard Keynes, the great economist and financial maven. Interesting as it was, it could not prevent Dalton from thinking about the extent of issues arising from the Elko mine find.

Certain things had been settled and the world was better off for it, he convinced himself. Israel had been taken down a notch or two, based on the rogue actions of Dr. Eli Weiss, Sang Huchara, and their friends. Weiss was forced into a total compromise, which gave President

Conner complete power to impose whatever punishment and sanctions he chose against the Israelis. All of the exceptional IEC applied research was stopped, summarized and sent to the U.S. for completion at Enertek. Secretary Dyan resigned, and a new man had replaced him who personally assured the President there would be no more clandestine agenda in his government that would undermine U.S. interests or activities.

Israel's successful bomb attack on Jefrah Iran was treated with a "wink and a nod" by U.S. officials. No request nor approval for the action taken by Israel was received nor acknowledged at the White House. *No harm no foul*, in the eyes of the President. Besides the whole world believed Iran got what they had coming to them, through their own actions, based on their avowed intentions to destroy Israel. Japanese Secretary Kytoma received a severe slap on the wrist, made to make personal, and public, displays of shame and regret for his ill-conceived actions.

The Knowledge Consortium Group, for all its power and connections, was now being reigned back in to appear as an "almost" legitimate company. The Justice Department was preparing indictments against Mitsui Mining, Inc., and its chief officers, including Sang Huchara. who were soon to be rounded up and questioned. In fact, Dalton expected that soon he would hear from Jack Tucker or even the President that

Huchara and his assassin squad led by Gilles Montrose were taken into custody.

Unable to eliminate the thought, Dalton reached for the satellite phone tucked in the side cargo pocket of his shorts and checked for messages - none. It was about 2:30 p.m. in the eastern Caribbean, so it was 1:30 p.m. in Washington, and 10:30 a.m. in Seattle, he reasoned. Attempting to redirect his mind to the beautiful, cuddly, almost naked beauty lying with him on the hammock, he closed his phone and shut it off. Looking out at the now distant image of St. Martin, Dalton thought, *Jack Tucker and Brad Ronet can handle this; let it play out.*

The next several hours were spent lounging on the boat, enjoying a fine late lunch prepared by the cook, a swim around the boat, and enjoying the eighty-six degree weather, full sun and warm gentle breezes.

The captain had been performing exactly as a bare boat captain should, managing the sail flawlessly, directing the crew and tending to the every need of the passengers. He also made his plans for the evening. Khamal had explained that reservations had been made at the outside balcony bar and restaurant at Frenchman's Reef Resort on St. Thomas at 7:00 p.m.

Dalton looked at Carolyn and studied her reactions. They had stayed at Frenchman's Reef two years earlier before being attacked by Yuri Tarasov, a mad Russian arms merchant Dalton investigated.

Carolyn sensed Dalton's concern, yet smiled and said, "That sounds great I would like to visit there again." Dalton was relieved that the horrific attack by Tarasov was not affecting Carolyn now.

Khamal arranged to take them over on a zodiac tender, from about a half-mile out in the harbor, straight to the restaurant dock and pick them up at 10:00 p.m., as they requested. The two crewmates were also going over and would stay the night on the island at the Shipwreck, an older, less expensive hotel located in the center of busy downtown Charlotte Amalie. They wanted some nightlife.

FRENCHMAN'S REEF BALCONY DINING

Dinner was extraordinary. They sat on a granite balcony that held about twenty tables, facing southwest and out to the sea about thirty feet above the beach. Open air with small candles and burning torches offered enough light to read the menu, although not spoil the ambience of the romantic setting. The meals were huge and largely set around lobster, mahi-mahi, and prime steak garnished with local vegetables and fruit. After dinner, while enjoying an after dinner wine, Carolyn studied Dalton.

"Are you enjoying yourself darling?" she asked with a definite grin on her slightly sun burned face.

Dalton was surprised by the question. "Why, yes, of course. Why do you think I'm not?"

"You're here and I love it, yet I sense your mind drifts away at times."

Looking as guilty as a small boy caught stealing a cookie, Dalton confessed, "I'm really sorry, I am so happy to be with you, here, on this vacation, but yes, I do keep thinking about the events of the last month."

Carolyn smiled at her insightfulness. "Well let's get back on the boat; I have some ideas that might hold your attention." She looked Dalton in the eyes, revealed a seductive smile and leaned into him to make her flirting clear.

Dalton caught the obvious invitation to a great evening of sex and love making "You've already got my attention, let's go."

It was nearly 10:00 p.m. and Dalton could see the zodiac plowing its way through the flat harbor waters toward the dock at the resort.

Khamal waited ready for his prey who were none the wiser, or so he believed. Both Dalton and Carolyn were so wrapped up in each other that the trip back to the boat went by quickly. A few light pleasantries and Khamal offered a gracious smile. "I'll retire for the evening then, unless there is nothing else I can get for you tonight."

"It's been a wonderful day Jacque, thanks; we'll see you in the morning. Good night." Dalton grabbed Carolyn by the waist, pulled her to him, and looked passionately in her eyes.

Thinking about his prey, Khamal could see his plan coming together very nicely now. They were alone, relaxed and unaware their assassin was on board.

Dalton changed down to his open collared flowered Caribbean shirt and shorts while Carolyn decided to change after taking a jasmine scented shower, just for Dalton. Not wanting to alter her plans one iota, Dalton said he'd have rum and coke on the deck as the last of the sunset rays shrank into the horizon. He would join her in about twenty minutes. The vision of Carolyn awaiting him in a sheer negligee, filling his senses with jasmine, in the main cabin bedroom suite became very compelling, yet for the moment, he felt a strong need to check his satellite phone again.

He retrieved his phone again stowed in his cargo pocket of his shorts and powered it, dialed up his voice mail and waited for a connection. The evening calmed, approaching complete darkness except for a bright strip of orange at the horizon. The boat floated in near perfect quiet, only slivers of light coming from the galley end, where the crew and captain Jacque had their cabins. The wind had died down to almost imperceptible. The boat gave very little hint of motion as it swayed slowly around the bow anchor.

Moments later Carolyn started the shower, laid out her special lounge ware for Dalton, when she felt a pull on her hair and a sharp sting near the back of her neck. As she dropped to the floor, she felt herself being carried to the bed. As her eyes gradually closed she heard, "Stay calm and quiet and all this will turn out okay."

The depth of fear Carolyn felt was unspeakable; she remembered the deep dark eyes of a few weeks before, although felt his words were not true this time. She quickly drifted into a light sleep.

On deck Dalton worked his phone. The screen lit up: *You have two messages.*

Dalton thought *it's about time I got an update.* Dalton brought up the first message from Jack Tucker. "Dalton, this is Jack. Just wanted you to know federal indictments came down today on Sang Huchara and Gilles Montrose, but as federal officers went to serve them the two were gone. None of Sang's staff knew anything about where he was or where he was going. Gilles Montrose was less known at the corporate office in Vancouver, and the only thing we found was a imprint on a note pad in Sang's office spelling out 'Gilles at Montreal cabin.' It appears they are on the run, but don't worry, we'll find them soon. Hope you are enjoying the vacation. Jack."

Dalton did not quite know what to think of this news. Sang appeared to be the type to fight not flee, although maybe he fell deeper into the dirt of the Elko matter than they presumed. In reality, it remained only a question of time before he was found, along with the mercenary Gilles.

Dalton pulled up the second message. This one was placed an hour after Jack's and was from President Conner. "JD, this is Jerome. I'm calling on the private satellite phone from my office to you directly because I didn't want to lose time alerting you. An assassin, named Hasim Khamal, we believe, has been contracted by the Iranians to eliminate Weiss, Huchara, and you for the Jefrah bombing. Somehow, they got to the asset, Mohammad Hatta, and he gave up a fair amount on the Israeli IEC and Weiss and you. We believe we have tracked Khamal's travels to St. Martin and have him arriving last week just after your vacation began. Be cautious, as we have no picture of this guy, but he is very thorough, with several presumed kills of high profile, protected targets. Call me ASAP and I will send a protection unit through Ronet to assist you."

Dalton sat numb struck for a moment. In all the

attention given to the Israeli's and to a lesser extent Japan, his team had just about forgotten the Iranians.

Sure, they were pissed, but what could they do? They must have gotten to Hatta and began figuring things out, Dalton thought.

He closed down his phone and thought to find Carolyn. He looked at the last bit of rum and coke in his glass, and raised it to take in the last swallow. As he rose the glass he saw reflected in the glass surface the shape of a man approaching him from behind. Instinctively, Dalton rolled to his left, just as Khamal lunged at him with a large combat knife, missing his right shoulder as he came down hard on the mahogany top deck.

Khamal flipped over, jumped to his feet, and made another lunge at Dalton. Fearing for his life, and Carolyn's, Dalton looked frantically for a weapon of some kind. In his cabin lay a nine millimeter Beretta, butit was no use now. Khamal moved closer, as Dalton backed up, guiding himself toward the stern of the boat, his hand slipped over a hooked object. Grabbing it firmly he retrieved a line gaff, used to pull a dock line to the boat when coming in to tie off. It was about six feet long, aluminum with a dull plastic two-inch hook on the end.

Better than nothing Dalton thought.

Khamal moved aggressively toward Dalton, slashing

and jabbing as he came close. Dalton jammed the hook end into Khamal's stomach, bending him over in some pain. However, he grabbed at the pole and nearly pulled it from Dalton. Khamal snatched a loose anchor line and twirled it around his left wrist to make a sort of whip. He flailed at Dalton trying to snare the gaff hook to no avail. Khamal stood barefoot and Dalton noticed the rear of the boat was wet as he moved away from Khamal.

Looking down, he saw Khamal had slacks, no shoes or socks, and a linen casual shirt. He waited for the next thrust from Khamal. It came at full force and Dalton grabbed his knife hand and held it off his chest as they tumbled to the deck and rolled near the safety cable running around the perimeter of the boat. Dalton took his free hand grasping Khamal's shirt and punched him hard in the throat, then once again in the face. Khamal never slowed his attack, he rolled over on top of Dalton and pressed his arm against Dalton's throat, then lifting his knife hand with Dalton still holding tight to it he thrust it down at Dalton, just missing his left ear, and burying it deep in the wooden deck. Dalton kneed him hard in the groin and Khamal fell off Dalton grabbing his crouch in one hand and trying to free the embedded knife with the other. Dalton quickly stood up and kicked Khamal hard in the stomach, throwing him against the safety cable.

Without a pause, Khamal jumped to his feet and slipped on the wet deck, falling backwards over the cable and hung by one hand over the edge of the boat. Dalton grabbed at the knife, pulled, and worked it out of the deck, just as Khamal started to come over the safety cable. In one fast, accurate move, Dalton spun around in a second, leading with his knife hand and caught Khamal, landing a deep gash extending from his right side collarbone, over the chest and through his left arm bicep. Khamal screamed in pain, released his hold on the cable and fell seven feet into the dark water. He sank out of sight.

Dalton looked at the six inch, serrated blade on the knife now shining bright with blood the entire length under a near full moon. He caught his breath, wiped his brow and then yelled, "Carolyn!"

Fearing the worst, he ran to the center galley opening, vaulted down the stairs and froze with his hand gripping the handle of the door to his cabin. He had not heard a sound from her during the struggle, he became worried. Was *she asleep, bound or dead?* He could hardly think the words, although knowing the answer lie beyond the door in front of him he rotated the knob releasing the door. There she lay motionless, sprawled on the bed, with only panties on, her back facing Dalton. He felt his eyes welling up, and he said a desperate prayer as he approached the bed, and gently rolled her toward him. There was no blood, although she appeared unconscious, mouth taped, feet and hands bound. He grabbed her arms pulling her to him, and she began to stir, gaining consciousness, opening her eyes. When she saw Dalton, the tears flowed and she shook uncontrollably.

40-NINE

Near Vancouver — Huchara's Private Airstrip

TED South had arrived early, checked out and fueled the six passenger Cessna for the flight. It was 6:38 p.m. and Sang Huchara arrived late, quite unusual for him. The flight plan amounted to a simple task for Ted to complete from the small private airfield Huchara had used for years to house his personal plane and two other aircraft available to move project teams around Canada and the States. This trip might be the last one for Ted South.

He had heard through Gilles of the trouble in Israel, the death of Dr. Weiss, and the strange events surrounding General Yong and his near death. It made him nervous, and he almost suffered the same fate as Jeff Harding during their ill-fated encounter with Dalton Crusoe. Things were getting out of control and he felt vulnerable. He knew it, Gilles knew it and, so did Sang Huchara.

The trip to meet Gilles at his cabin would be the last meeting the three would have for some time. Sang would try to get to Japan before the federal authorities could locate him and from there he could run the Mitsui operations through his officers and managers even if he wasn't in his world headquarters in Vancouver. He wanted enough time for all the claims and charges to come out, and hopefully deny involvement of his company, or himself directly in the events which started at Elko; after all the list of knowledgeable players were dropping fast. Weiss was dead, as was Toro Nagama, and Jeff Harding.

All the others like Secretary Kytoma and Defense Minister Dyan were removed from their cabinet posts and were not able to be placed at the times and locations where the killing and other crimes took place. He hoped for himself that he could maintain his distance from the most incriminating matters by securing the silence and allegiance of Ted and Gilles. That had pretty much been done with Gilles through his now fully paid fee for his services, even though Crusoe remained alive and still in charge. Ted would get $500,000 USD in cash after the trip to Montreal and the final meeting to discuss their escape plans.

The biggest risk, reasoned Huchara, was General Yong. His story seemed too mired in the failed first attempt to destroy the North Korean Missile Research Complex — his apparent accidental death, and then his re-appearance in Saigo, requesting equipment, men and vehicles to complete the mission. Days later the world learns the NKMRC is destroyed along with many high-ranking North Korean leaders, including the Prime Minister and no one knows the cause except those in the Knowledge Consortium Group. His connection to the mission Yong successfully accomplished was going to be hard to hide. Nevertheless, if once back in Japan the benefits to the country and the world should be clear, it would be a big help in getting his actions forgiven, if fully exposed — or so he hoped. He felt certain Crusoe somehow had compromised or convinced Yong to participate.

Ted was an experienced pilot and had flown this plane many times for Sang Huchara and others in Mitsui. It took off with the two men, several suitcases including a weapons case and cash. They were to fly to just outside International Falls, Minnesota, refuel, and continue on to the small airstrip just outside Montreal, only twelve miles from Gilles's place. They expected to arrive at the cabin about noon local time. The trip manifest did not list Sang Huchara as a passenger, rather it identified a Jeff Harding, and they surely would not be able to track him down for questioning.

Ted and Huchara said very little on the flight except that the meeting with Gilles was very important to the survival of each man. As the plane rose to 21,000 feet and cruised through the large clouds Sang watched the fading orange and red sunlight streaming off the clouds

344

below slowly give way to a clear black sky speckled with stars. Huchara reflected, *If only they had been able to get to Crusoe before he got to the technology, my future would be looking and feeling very different.*

OUTSIDE MONTREAL, CANADA

The weather had taken a turn to the cold side. Gilles worked outside for the second time since his arrival four days earlier, splitting wood for his fireplaces. The temperature at 9:54 a.m. steadied at forty-eight degrees, and expected to rise to the low sixties by mid afternoon. The cloud cover present at dawn started dissipating to just a few large clusters moving to the southeast. Gilles wanted to keep at least a three-day supply of dry, split wood in the cabin.

With its six thousand square feet of space, the place was best described as a lodge, although Gilles always referred to it as a cabin. He had it built five years ago just after he began working for Mitsui and Sang Huchara. He always expected to live out his retirement summers at the place where he loved to fish, hunt, and escape from the world.

It also gave him a sense of isolation and security as it was a mile off the nearest blacktop road, tucked in the woods and perched on a hill, overlooking a vast valley of pines, rivers and grasslands. It looked northwest, affording nice sunsets, and a view of a distant low mountain range reaching a respectable 3,200 feet in elevation.

Gilles was not one to bet on nature alone for his isolation and security. So, he surrounded the 350 acres he owned with the top surveillance systems, perimeter cameras, and a security system that, based on a perceived threat, would automatically lock down the lodge, and operates on a full internal standby power unit housed in his attached garage.

Preferring a natural fire to propane heat, he usually ran the fireplaces first to heat the place, and only when the weather got below thirty-two degrees did he activate the furnace system as a supplemental heat source. Very few people had ever been to his lodge, although Sang Huchara had and Gilles expected he would appear again one day.

Gilles felt that, even though his work had been fully paid for, he still owed Huchara the Elko disks and a death certificate for Dalton Crusoe. He was anxious about the recent news; the suspicious death of Weiss, Sang's jittery nature on the phone, and the status of Mitsui at the Elko mine. He knew he had covered his tracks, and with Jeff dead and Ted a trusted comrade, he did not feel a particular need to disappear, just stay out of the action for a couple of weeks.

RICHARD TREVAE

Huchara was a different matter however; he was extremely visible, what with forty or fifty large construction projects going on throughout the world, and his tendency to travel anywhere, anytime. He wondered how the Knowledge Consortium Group would restructure itself with Weiss gone.

The main fireplace took hold warming the large main living room, and the heat began rolling out the opening into the lodge. Glancing out the southern windows, Gilles could see a grey Hummer H2 moving up the gravel road to his lodge. It had to be Sang Huchara. He grabbed a nearby loaded Marlin 30-30 for companionship as he walked out to his rear porch.

"Got some hot coffee in there?" yelled Sang as he jumped out of his H2.

"Could be, are you alone?" Just then, Ted South opened the passenger side door and looked up at Gilles. Ted waived, grabbed a back pack and shut the doors to the H2.

"Just me and Ted. We've got some plans to make."

After a few minutes of adjusting to the coffee and fire, Huchara began recanting to Gilles what he believed had happened in Israel. Ted South wasted no time opening the metal suitcase filled with neatly bundled stacks of $50 and $100 bills promised to him by Sang.

Gilles finally said, "Well, I'm up at my cabin, like you

asked, and you've had some time to think. What's the plan?"

Sang began by reciting to Gilles, and himself, the recent events. His old friend and clandestine fellow member of the KCG had delivered some strange messages over his last days. General Yong resurfaced and was ready to complete the earlier failed mission. He was asked to deliver personnel, equipment, and transport to Yong and a small insertion team back into Hyesan. Not long after that Weiss responded in text a message indicating he was "fully compromised. Not in control."

"What the hell did all mean?" Sang asks in frustration. "Then the North Korean Missile Research Complex is blown up, as we had hoped. Then a few days later Weiss dies — unexpectedly." Gilles and Ted were surprised how a man of Huchara's toughness was made to sound like a confused teenager.

"Who the hell is running things?" asked Sang rhetorically and in a state of frustration.

During the monologue, Gilles had located a bottle of Glen Livet and poured each of them a rock glass filled with ice and scotch. Gilles walked to the large glass window displaying the endless forest beyond and sipped his drink. "Could this Dalton Crusoe be playing us?"

"That's what I'm wondering too. I heard from my staff in Vancouver yesterday that federal agents came to my office with indictments against me and Mitsui. They were also looking for you."

"Oh damn it, I should have taken more precautions against Crusoe and his woman when I had them in my sights," growled Gilles, looking disapprovingly at Ted who had now counted his money twice and just started to join in the conversation.

Sang stood and studied his drink. "Well, just relax and listen a minute. I emailed my attorneys and they will meet with the federal agents and find out what they have. If it is a fishing expedition, they will tear their indictments apart. If not, I may have to disappear for a while. The charges against you must be circumstantial, unless you left a calling card during your visits to Elko."

"He never knew I was there until I went for him, and he had no clue I was coming at him. Jeff's dead, and Ted is not named, right?"

Sang set his scotch down and pointed a finger at Ted. "I have not seen or heard of anything formal looking for you, Ted, but get lost after this meeting. Clear?"

Nodding his understanding Ted said, "Clear."

"Yeah, this may blow over or at worst Mitsui gets a slap or fine," scoffed Sang.

"Our real concern is whether or not all the events of the last two weeks or so have been run by Crusoe and his team, whoever they are. That would mean they know a lot, and have piles of information, which could only have fallen in their hands if Weiss was 'fully compromised,' as he said in his text email."

"Maybe he was trying to warn you, and the KCG, with that text message," supposed Gilles.

"Well, we will know soon enough. Let's think about a short term plan."

As the evening went on and darkness approached, Sang explained how he thought the next few weeks would unfold. He told Gilles to stay retreated near his cabin, even taking some time to travel the local area or plan a hunting trip to the north. Ted was told to leave the States for at least six months, preferably somewhere he would not likely be recognized. Ted already knew he would head to Argentina to visit an old girl friend recently divorced and anxious to re-start their past relationship. Sang would head to Japan leaving through Canada in the next day or so, depending on how he could best disguise his escape.

After four weeks, they were to contact Sang at a new email address: rh1128@yahoo.com. This seemed simple enough and only a very distant connection to Sang Huchara for it used his dead father's initials together with his birthday and month. Clever enough and quite safe, Sang thought. Once Sang knew more of the government's case against the KCG and him, he would contact them with more plans. The drinking continued.

TOKYO, JAPAN — U.S. EMBASSY

GENERAL. Yong sat nervous and somewhat on edge without his full dress military uniform he typically wore. The first meeting with the State Department officials went well he thought — no criminal prosecution, no jail time, asylum in the west, all in exchange for complete information on the KCG and its passive supporters, Japan and Israel, and associates. By most measures, it came off well for everyone directly involved with him, except of course for the North Korean regime, now without a Prime Minister, six cabinet members, three other very high ranking generals in the military, and two top scientists overseeing the work at the NKMRC. Major Roh Kunghee, as promised by Dalton, was also given asylum in the west. The regime collapsed so broken apart that no one emerged positioned to muster the attention of the world to blame the West for their problems. As Dalton envisioned, the cause and timing of the blast were perceived as a critical mistake by a rogue regime out to test its military muscle.

Yong watched events in North Korea daily and the

State Department had connected him with other sympathizers in the south seeking a reunification of the two Koreas. South Korean officials felt it best to keep his false death hidden from those in the north until some initial attempts to open discussions came forth. Yong felt hopeful that within a month he could be the link to beginning reunification.

The next interview with Jack Tucker had much more focus on the KCG and how much the group and its members interfered with research at Enertek, what had been learned from Toro Nagama over the years, and who may have had access after Huchara received the data. At this point Yong was grateful for the quick, creative thinking of Dalton Crusoe and the trust President Conner and Colonel Ronet had in the plan he devised. In a strange sort of way, very different from the early thinking within the KCG, Yong had achieved his most sacred desire; toppling a corrupt tyrant leadership holding North Korea hostage and denying its people the benefits of a modern society integrated into the western world. He would hold back nothing about the KCG and its dealings.

50-ONE

OUTSIDE MONTREAL, CANADA

THE rain started to freeze and small crystals of snow began falling on the communications equipment. Ronet ordered his team of eight to complete their photography and scanning for laser security fences around Gilles lodge. They had followed Sang Huchara's travel across Canada from Vancouver to Montreal during the last twenty-four hours. The federal agents missed him by an hour and it was just luck that a satellite could be re-tasked quickly, and found his licensed sports car driving to his private hanger outside the city.

Once in the Montreal area they lost track of his trail, except for the note pad imprint in Sang's office that left the words "Gilles at Montreal Cabin" which gave a fresh start to the search. Ronet had actually been able to secure satellite photos off the internet of the wilderness area surrounding Gilles's land.

He took a chance and moved his team to within a quarter-mile of the only cabin showing on the images and attempted to scan it with long-range cameras. Ronet's team set up early in the pre-dawn hours and was prepared to wait until Huchara found his way to the cabin. They did not have to wait long. By 11:00 a.m., a vehicle approached the dirt road and turned in toward the cabin. As the man drove up in a Hummer and stepped out, a clear photo was taken which confirmed it was Sang Huchara along with Ted South. Moments later, Gilles Montrose stepped outside, noticeably carrying a rifle, and his identity was also confirmed. Ronet decided to wait until dark and attempt a raid on the cabin to catch them by surprise and limit casualties if possible.

The rain and snow mix did turn into an intense snowfall as the temperature dropped to thirty degrees. At 1:30 a.m. Ronet's team was preparing for the mission; snow cover camouflage suits, full communication gear to talk with each other, live video feed to their mission coordinator station on the hillside where they set up in the afternoon were all ready. Ronet's veteran team located the laser security fence and positioned a pair of reflectors to break the beam, yet not trigger the breach alarm. It was set up to provide a ten-foot wide gap in the true laser beam through which Ronet and his two-man assault team passed. The remaining five men stayed at the surveillance location they had established and functioned as the control and command data center.

Once aware Huchara was heading to Montrose's cabin Ronet had ordered a sleek, quieted Apache helicopter to transport the eight men from a small military airfield and training camp in northern Maine to the Montreal perimeter. From there two civilianYukon SUV's were waiting to take them to the area of the cabin. Moving swiftly at the rear of the cabin, Ronet's team spread out to about thirty yards apart and focused on the main door entrance.

Sang Huchara and Ted South had fallen asleep in spare bedrooms and Gilles had just gotten up to fetch a brandy as he became unable to sleep with a painful throbbing in his injured leg that appeared each night, as well as re-hashing all he had learned earlier in the evening. Moving in the dark through the living room to the bar area, he could see a man crouching, moving toward the porch, armed and dressed for combat — clearly not your local thief.

He turned and went to activate the security system; a second later all the doors locked, outside lights lit and security cameras focused on all possible entry points to the cabin. Gilles went to his decorative gun case displaying shotguns and hunting rifles, pulled the false cabinet back open, entered a five number code into the keypad, opened the hidden gun safe, and grabbed one of six assault rifles among the stashed handguns, grenades, knives, and ammo packs. He ran by Sang Huchara's room, still sound asleep, banged on the door and said, "We've got visitors."

Ronet held his men in position, waiting to see what Gilles was going to do.

"What the hell is going on?" growled Huchara as he tried to wake. Ted came out of his room and instinctively grabbed an assault rifle and an automatic handgun, which he tucked in his jeans he pulled up as he sprang to his feet.

"We've got two; no make that three, at least, coming up on the front side of the cabin, all with heavy firepower. Get your ass out of bed and take this Uzi," said Gilles as he threw Sang the weapon.

Catching the weapon in mid-air, Huchara woke immediately, his adrenaline pumping. He crouched nearby Gilles as they looked out into the brightly lit front and side of the cabin. Ted crawled to near the front door, stood up beside it flat against the wall and awaited instructions from Gilles. No one could be seen now, yet Gilles knew they were planning to attack without warning had he not noticed them approaching.

After a few anxious moments, a bullhorn sounded. "This is U.S. Marine Colonel Ronet, and I have your cabin surrounded. We are here with arrest warrants for Sang Huchara and Gilles Montrose on charges of murder and acts against the United States of America. Come out with your hands empty and held high."

Sang Huchara was a powerful man in business, and as such had always hired the brightest and best lawyers.

He began to think how a U.S. military man could enforce a warrant on Canadian soil without the Canadian police, Mounties, or whatever calling the shots. Emboldened, he said, "You have no jurisdiction in Montreal Canada to arrest me."

Gilles looked at him and almost laughed, "You think you can legally argue them into going home?"

"No, but I'm sure not giving in to this group; they are probably still operating through Crusoe, and have no authority to arrest us here."

"Better get ready to fight our way out." Gilles offered mockingly.

Ted snapped the thumb lever and loaded a round in the firing chamber of his Uzi.

"Sit here, I'm going up to the loft where I can see all around the cabin and get an idea as to how many there are." Gilles motioned to the spiral staircase heading up.

Ronet did not expect them to come walking out sorry for all their bad deeds, and he surely didn't expect Huchara to try to claim protection under some jurisdiction issue. Still a Japanese citizen, Huchara lived all over the world and felt no particular obligation to recognize an authority based on what he had heard so far. Gilles chose a dual citizenship in Canada and the U.S. so his problem became more complex.

Gilles reached the loft, scanned the area, and looked down to Sang and then Ted, while holding up three fingers to indicate he located Ronet's assault team. As he looked back outside, he could see a man standing, aiming his weapon, and preparing to fire. Gilles yelled for the others to take cover, just as the smoke and tear gas bomb broke through the living room window and filled the air with a dense fog. Seconds later the door came crashing down as one of Ronet's men bashed it in and dove inside the cabin; automatic rifle in shouldered position ready to fire. Gilles swung around from his loft location and found the marine in his sights. Three quick rounds and the soldier lay bleeding, yet conscious, just inside the front door.

Falling to the ground, the marine saw Ted taking aim at him and got one accurate shot off hitting Ted in the center of his neck. He clutched his throat in pain and collapsed on the floor, bleeding heavily. Ronet and his second man were right behind the first and opened fire throughout the cabin. Gilles felt this was the time to make his stand, for he sprayed the entry door opening with automatic fire from his 6.52 mm Uzi. Ronet wheeled to his left and fired seven automatic rounds, three hitting Gilles in the neck and shoulder. Gilles was hit badly, he could not move and the third man in Ronet's team jumped on him in an instant, stripped him of his weapon and put the rifle to his temple. Ten seconds later Gilles died, having bled out from his wounds.

At this point, Sang shook, completely traumatized, hiding behind a huge couch as he kept yelling, "Don't shoot, I am not armed." Silent and now appearing quite meek, Sang Huchara let his head fall to his chest in fear for his fate. Ted South never regained consciousness and bled to death.

Ronet grabbed Sang, threw him to the floor and held his foot on his throat until the third marine came over and secured Sang with plastic wrist straps and tape. Huchara looked bewildered as Ronet quickly took charge of the situation and tended to his injured marine. Gilles hung slumped over the short loft wall leading to the staircase. His dream of a quiet retirement in the Mediterranean during the winter and his woodsy cabin in the summer would never be realized.

Ronet called in to the fourth marine operating the communications at base camp for the operation. "Target one secured, target two and three dead, one marine wounded, call in the helicopter from Maine to airlift out the dead and our wounded."

An official prompt answer came back. "Roger that, Helo should arrive in twenty."

The third marine and Ronet took Huchara and secured him in their vehicle while they packed up everything they had brought. A special detail of marine military police would escort Sang Huchara back to Washington D.C. where officers in the NSA would take over the legal actions against Mitsui and Sang Huchara.

50-TWO

St. Thomas — Harbor at Frenchman's Reef

JACK Tucker looked like a misplaced businessman, wearing a dark tan suit and tie, brown captoe lace shoes, and sporting a briefcase. His lack of color easily marked him as newcomer to the island's powerful sun and gleaming waters. Forgetting to bring sunglasses, Tucker squinted and rubbed his eyes as they tried to adjust to the intense sunlight. Sheltering his forehead and eyes, he meandered awkwardly walking around the harbor looking for Dalton's rented sailboat the "Sea Gypsy."

Just as he turned the corner at the far end of the marina, Jack waved vigorously, indicating he found them, after seeing Dalton and Carolyn motioning to get his attention. It had been almost thirty-six hours since that fateful evening when Khamal made his attempt to assassinate Dalton, and presumably Carolyn as well.

The morning after the attack, Dalton and Carolyn took the zodiac to shore and waited for the two crewmen who spent the night in Charlotte Amalie. It took some time, however Dalton was able to get them to understand what had happened. The two baffled crewmen explained that Khamal presented himself to Captain Mastil as Mr. Crusoe and that his nickname was Jacque, just like the captain's. Then "Jacque" informed all that for the first part of the trip a friend and his fiancé would be joining them on the trip to St. Thomas where they would depart back to the states. The two crewmen assumed they were to take the arriving zodiac back to the boat in the morning after Dalton and his fiancé motored it to the island to catch a cab to the airport.

Further proof of the events received confirmation by Dalton when he produced his copy of the rental agreement with Captain Mastil, which the Captain later verified over the ship radio to both crewmen. As instructed by Captain Mastil, the crew was to sail Dalton and Carolyn back to St. Martin where U.S. authorities would meet them.

Dalton had called the President late the evening of the attack and gave him the details of what had happened. Thankful Dalton and Carolyn were safe; he authorized Ronet to dispatch a special Coast Guard unit in Puerto Rico known as the Kidnap and Rescue Team (K&R) to provide security for Dalton as he returned to St. Martin while the team looked for Khamal's body. The St. Thomas police weren't much good on open sea crimes, only matters on the island itself. The local leaders on the island were told practice naval maneuvers were planned for a week. It fell to the Coast Guard K&R team under Ronet's direction to handle the search effort and protection for Dalton and Carolyn. With two of Ronet's handpicked men on the boat during the return sail, Dalton and Carolyn felt well protected.

Two Days Later
The Oval Office

The President was busy, yet he insisted Dalton join him for lunch at the White House. Dalton had already briefed the President and the Secretary of State following his return from the Caribbean with Carolyn. Tucker and Ronet had filed a complete report, identified as "Project Return Strike — Top Secret," which compiled all the intelligence gathered, video and voice data, documents, confessions, and agreements negotiated. Only the top leadership in Congress dealing with terrorism and other global threats were privy to the summary report.

The Joint Chiefs had been brought up to speed on the entire episode and applauded the President for his quick thinking and resourcefulness. He was now winning broad spread congratulations from those allowed to know the details of the last six weeks. Events were still unfolding overseas and the Japanese, Israeli, and South Korean governments were confidentially brought up to speed on the recent history of the Knowledge Consortium Group; which led to the ambitious plan conceived and executed by Dalton ultimately taking down the organization.

Again, sitting outside the oval office Dalton looked at his watch, and began to reflect on the various outcomes. He was pleased to learn Ed Kosko came out of his coma, had some memory loss, which all involved thought would return in a matter of months. He would return to work soon, Dalton hoped.

Dr. Eli Weiss was dead, with suspicions whether from natural causes or a murder. Gilles Montrose was dead from his shootout with Ronet, and Sang Huchara was under the custody of federal officials. Israeli and Japanese cabinet members were removed from the international scene and received a private berating from their governments. The leaders of both Israel and Japan were paying their homage to President Conner for sequestering the report resulting in damaging public humiliation, which would surely have dogged each country for years. Neither country wanted to be seen as trying to undermine the supportive relationship with the U.S. That would be political suicide for Israel and something just short of that for Japan.

On a more pleasant note, General Yong was being mentioned more and more as the leader to make re-unification of North and South Korea a reality. The North had fallen into a confused state of desperation and many low level party officials were openly calling for talks with the South.

Carolyn had poured herself into her teaching work-load, now into the fall semester. Dalton planned to visit her for an evening dinner, talk about their future, and to make sure she felt safe.

Dalton tried very hard to avoid giving press state-ments, being interviewed on news talk shows, even foregoing an interview with Larry Kudlow on his busi-ness roundtable show to discuss the implications of the technology. Most of that stuff he pushed off to the press secretary of the President with a few quick oversight comments by under secretaries now all at Dalton's dis-posal.

However, the buzz started about the vast implications of the discovery, and the President, now late in the third year of his first term in office felt a responsibility to hold onto office for another four years and take this new technology from its infant stage to that of a tod-dler. Clearly, from the President's perspective, Dalton played a key role in the effort. The President had gen-uinely come to appreciate the intellect, skills and potential of Jameson Dalton Crusoe. He wanted him near at hand.

The President's Chief of Staff opened the door to the oval office, came over to Dalton and shook his hand with obvious enthusiasm. "The President can receive you now, Mr. Crusoe," he said with a broad smile. Escorting Dalton through the door, he patted him on the back gently and closed the door once he was in.

"Dalton, come over here with me." The President was smiling and almost joyous at seeing Dalton. The White House official photographer took at least ten photos of the President and Dalton in various stages of conversation and hand shaking. One had the President with his right arm around Dalton's shoulder while shaking hands with his left. Just as quickly as the photographer performed his work, he was dismissed, leaving the President and Dalton alone.

"I've told the kitchen staff to bring us a light lunch of sandwiches and fruit, is that okay?"

"Yes, of course Mr. President, that's fine."

Sitting across from each other on opposing couches, the President went on to say again how much he appreciated his strong, decisive decision-making and intuitive skills in handling this Enertek matter. He felt Ed Kosko would eventually be able to resume his normal duties, although for the time being he wanted Dalton to report direct to him and oversee the ongoing activities at Enertek with the research Jane Homan and her top scientific team were undertaking. He also wanted Dalton to take charge of the Elko mine area, maintain security, and organize a plan to proceed with the excavation, storage, refinement, and safe inventorying of the energy ready catalyst created from the ore.

This expanded role would be handled under the title of Special Deputy Assistant Secretary of Energy. As the technology became fully understood, Dalton would likely oversee a new department dealing with the security and deployment of the source of energy throughout the world.

Dalton took a deep breath. "Mr. President, I am very flattered, but I'm not sure I'm the right man for the job. I've never been much of a success at being a political type." Dalton offered with a deprecating message.

"Nonsense," said the President. "You know the technology and big picture implications better than anyone and Ed will have his career deputy under secretaries do all the mundane stuff for you."

"May I have a few days to consider this Mr. President?" Dalton asked sheepishly.

"Yes, of course, yet I won't easily take no for an answer. Dalton, you and Ronet made a great team under remarkably tight schedules with enormous political risks for the country if you failed, and you pulled it all off! This country needs more men like you two."

"All right, I hear your reasons, Mr. President but I'd still like a little time to think this out."

"Fair enough JD, let's have some lunch."

The rest of the next forty minutes were spent enjoying the lunch and filling in a few juicy details of how Eli Weiss reacted to the inquisition of him in Israel by Dalton. The President truly enjoyed the images of Weiss being trapped in his own plan after he smugly went about stealing and capturing what he thought was the technology to raise Israel to the status of the U.S., and beyond, in the eyes of the world.

The President expressed, "It's an unusual feeling to be so critically involved in a truly epic event like the energy issues of the world and yet remain a silent spectator to the general population."

Dalton agreed, "I feel the same way sir. It's kind of like we were driven by unforeseen events which demanded we act to avoid world disorder." Dalton also wondered if another President had been in office and not had the backbone and sense of achieving the greater good President Jerome Conner possessed, would the results have been so outstanding. Dalton didn't know and was glad he had a man like President Conner to rely on and stand behind the planning and operations he had led for the country.

"Mr. President, I can't express how much your confidence and support in me made my decision-making easier."

"Ed was correct Dalton, you proved to be the right man at the right time."

Dalton felt a real connection to this President, and found him hard to resist when he was called upon to do his bidding. He felt certain whatever he decided to do; President Conner would not hesitate to call on him for advice.

Dalton left the oval office with many issues on his mind, and a dinner with Carolyn would help him sort out what to do, he thought.

PAGANELLI'S ITALIAN RESTAURANT, NEAR THE WHARTON SCHOOL.

Dalton could not easily shake a wired-feeling as he enjoyed the excellent meal at Paganelli's with Carolyn. Beyond the great sea bass and scalloped potatoes attractively displayed on the entrée dishes, Dalton also enjoyed his favorite pinot noir, as he bounced between the thrill of being with Carolyn and the rush of the day at the White House. He went through the meeting with the President and asked her to give her impressions. Dalton spared nothing, including the details of how much the President enjoyed having the real upper hand with Israel and Japan when all the cards were played out.

"Is this the kind of work you want to continue doing?" Carolyn didn't know what she wanted to hear for an answer. Clearly Dalton was at the top of his game during the crisis and all in power knew it. Yet she feared for his life and the intense stress that a role in the NSA similar to the last six weeks would bring.

Looking at Carolyn with a clear sense of her concern, Dalton reminded her, "This isn't the first time we've both been in trouble and survived, right?"

"Yes, that's true. I just don't want to always worry this is what life holds for us."

"It won't, I promise. Soon I'll look like any other bureaucrat." Dalton smiled and touched her hand to lighten the mood.

"I truly doubt that my love." Carolyn had to smile at the obvious half-truth he tried to sell.

Carolyn was excited for Dalton and not surprised the President would make Dalton an offer to emerge from the rather hidden and obscure role as Consultant to Ed Kosko, and become a more involved political ally of the President. She encouraged him to accept, and hoped it would lighten his travel to a more predictable schedule so they could spend more time together and plan their future as a couple. In his own mind, Dalton knew he would likely take the position although didn't want to isolate Carolyn from the reasoning process leading up to his decision. He valued her input and wanted her support for his decisions. Losing her, while gaining this opportunity, was not on his agenda.

They finished dinner; he embraced her warmly then had to catch a late flight back to Washington for meetings with Ed the next day.

As Carolyn felt he was ready to depart, she asked, "Promise me you will call when you arrive. I worry every time we are not together."

"I will and soon we must plan another weekend away."

She also made him promise to call and tell her how he decided to answer the President's call to join the administration.

Taking his seat on the small jet shuttle between Pennsylvania and DC, Dalton worried that the Coast Guard had not yet found Khamal's body or remains. The chance of Khamal surviving the deep wound Dalton left him seemed very remote, yet unnerving. His mind would not close out the terrifying events outside St. Thomas until he knew Khamal was dead.

ABOUT THE AUTHOR

Part adventurer, part businessman, part author, Richard Trevae is a chemical engineer with an MBA in Finance and Management. Trevae matured a startup design/construction/development firm into a publicly traded company that later merged with a parent corporation generating four billion dollars in annual revenues. His articles concerning business valuation, mergers, acquisitions, and management practices have been published in various trade associations and business newspapers. Writing "reality inspired fiction" has become his latest passion, commencing with, "THE FUSION BREAKTHROUGH," followed by the prequel, "THE TARASOV SOLUTION." His extensive world traveling has provided a rich backdrop for the exotic locales featured in his novels. Mr Trevae lives with his wife along the picturesque shores of Lake Michigan where he is working on his next novel.

CPSIA information can be obtained at www.ICGtesting.com
Printed in the USA
266665BV00001B/1/P